·CORONATION ST.·

Snow *on the* Cobbles

Also by Maggie Sullivan

Christmas on Coronation Street
Mother's Day on Coronation Street

·CORONATION ST.·

Snow *on the* Cobbles

MAGGIE SULLIVAN

HarperCollins*Publishers*

HarperCollins*Publishers*
The News Building,
1 London Bridge Street,
London SE1 9GF

www.harpercollins.co.uk

First published by HarperCollins*Publishers* 2019
2

Coronation Street is an ITV Studios Production
Copyright © ITV Ventures Limited 2019

p.337 Archive photograph
© ITV/ REX/ Shutterstock

Maggie Sullivan asserts the moral right to
be identified as the author of this work

A catalogue record for this book
is available from the British Library

ISBN: 978-0-00-835475-6 (HB)
ISBN: 978-0-00-835637-8 (TPB)

Typeset in Sabon LT Std by Palimpsest Book Production Ltd, Falkirk, Stirlingshire

Printed and bound by CPI Group (UK) Ltd, Croydon CR0 4YY

MIX
Paper from
responsible sources
FSC C007454

This book is produced from independently certified FSC™ paper
to ensure responsible forest management.

For more information visit: www.harpercollins.co.uk/green

Acknowledgements

Special thanks to the two most important people who made the book possible, my editor Kate Bradley and my agent Kate Nash, for their unstinting help and support.

Thanks go to all my friends and family for their continued support and encouragement with specific thanks to those whose endless backing helped to guide me over the finishing line. To bestselling author Sue Moorcroft who was always available to offer guidance and help regarding all aspects of the writing process as well as introducing me to the delights of Malta. To Pia Fenton (who writes as Christina Courtenay) who opened her home for me and Sue Moorcroft to use as a retreat at a critical stage of the process that enabled me to forge ahead with the writing. To Ann Parker for always being at the end of a phone offering practical solutions, such as bringing me down from the ceiling when my computer swallowed my manuscript whole and refused to give it up. Thanks also to my nieces Avril and Masha and my sister-in-law Rita for allowing me the time and space to finish the book even when I was supposed to be on holiday and should have been giving them and their wonderful families my full attention.

Thanks also to Shirley Patton and Dominic Khouri at ITV for their invaluable knowledge and advice regarding *Coronation Street*.

To my wonderful nieces Avril and Masha

Chapter 1

Weatherfield, January 1945

Hilda Ogden blew the dust off the photograph frame.

'My Stan,' she sighed. She pursed her lips in the direction of his cheek only drawing back when they touched the cold glass. 'Come home soon, chuck,' she whispered as she placed it back on the tiled mantelpiece. 'The bed's cold without you.' But she had no time to dwell on her prisoner-of-war husband right now. While he remained stuck in Italy there wasn't much he could do to help her, but here at home it was Monday morning, the start of a new working week, time for Hilda to brave the spell of wintry weather that had suddenly hit Weatherfield, and hope that the thin dusting of snow that had already stuck to the wet cobbles overnight wouldn't seep through the canvas of her shoes. It was time for her to venture out to find a new job.

'We won't be needing all our workers now, so it'll be last in first out,' Al Martin the supervisor at Earnshaw's munitions factory had said last Friday when he'd handed over her wages, her notice, and a few additional hours' pay for some extra time she'd put in. 'Consider yourself lucky the boss was feeling generous enough to give you a few bob besides.' Hilda had looked down at the added coins, wondering what she might be able to treat herself to from the corner shop on the way home.

Al was one of the growing number who were convinced the war was going to end very soon now since the Home Guard had been disbanded in December and the Civil Defence was gradually being stood down and Hilda could only hope he was right. The occasional unmanned rockets were still falling in the south but things in Weatherfield had been quiet regarding bombs and sirens for several weeks now and rumour had it that it would all be over in a few months. Not that it would make it any easier for her to find a new job if all the soldiers came rushing home, but Hilda was willing to take on the kind of jobs that most men would avoid, like doing a spot of cleaning, especially if the money was put directly into her hands, no strings attached. She had shrugged as she turned to leave the office, humming in her usual tuneless way.

She'd wondered about trying for a job at the pub in Coronation Street, The Rovers Return, as it was not far from Charles Street where she and Stan were renting rooms; well, she was renting the rooms – Stan had never even seen them, of course. She'd had the occasional drink in the Rovers, met a few of the locals, but she wasn't sure about working with the stuck-up landlady, Annie Walker. The Tripe Dresser's Arms, on the other hand, around the corner from the Rovers, was more Hilda's style with its bare brickwork, sawdust sprinkled on the stone floors, and its rough-and-ready customers. It had been closed for a while but Hilda had heard it would be opening again soon with new landlords. According to one of Hilda's friends, they were doing it up and would be needing staff, so she should get down there quick.

Hilda pulled her well-worn coat round her skinny frame and shivered, watching through the windows as further flurries of snowflakes settled on the slushy paving stones. She knew the thin, unlined material wouldn't provide much protection against the chilling wind but it was all she'd managed to find in the Red Cross charity shop this winter and she hoped her thin-soled shoes wouldn't send her slip-sliding across the shiny cobbles. She shook her tightly wound curls free from the curlers she'd wrapped them in overnight and covered them with a headscarf that she tied under her chin. Checking her reflection in the wide oval mirror over the empty fireplace, she pulled up her coat collar and, with a hopeful smile, set off in search of work.

Lizzie Doyle looked down at the piece of paper in her hand, then up at the house in the middle of the terraced row. Number nine Coronation Street. It looked a lot crisper and cleaner in the black-and-white photograph than the real thing. She peeked into the folds of the blanket-wrapped bundle she was holding closely in her arms and rubbed her finger gently against the baby's pink cheeks. She felt proud that despite all the shortages the family had suffered recently at least they were as smooth and plump as any six-month-old's should be. 'Nothing a bit of soapy water and a touch of elbow grease won't shift, eh, Sammy?' She stared directly into his dark-blue eyes. 'So, how do you fancy living here, then? It doesn't look so bad, does it? And by the time our ma and the boys are installed and we've run up some bits and pieces of curtains and the like, I'm sure we can make it really nice.'

She put the key in the lock and pushed open the front door. She was about to step inside when the door to number eleven swung open, revealing a young redhead, dressed in a short skirt and brightly coloured home-knit jumper. She looked to be about twenty or twenty-one, the same age as Lizzie. The woman drew on the cigarette she held between two nicotine-stained fingers and blew the smoke high into the air.

'Morning,' she said peering beyond Lizzie into the hallway of number nine. 'You movin' in?'

'When me ma and brothers gets here with the cart, we will be, yes. You live next door, then?'

The young woman put out her hand. 'Elsie Tanner's the name. And I do indeed live here at number eleven. Welcome to Coronation Street.'

Lizzie transferred the baby into the crook of her other arm and shook Elsie's hand. 'Ta,' she said, 'I'm Lizzie Doyle.'

'We was all wondering who'd be brave enough to take it on,' Elsie said.

'Why's that?' Lizzie felt a jolt of alarm. 'What's wrong with it?'

'Oh, there's nowt really wrong, I can assure you. And I'd know as I've lived next door for nearly six years now. But you know how it is, when a house has been empty for a while – folk like to make something of it, and by the time everyone has put their two penn'orth in there's all kinds of rumours flying around, even when there's no truth to them.'

'Has it been empty that long? No wonder it smelt musty when I opened the door.'

Elsie leaned back against her own front door. 'Nowt to fret about, the last of the Todd family departed not long since.'

Lizzie didn't say anything. They couldn't afford to be choosey. They needed this house and her ma would never let any neighbourhood gossip put them off. 'I suppose folks need to keep themselves entertained,' she said eventually. 'There is a war on.'

'Aye, though maybe it'll be over soon, eh? Let's hope.' Elsie pulled herself upright. 'And let's hope you'll bring a bit of luck to the place.' She grinned, and coming down off the front doorstep, tried to peep inside the blanket. 'That your nipper?'

'My baby brother,' Lizzie said quickly, pulling the blanket back from Sammy's face. Elsie chuckled him under the chin.

'And the rest of the family are following on with all your stuff, then?'

Lizzie nodded. 'All our worldly goods. Not that there's much to 'em, but we manage.'

'How many of you is there?'

'There's me ma, Cora Doyle, the twins Seamus and Tommy – they're seven – and little Sammy here; he's not yet six months.'

'Gosh, your poor mum's got her hands full there.' Elsie laughed. 'I've got two little 'uns, so I know what it's like. They're five and two and they're always getting under my feet. No doubt you'll hear us all yelling at each other – the bricks are not so thick.' She knocked on the wall that joined the two houses to prove her point.

Lizzie grinned. 'I don't think we'll be any better. The twins are quite a handful when they've a mind. At least, Seamus is, though they think I can't tell the difference between them. And this one can do his fair share of screaming.' She beamed down at the baby who rewarded her with a toothless smile.

'Have you come far?' Elsie asked.

Lizzie hesitated, unwilling to go into detail about the family's comings and goings. 'The other side of Weatherfield,' she said eventually.

'I tell you what, then,' Elsie said, 'when your lot get here why don't you all pop in for a quick brew? I don't suppose a kettle, or coal for the fire will be the first things you'll have to hand.' She turned to go back indoors. 'I'll go and get the water up. You knock on when they arrive.'

Elsie's house looked well lived-in. There were several chairs and a large wooden table and every surface was covered with toys or discarded clothing. Elsie was tending the fire at the kitchen end of the long room when they arrived and she went to the bottom of the stairs and shouted up the stairwell, 'Linda, Dennis, get your arses down here now! We've got visitors and there's nowhere for 'em to sit. How many bloody times do I have to tell you?' She gave a resigned smile and threw her hands up in a gesture of despair.

Lizzie looked round the cluttered room. It was the

same shape as the one they had just piled their few belongings into but Elsie had made some changes, like the wall behind the two-seater couch in the living area that was papered from floor to ceiling with pictures of film stars cut from magazines.

'Don't you just love him to death?' Elsie said, making a brushing motion on the moustache on the enlarged face of Clark Gable. 'My Linda would have been called Clark if she'd been a boy. But I had to settle for Linda Darnell. Which was just as well, I'm not sure Clark's quite right for a kid to be saddled with round here and he'd certainly not have thanked me once he'd got to Bessie Street school.' She gave a throaty chuckle. 'Here, don't mind these.' Elsie picked up a little girl's vest and a liberty bodice and stuffed them behind a threadbare cushion that looked as if it had been punched into a corner of the couch.

'Sit anywhere you like,' she said, gesturing aimlessly round the room. 'The kids won't care what you do with their things. They never know where anything is anyway.' As she spoke, she swept the items from two of the chairs onto the floor before hurrying back to where the kettle had begun to whistle on the hearth. Lizzie removed the dubious remains of a knitted bunny and what was left of its fluff-ball tail from the upright chair that was closest to her and sat it down on the table, indicating that her mother, who'd taken charge of baby Sammy, should sit down.

'Linda!' Elsie shrieked from the scullery. 'What have I told you about leaving that mucky old rabbit lying around? If I find it down here one more time I'm going to chuck it straight into the dustbin.'

A little girl with sandy-coloured hair wound round strips of rags, had come down the stairs and was busy putting a one-armed doll to bed under a handkerchief. At the sound of her mother's shriek she grabbed the offending animal from the table. 'He's mine,' she said, pushing the stuffing back into the rabbit's chest, 'and you can't have him!' And she abandoned the doll and bounded back up the stairs.

'Tell that brother of yours to come down and shift his bloody things before I give 'em all to the rag 'n' bone man,' Elsie yelled after her. 'Honestly. Kids!' She turned to her visitors and shrugged in frustration.

Cora grinned her agreement. 'Don't let these two fool you, them looking as if butter wouldn't melt,' she said, indicating the twins. Elsie put down two steaming cups, not seeming to care about the new scorch rings they seared onto the table. Then she brought in her own drink and sat down to join them. There was no milk or sugar on offer.

Lizzie's gaze was drawn to a photograph of a young couple that stood on the mantelshelf in a wooden frame. She recognized the woman as Elsie, though in the picture she looked no more than a girl. She was smartly dressed in a tailored costume and was smiling confidently into

9

the camera. Her hair was coiffed in the latest style and she was holding a small bunch of flowers. The man was considerably taller, with broad shoulders that were made to look even wider by his double-breasted suit. He had a moustache that drooped over his scowling mouth.

'That's Arnold, my lumbering hulk of a husband,' Elsie told Lizzie. 'Though thank goodness, he's been away at sea since the start of the war. He says he likes me to keep the photograph on show to remind me I'm married.' Without thinking, she rubbed her arm ruefully. 'But not for much longer, if I have my way.' She picked the frame up and stared at it for several moments. Then, with a defiant look, she put it back on the mantelshelf, face down. 'But I'm sure you don't want to hear about my family nonsense.' She turned to Lizzie's mother. 'So, Cora, is your husband away fighting still?'

Lizzie was about to cut in but she had to bite her lip to stop it quivering.

'No, I'm afraid not.' It was Cora who answered, the hint of her Irish brogue still apparent. 'He'll not be coming home no more, at all.'

Elsie's cheeks coloured. 'Me and my big mouth. I'm sorry I didn't mean to . . .'

'No, it's all right,' Cora said softly. 'You weren't to know. And it's something we're all learning to live with since we got one of those dreaded letters from his captain. It was at Christmas, would you believe,' Cora said, looking away as she tried to stop her voice trembling. 'It was filled with all the usual nonsense. Died bravely, didn't suffer, blah, blah, blah. I'm sure everyone's told the same thing.'

'And just so's you know, my Joe was taken the year before,' Lizzie added quietly and she couldn't look at Elsie either as she struggled to control her breathing.

It was Seamus who broke the momentary silence. 'But that wasn't the same as losing me dad. Yous wasn't even wed yet, so it doesn't count.'

Lizzie's cheeks flamed.

'And he was American.' Tommy joined in now.

'Actually, he was Canadian,' Lizzie said, her voice cold. 'And let me tell you, every single person who fights for us counts when there's a war on.'

'But it wasn't as though he was like, one of us,' Tommy said.

'No, he was a whole lot better than either of you two! Honestly, you do say some of the most idiotic things Tommy Doyle.' Lizzie's voice had begun to rise.

'Will you shut up, both of you!' Cora suddenly shouted. She pointed a shaking finger at the twins. 'As you two don't know what you are talking about, as usual, I'll thank you to keep quiet and to show a bit of respect to your sister. You were far more interested in going out to play and causing havoc than paying much attention to Joe. Not that you saw much of your da either for that matter, except when he was home on leave, which was hardly ever.'

'You always say that,' Seamus said with an angry toss of his head, though his eyes were filling as he spoke. 'But you'd be surprised what I remember.' He scowled at Lizzie, who stared at him in alarm while Cora glowered angrily. 'I'll thank you two boys not to interfere in grown-ups' conversations, so sit down and be quiet.'

'But you always said Joe wasn't really—' Tommy persisted.

'Enough!' Cora cut in, her voice sharp now. 'Mrs Tanner doesn't want to be hearing any more of your nonsense and I won't have you upsetting our Lizzie.'

'I suppose we've all had it tough,' Elsie said. 'One way or another, we've all lost loved ones at some point.' Elsie sighed. Then her lips twisted into a smile. 'Though as far as I'm concerned, I can't pretend I'm sorry my man is overseas. I don't care if he stays there. I'm lucky I've got my kids. They make up for a hell of a lot.'

'Yes, they do,' Cora said, suddenly hugging Sammy close to her. 'When they're not trying to get above themselves,' she added rubbing her finger under her eyelids.

'But it's because of my dad that we've been able to move here,' Lizzie said. This time she was unable to stop the tremor in her voice. 'We couldn't pay the rent at our old place without my dad's wages coming in.'

'Then we found out that we were due something through the benevolent fund at Hardcastle's Mill,' Cora added. 'Archie had worked there since he were a lad, so they said on account of that they could offer us number nine Coronation Street at a much lower rent. We could hardly say no, we was getting that desperate.'

Lizzie put her hands out to Sammy, who began cooing with delight. He struggled to sit up in Cora's lap and stretched his arms towards Lizzie. She gathered him up and held him aloft, her arms high over her head. Then she lowered him back down into her lap and repeated the game several times until Sammy was beside himself with excitement.

'I don't imagine you've been able to go out to work since he was born?' Elsie said.

Lizzie opened her mouth as if to say something, but it was Cora who shook her head and then spoke. 'I can't be getting a job on account of having to look after this little one all day.' She stroked the top of Sammy's head. 'So Lizzie's the one that'll be looking for work. I used to work while she was at college and we all had such high hopes . . .' Her eyes momentarily flashed with pride. 'She was training to be a teacher, you know, before all this war business got in the way, but of course, these last few months what with the baby and all, I've had to stay home to look after him, same as I looked after the other two.'

Lizzie bit her lip. 'College was a long time ago, Ma,'

she said. 'I reckon I've earned my keep well enough since I stopped going.' She turned to Elsie. 'I was last working in a dress shop near to where we were living on the other side of Weatherfield,' she said, 'but it's too far to get to from here.'

'How would you fancy working behind a bar?' Elsie asked.

'I don't mind what I do so long as it's local and pays me a wage that'll help to keep us all going.' Lizzie sat up.

'Then you might want to try the Tripe Dresser's Arms,' Elsie said.

'Come again?' Cora laughed.

'Seriously, it's the pub at the other end of Rosamund Street and it's called the Tripe Dresser's Arms.' Elsie laughed too. 'For now, at any rate, though probably not for much longer.'

'Why's that then?' Lizzie asked.

'It's been taken over by Warner's brewery and it's being done up. Rumour has it they'll be changing the name and I reckon they'll be looking for new staff pretty soon too; before they open, at any rate, which shouldn't be too long from what I hear. And then sparks will fly.'

'How come?'

'It'll be in direct competition with the Rovers Return, the main pub on the corner of Rosamund and Coronation Street. Once the war ends, folk will be looking for bright new places to have some fun. A newly done over pub should fill the bill – and won't that be one in the eye for the lardy dah Lady Walker.' Elsie gave a self-satisfied smile.

'Who's she then when she's at home?' Lizzie wanted to know.

'Annie Walker is the landlady at the Rovers. And let me tell you, a spot of competition won't do her any harm. Mind, she's done a good job keeping things going while her husband Jack's been away in the army, I'll give her that. But the trouble is she thinks she's the bee's knees – conveniently forgets we've all had to pull our weight, one way or another. It'll do her good to be taken down a peg or two.'

'Why wasn't the Tripe's Arms, or whatever you call it, competition enough?' Lizzie was interested.

'I suppose you could say it was a bit rough. Far rougher than the Rovers. Though I would never have admitted that to Annie Walker. She liked to think the Tripe wasn't in the same league as the Rovers. Spit-and-sawdust they call it round here. But it wasn't so bad. I've drunk there on occasion. But now there's to be a new landlord and I've heard he wants to smarten it up some, so there could be fireworks between him and Mrs Walker.' She rubbed her hands together. 'Bit of rivalry could be good for business.'

'Sounds like it might even do us a bit of good too,' Cora said. 'So?' she said and turned to Lizzie. 'You'd best get in there quick if you've half a mind to land yourself a job. What do you think?'

Lizzie nodded her head in agreement. Serving behind a bar was not what she'd planned to be doing when she'd first left school, but then life had turned out so differently that now she really had no choice. Beggars can't be choosers, as her ma so often reminded her, so she said, 'I think I should get down there as soon as possible, and find out when they intend to start hiring.'

There were ladders up outside the pub, in front of the large plate-glass window, and when Lizzie arrived two men were wrestling with a freshly painted sign that read, The Pride of Weatherfield. An older-looking man, who not so long ago had probably been part of the Home Guard or one of the firewatchers, was slowly applying a coat of glossy black paint to a side door. He was obviously in no hurry and was alternating swipes of the paint brush with long draws on his cigarette when Lizzie approached him.

'Excuse me, but do you know when they'll be opening for business?'

The man took the opportunity to rest the brush in the paint pot and suck an extra few puffs from his cigarette as he eyed her up and down.

'Desperate for a drink, are you?' He gave a phlegmy laugh.

'No,' Lizzie retorted, 'but I wouldn't say no to a job.'

'Well, put it this way, they can't open before I've finished this,' he said waving the paintbrush in the air, 'an' I've to make this here pot go as far as I can, so you can work it out yourself.' He coughed and laughed again.

Lizzie turned away as he went back to his work, chuckling.

A young woman in a headscarf was passing by the large frontage, her lips pursed so that she looked as if she was whistling quietly. She stopped when Lizzie spoke to the workman and glanced up at the sign, interested in his reply.

'Glad to hear you ask that,' she addressed Lizzie. 'Cos I've been wondering the same thing.'

'You a barmaid an' all?' Lizzie asked.

'Oh no! I tried it once but I'm not quick enough at making change. I'll stick to my cleaning. At least I know I'm good at that. My name's Hilda Ogden, by the way.' She extended a hand in Lizzie's direction.

Lizzie shook it. 'Lizzie, Lizzie Doyle,' she said. 'Where've you been working till now, Hilda?'

'I've been up at the moonitions place up the road. Very important we were, once upon a time, making bullets and the like, but they're beginning to lay folk off now, starting with me! I thought I should get down here quick to find out when they might start hiring so's I could get a new job. Perhaps one more suited to my talons.'

17

Lizzie smothered a smile at Hilda's unfortunate mischoice of words. 'It looks like we might well be first in line,' she said, 'though I'm sure we won't be the last.'

'You live round here then?' Hilda asked.

Lizzie nodded. 'I've just moved into Coronation Street with my ma and . . . my three brothers. And you?'

'I'm living in Charles Street, not very far away,' Hilda said. She pointed in the general direction of the next set of terraces. 'At least, I'll be there until my Stan is mobbed and comes home from Italy. It would be handy to work here. Whereabouts in Coronation Street are you?'

'Number nine'.

'Like it?'

'We've not really settled in yet, though everyone I've met so far seems very friendly. In fact, it were our next-door neighbour as told me about this new pub.'

Hilda gave a short laugh. 'She obviously didn't want the job then,' she tittered. With a nervous gesture she retied her headscarf under her chin, pulling the knot away from her throat, then she patted the curls that stuck out at the front as if for reassurance.

'I suppose not,' Lizzie said. 'But she seems nice. Like she enjoys a good laugh. I reckon she needs it with two young kiddies to look out for. But, no, she didn't seem to be interested in the job herself.' Hilda tapped the side of her nose. 'Maybe she's one of them who finds other ways of putting a bit of extra food on the table, treats for the kiddies and the like, if you follow my meaning. I've heard talk of some round here who liked to hang around them Yankee soldiers, always cadging ciggies or chocolates or the odd pair of nylons from them.' Lizzie looked at her sharply, but Hilda had turned away and was using the window as a mirror, a benign smile on her face.

The two men had successfully managed to string the banner announcing The Pride of Weatherfield above the plate-glass window and were fastening a smaller brewery sign for Warner's Ales to the wall.

'What do you say we knock on and see if anyone's at home yet?' Lizzie suggested.

'Good idea, chuck,' Hilda said, and she immediately linked arms with Lizzie as they faced the front doors. But they were saved the bother of knocking, for at that moment one of the doors swung open, like in the Western saloon bars Lizzie had seen at the pictures, and it nearly knocked over the painter. A large man with a balding head, his lumberjack shirt barely fastening over his corporate-sized belly, emerged. He didn't look in her direction, but she could see how he stood his ground, feet planted firmly apart, his features set in a no-nonsense stare as he folded his arms and addressed the man with the paintbrush.

'How's things going, Fred?' he barked. 'How much longer?'

'All under control, Bob. No need to fret. We'll soon be done and out of your hair.' Fred took a particularly long drag on his cigarette and nodded towards Lizzie and Hilda. 'I think these young ladies might be wanting a word with you.'

Bob looked at them then and Lizzie immediately felt she was under close scrutiny. She disengaged her arm from Hilda's and tried to meet his fearsome gaze with a confident air. 'Are you the landlord here?' she said.

The man's eyes narrowed. 'I am that. Who wants to know?'

'My name's Lizzie Doyle and I came to ask when you're likely to be hiring new staff?'

The man clicked his heels, smiling suddenly. 'Bob Bennett at your service.'

She hesitated, then said, 'I'd like to apply to be a barmaid.'

'Would you now, Miss Doyle? And you've worked behind a bar before, have you?' he asked in a mock-Irish accent and Lizzie could feel her hackles rise.

'I'm not actually Irish,' she said. She looked at him directly now, in a show of bravado. 'That would be my mother you'd be confusing me with.'

'No offence,' he said, putting his hands up as if she were holding a gun on him. 'I'm always one for a little joke. Why don't you come inside? We've no need to conduct this little interview out in the cold, now have we?' He put his arm round her waist and gave her a squeeze as he made to usher her inside. Lizzie wriggled out of his grasp and turned round quickly, grabbing hold of Hilda's arm again.

'Oh, but my friend Hilda's looking for a job too. She's an excellent cleaner and comes highly recommended. You might be interested in hiring the both of us at the same time.'

Bob didn't reply but flashed a disdainful glance at Hilda before turning his attention back to Lizzie. Hilda gave a nervous giggle and hung on to Lizzie's arm as Bob beckoned them to follow him indoors.

Chapter 2

The refurbishment of the old pub, now to be called the Pride of Weatherfield, had almost been completed, and according to Bob he was preparing to open the doors to much razzmatazz on 14 February, St Valentine's day.

'After that,' he said, 'there'll be live shows every Saturday night with a variety of up-and-coming cabaret artists and me, of course, giving them the benefit of my old magic act in between.'

There was no doubt the builders had done a good job on the refurbishment and Lizzie liked what she saw when Bob gave her and Hilda a brief tour of the premises. He didn't seem concerned that she had no actual bar experience. 'I'm sure you're a fast learner,' he said with a wink. So, despite any reservations she may have had about his somewhat over-familiar behaviour, she couldn't afford to refuse when he put his arm around her shoulders and offered her the job as a full-time barmaid.

'Play your cards right and pretty soon you could find that you're in charge,' he said. 'I need someone I can rely on and you look like that kind of someone.' But before Lizzie could respond he'd moved on to Hilda, officially hiring her as the Pride's new cleaner.

'I have to say, this year's starting out a lot better than the last one. Don't you think?' Hilda interrupted Lizzie's thoughts as they left the pub together after their successful interviews. 'I call that a good morning's work.' She swiped one hand across the other several times in quick succession to indicate her satisfaction.

Lizzie nodded; she didn't want to dampen Hilda's enthusiasm voicing her reservations. She was just thankful that she had a job, and that at least it wasn't in a munitions factory.

'What with the war ending and all the soldiers coming home, the future's looking right exciting, isn't it?' Hilda continued to bubble as she stared ahead dreamily, but Lizzie was too bound up with her own thoughts to answer. Suddenly Hilda giggled. 'Fancy, live shows with singers and comicals in Weatherfield every Saturday night, whatever next? I think I'm going to like working there,' she said. 'What about you, Lizzie? You're very quiet. What do you think?'

'Hmm,' Lizzie said, 'I was thinking about what it might feel like actually pulling pints. But at least I shan't have to worry about putting food on the table at home for the next little while.'

Bob organized a meeting for the newly hired staff the day before the Pride officially opened its doors and it seemed fitting that he addressed them from the stage, for he had a showman's air about him in everything he did. And Lizzie could see from the start that he was not a man to be challenged.

'I've already started developing a weekly entertainment programme as you can see from the flyers I've left on the tables,' Bob informed them all. Then he gave a brief introductory welcome to Lizzie and Hilda, Pat Evans and several other young women who he'd hired as part-time barmaids, and a couple of shifty-looking older men who were helping out on a casual basis in the cellar. 'And for our first night I've booked a local singer who's recently returned from a tour abroad where she's been one of the star acts entertaining the troops.' Lizzie looked with interest at the leaflets that were being passed round, but was disappointed to find she'd never heard of the singer despite the build-up. She whispered as much to Hilda.

'Me neither,' Hilda responded. Her voice was well

above a whisper and she received a glowering look from Bob.

'On show nights, I'll be acting as compere,' Bob continued, expanding his chest as he tucked his thumbs under his braces and strode back and forth across the stage. 'So, I'll introduce the acts, tell a few jokes and perform the odd magic trick or two like I used to in the good old days in Blackpool.' He was beaming now.

'The one thing I'm asking everyone else to do, as you can see from the leaflets, is to wear something special for opening night,' he said. 'I would say wear your Sunday best, but that might be very dull.' There was a titter from the floor. 'So, let's see if we can find a way to brighten things up and really let our hair down.' He gave a lurid wink. 'If you know what I mean. I'm offering a prize for the brightest and best so let's see what you can do.'

'Does that mean I'll have to take my curlers out?' Hilda chuckled. 'Only he didn't say anything about hairdos,' she said and Lizzie had to stifle a yelp as she felt Hilda's elbow in her ribs.

'If we show the punters on the first night that this pub is really something out of the ordinary, then the whole neighbourhood will want to come to see what's going on. And once they're through those doors,' he pointed, 'all we have to do is to make sure to keep the beer flowing. In one night we'll become more than the Pride of Weatherfield – we'll be the *talk* of bloomin'

Weatherfield and we'll knock our rivals, as the saying goes, into a cocked hat.' This time he winked in Lizzie's direction and she felt the blood rise to her cheeks.

'Good luck, everyone!' He raised both his arms high over his head in a sort of triumphal wave. 'See you on Wednesday.'

Lizzie grumbled to her mother about the idea of dressing up for the opening. 'What do I want to waste time and money getting dressed up for? It's not as though I'm trying to get a new boyfriend or anything,' she said. 'Who'd want me anyway?' she added.

'Lizzie, you've got to stop talking like that. You can't keep hiding away,' Cora said, trying not to show her exasperation. 'You're young. What's wrong with dressing up once in a while? You've got to look to the future and stop dwelling on the past.'

'It's not as simple as that, as well you know.' A tear trickled down Lizzie's face. 'I won't ever be able to let go of the past.' She wiped the end of her nose with her handkerchief. 'Besides, it's not as if we've got enough money or sufficient clothing coupons to buy any new material, so what am I going to do, even if I wanted to go along with it? I've not even got anything I could alter.'

Lizzie pulled her only smart dress off the clothes rail in the bedroom they shared and held it against her while she peered down, trying to gauge its appropriateness. She shook her head. 'I can't wear this. It's far too old-fashioned, too big, and the grey looks so dull.' Her voice was close to tears again as she threw it down on the bed, then she shut her eyes quickly as she remembered the last time she had worn it. She had to breathe deeply before she could risk opening her eyes. Then she saw Cora had picked it up and was scrutinizing it.

'It's not as though there's enough material in it to be able to turn it into something different,' Cora said as she hung it back on the rail. 'But I tell you what, why don't you try on that green taffeta dress of mine? There's lots of material to play with in that.'

'You mean the one you hired for that big dance you went to with Daddy before the war?' Lizzie turned to her mother.

Cora laughed. 'You make it sound like I stole it, which I never did.'

'I know. The shop closed down before you could return it after the do.'

'Well, it's true,' Cora said. 'So what was I supposed to do with it? Besides, it was well worn by the time I got it. But you're welcome to have it if you'd like, so you are. Let's see what we can do with it.' Cora was already standing on a chair and, lifting down one of the boxes from the shelf above the clothes rail, she set it on the bed. There was a rustle of tissue paper as she removed the lid and a strong smell of camphor rose from inside. The anti-moth crystals had evaporated and all that remained were the slender chains of lavender-coloured thread. She carefully unpacked the emerald-green, shot-taffeta gown, standing back to admire it while Lizzie looked at it critically.

'I suppose I could take out one of the panels in the skirt, nip it in at the waist on either side, and then shorten it. That would make it quite stylish,' she said. 'Providing Gran's sewing machine still works, of course.'

Cora laughed. 'It better had, or else we've been carting it about with us like a dead donkey. I was hoping to run up some curtains if I can find enough bits of material at the charity shop.'

Lizzie pulled the dress against her and tried to look at her reflection in the broken fragment of mirror her mother held up for her.

'It's a bit worn under the arms, but I could take a tuck there to get rid of the faded bits, if you really wouldn't mind. I'd hate to spoil it by playing about with it too much.' Lizzie sounded uncertain now as she looked to her mother for approval.

'It really doesn't matter what you do with it,' Cora said. 'I think there might even be some beads in the sewing box. You could dress it up a bit and it'd look really pretty, so it would.'

Lizzie turned to her mother and smiled. 'If you're sure?' Then she leaned forward and, grabbing her by the shoulders, kissed her lightly on the cheek. 'Thanks, Ma,' she said.

Cora laughed. 'You might as well enjoy it. I'll certainly not have any use for it again.' She stroked her hand gently over the material and it seemed to change colour as she touched it. Tears were in her voice as she spoke and Lizzie put her arms round her, holding her close for a moment.

'Oh Ma, don't say that.'

'Why not? It's true. I'm not likely to need it again, now am I? When will I go dancing? Besides which, I'd never be able to fit into it; and if I did, it would only make me look like mutton dressed as lamb.' She laughed ironically then immediately became serious again. 'No, my love, you've still got your whole life in front of you and it's important you remember that. I know it's hard, because of – well, because of everything that's happened, but you mustn't hide yourself away.'

'Ma! I hate when you talk like that when you know that I can't—'

'Yes, I know that it still hurts but it doesn't mean you can't have some fun sometimes. Your life can't stop because of . . . because of what happened. So, you wear it and enjoy it.' To her relief, Lizzie began to peel off her clothes and prepared to try the dress on.

Lizzie was pleased with her sewing efforts and on the afternoon of the opening night paraded her new dress for Cora's approval.

'It looks far better on you than it ever did on me,' Cora said, generously.

Lizzie secretly agreed and she had to admit that the new outfit made her feel more light-hearted than she had done for a long time. 'It looks very posh, doesn't it?' Lizzie chuckled. 'Though it feels very strange getting dressed up in an outfit like this only to go to work.'

'I'm sure it does, but maybe that means you're ready to have some fun. It's put a real smile on your face.'

'You know you don't have to worry about me, Ma,' Lizzie said, with an optimism she didn't really feel. 'I'll get through somehow, even though it's not easy right now.'

'But I do worry. You're too young to—'

'Oh, no, not tonight, Ma, please. It's going to be hard enough on the first night in a new job and all that.'

'I know, love, and I'll be thinking of you.' Cora stood on tiptoe and, taking Lizzie's face between her two hands, kissed her daughter's forehead. 'Safe home. That's all I'll say. I look forward to hearing all about it.'

Lizzie arrived at the Pride well before opening time and she had to ring the bell in order to get in.

'Now there's a corker if ever I saw one!' It was Bob who opened the door, an admiring look on his face when Lizzie's coat fell open as she stepped inside. He gave a long, loud whistle and Lizzie blushed. Normally she would have reciprocated the compliment without thinking, but when she glanced up at Bob it was all she could do not to laugh because he looked like he'd stepped out of a circus ring. His red master-of-ceremonies jacket had seen better days and it was obviously some time since he'd been able to fasten together its gold braided edges.

'Staff coats this way,' Bob said, indicating the passageway between the bar and the kitchen, and Lizzie did her best to squeeze past without touching him. As she stepped into the bar she was impressed by the amount of work that had obviously gone into the decoration, even if it did look rather gaudy, for the whole room was festooned with streamers and balloons and cut-out red hearts.

'I only hope the punters appreciate the effort we've put into all this,' Bob said behind her.

'I'm sure they will,' Lizzie said.

'Well, you'd best get settled in behind the bar, then,' he said. 'We can't afford to open late on our first night.'

Hilda, too, made an effort with her appearance for the opening-night celebrations, although in her position as cleaner and general charlady she didn't imagine anyone would expect her to come dressed in anything too fancy. She chuckled at the thought. Just as well, for she didn't possess anything fancy!

The only smart thing she had in her wardrobe was

the pale-green serge suit with its pencil slim skirt and nipped in jacket that Stan's mother had given her for her wedding two years before. She'd worn it then with a plain white cotton blouse that she'd tucked in at the waist and she saw no reason not to wear the same blouse now. She abandoned the headscarf that she normally wrapped round her hair like a turban and discarded the curlers that were usually hidden underneath. Instead, she brushed out her fair curls and styled them into a victory roll that she tucked in and pinned like a pie crust around her head. She had suggested that she and Lizzie might walk down to the Pride together but Lizzie had persuaded her otherwise.

'It won't be necessary for you to be there so early, Hilda,' Lizzie said. 'I'd wait till things warm up, if I were you. You're not on duty, so if you time it right you can make an entrance like a lady.'

'Ooh, just imagine,' Hilda said, 'someone announcing: "The Right Honourable Hilda Ogden",' She put on a high-pitched voice which was how she imagined a posh voice might sound. 'But I suppose you're right, there's not much point, and I will have to be there bright and early the next morning.'

Lizzie laughed. 'Not in your best togs! I'd rather not think about what the place might be like by then.'

By the time Hilda arrived, the newly decorated lounge bar was filled with people from the surrounding neighbourhood and it took her several minutes to push her way through to the bar to claim her free drink with the voucher she'd been handed at the door. She saw Lizzie manning the pumps at the far end of the counter while Pat Evans was serving at the other. Both girls seemed to be rushed off their feet so she could do no more than wave at her friend and find a place in the queue. It was Pat who eventually exchanged Hilda's voucher for a port and lemon, though Lizzie did look up long enough to point to Hilda's hair and give her the thumbs-up sign of approval. Bob was nowhere to be seen. Hilda bumped into Phyllis Bakewell, an old work colleague who she'd shared a bench with in the munitions factory, and she smiled at her and said hello. Phyllis didn't seem to recognize her at first and Hilda didn't know whether to feel pleased or offended.

'It's Hilda. Hilda Ogden,' Hilda said.

'Of course!' Phyllis said, after staring for several moments. 'Sorry, you must have wondered why I was ignoring you, only you look so – so different.'

Hilda patted her hair as if to indicate what the difference might be and was pleased to feel that not one curl had moved out of place.

'I'd never have known it was you until you opened your mouth, and then I'd have known that voice anywhere,' Phyllis said.

When Phyllis added her own inimitable loud cackle of a laugh, Hilda was taken aback. 'Likewise, I'm sure,' she said, not really knowing what else to say.

'I meant, I'm only used to seeing you in your work clothes. You look quite different dressed up like that and without your headscarf.' Phyllis tried to make amends. 'You look very smart, if I might say so.'

'Ta very much,' Hilda said. She decided Phyllis had meant it kindly and managed a smile. 'I always like to get dressed up for my Stan,' she added.

'Is he here? I didn't know any local lads had arrived back yet.' Phyllis's gaze surveyed the room. 'Thankfully my Ron never went away.'

'No, no. He was still in the prisoner-of-war camp in Italy, last I heard. But hopefully it'll not be long now.' Hilda gave a dreamy smile. 'He likes to see me dressed up, does my husband – and he's especially fond of this costume,' she went on, not wanting to admit that she had only worn it on the one previous occasion. 'So I thought I'd give it an airing before he actually gets here.' With that, Hilda pressed her lips tightly together, made a slight humming sound, and moved away to one of the chairs that seemed to be vacant. She found she was sitting next to a glum-looking man she reckoned must be one of Lizzie's neighbours in Coronation Street. Hilda had seen him before, she recognized him from his days as a volunteer air-raid warden, though he didn't seem to know her. She remembered that in those days she'd thought of him as 'a proper gent' and he had taken his job very seriously. He was always shouting at people about the blackout and he'd never smiled much. She was surprised to see him at the new pub, for as far as she knew he was one of the regulars at the other pub in the area, the Rovers Return. But tonight he was nursing his free pint at the Pride, waiting for the entertainment to begin.

'I don't think you're the only one deserting the Rovers tonight,' Hilda said with a mischievous smile.

The man stared at her blankly as she sat down. 'I remember you with your tin hat when you was a warden,' she said. 'I was the one you were always shouting at for being the last to clear off the street when the sirens went.' She giggled. 'I always seemed to be forgetting something when the doodlebugs were practically over-head.' He still showed no signs of recognition, so Hilda said, 'There's quite a few others as I recognize from the shelters here tonight, folks who said they drank at the Rovers,' and he finally nodded. 'Happen like me they've come to check out what all the fuss is about, now they've done this place up. I wanted to see what they've made of it, because I remember when it still had the reputation of not being a place you could take a lady.'

Hilda pursed her lips, not wanting to admit Stan had brought her here on several occasions when it was still called the Tripe Dresser's Arms. 'You don't have to apologize,' she said stiffly. 'It doesn't matter to me where you choose to drink. It's the landlady up at the Rovers I feel sorry for. She's the one who'll be licking her wounds tonight.'

'If I pays me money I can take me choice of where I sup,' the man said, and he took a long drink from his pint. 'Happen Annie Walker will have to look sharp if she wants to keep hold of all her regulars on a Saturday night.'

'I, of course, have the privilege of working here,' Hilda said, unable to keep the boastfulness out of her voice, 'so I've come here tonight to offer my support.' Her hands strayed to the nape of her neck where she detected several loosened strands of hair and she wound them nervously round her finger into a small roll. She gave a satisfied smile. 'At least, that is, until my Stan gets back from Italy. He's a prisoner of war over there, been there a while, but if the news is anything to go by, I reckon he could be coming home soon.'

'I'm not so sure about that,' the man said. 'Haven't you heard what's been going on in Germany? Our boys have been involved in some kind of bombing raids over there, a place called Dresden. That could set things back a fair bit, so it's not over yet.' Before he could say more, Phyllis Bakewell had pushed her way through the crowd and had come to sit with them followed by an even larger lady with a strident voice who, it seemed, ran the corner shop where Phyllis was registered with her ration coupons. From their ongoing argument it seemed the two had had many a clash with Phyllis having strong words to say about the lack of availability of certain food items for the shop's regular customers.

37

She practically accused the shopkeeper of running a black market, but before the larger woman could reply, Phyllis suddenly changed tack and turned to Hilda.

'So, you say your husband's still overseas. Stan Ogden you said his name was? – how can you be sure they'll let him come home soon?' she said as she set down her Campari and soda on the little table between them and chortled as she tried to twist her outsized body in the chair so that she could face Hilda.

'Of course they will, and don't you be saying otherwise,' Hilda said, shocked at the suggestion.

'I'd be careful what you wish for,' another voice said, 'for you may not want him home if it's the Stan Ogden I remember.' Hilda looked up, horrified, particularly as she didn't know the man who now joined the group, but it seemed it was Ron Bakewell, Phyllis's husband, and that he'd known Stan as a young lad. Ron sat down. 'Well,' he said, 'I hope you've got a job that pays well, cos otherwise you'll be hard put to keep his body and soul together as well as your own.' There was a general titter of amusement among the group and Hilda bristled. She was about to respond with a sharp-tongued reply but Ron turned away from her as he pulled up a stool so that he could sit next to his wife.

'If you've not, maybe he won't want to come home after all,' Phyllis said as he joined them. 'It might dawn on him that he'd be better off staying where he is with guaranteed sunshine and regular meals.'

At that, everyone in the little group laughed and Hilda, uncertain at first, decided to join in, somehow managing to reassure herself that it was just a joke and that they meant no harm. Over the years she'd often been the butt of others' jokes, but she had found that if she smiled and didn't object, their playful banter would sometimes make her feel as if she was one of them, even if she wasn't.

It had been like that with the kids she went to school with, when she'd tried so hard to be one of the gang. They'd teased her mercilessly, always picking on her faults and shortcomings, never seeing any good in her. They used to call her 'two planks'. 'Cos that's what you're as thick as,' they'd chant when they were out in the schoolyard during playtime or racing off home at the end of the day. Then they would scamper away, leaving her on her own with no way to defend herself against any of the gangs from other schools and with no chance of running fast enough to catch up with them. How she'd hated those children then. Most of them were worse off than her family was, though it was hard for her to remember that when they tried to lord it over her pretending that they weren't. But unlike many of the others, she and her two brothers at least had something to eat most days and they had clothes to wear, even if they didn't always have shoes. She'd also consoled herself that her mother and father had shown her some love –

when they weren't drunk. But it wasn't in her nature to call the other kids bad names, however poor or stupid they were.

In the end she'd had the last laugh over those she considered to be 'uppity', because here she was now, a married woman with an important job in a new pub. A job that paid her enough to rent two rooms in the heart of Weatherfield. Sadly, so many of the young lads had been killed or injured in the war, while most of the girls she knew had made disastrous marriages that usually involved a trail of children, even at their young age. 'I wasn't too thick to recognize a good 'un when I met my Stan,' she reminded herself whenever she thought back to those difficult school years. 'I spotted him as the man for me right from the start, and even if he didn't exactly match up to Clark Gable, he was smart enough to live out most of the war in a prisoner-of-war camp in the sun.'

Suddenly a loud voice was calling for hush and Hilda, remembering where she was, saw that her new boss, Bob Bennett, was banging on an empty pint mug with a spoon. He had come on stage wearing a top hat that looked as old as his master-of-ceremonies outfit and was perched uncomfortably on the top of his head, but as he began to speak he took the hat off and stood it upside down on a chair by the microphone.

'Ladies and gentlemen, if I could take a few minutes of your time,' Bob began. 'I'm afraid I'll have to shout while they're still playing about with the electrics back there, so I hope you can all hear me.'

There were shouts of, 'Get on with it before the lights go out,' and 'Anyone got a spare bob for the meter?' but Bob was not a stranger to projecting his voice.

'It might seem strange to be celebrating the reopening of our lovely new pub on a Wednesday night,' Bob continued, 'but then as you know this is no ordinary Wednesday night.' He paused while he scanned the room, taking in the large crowd. Then he lifted the tankard and shouted, 'This is Valentine's night.'

'I'll drink to that!' someone called out.

'Indeed!' said Bob, raising his pint pot in the air once more. 'So let's have a toast to all our brave soldiers, especially to our absent loved ones to let them know we're missing them and waiting for them to come safely home.' Then he turned his head in different directions as he mouthed the words, 'and we're keeping the bed warm' with an exaggerated wink, and several individual cheers went up. 'And let's have another toast,' Bob went on, 'to all those who've made it here today, on this very special, romantic night. Let's raise our glasses to Saint Valentine.' He turned towards Lizzie as he lifted his glass.

'To Saint Valentine!' everyone in the room responded.

'To the end of the war!' someone else called out and a rousing cheer went up again. As the room quietened, Hilda could hear Ron Bakewell muttering to his wife about possible delays to the war ending because of Dresden and the RAF bombers and Phyllis passed the news on like the Chinese whispers game they used to play in school. But Hilda had set her mind on the thought that the war was ending and that Stan would be home soon and she didn't want to hear anything to the contrary, so she stood up and began edging her way towards the other end of the counter where she could see Lizzie was still swapping vouchers for free drinks.

'All we want now,' Bob was speaking again, 'is for the war to end sooner than they've been forecasting recently.'

For a moment Hilda paused as people cheered and banged their fists on the tables.

'For when that happens, an even greater celebration will be in order,' he said.

'How about a free jar every night of the week?' a voice called out, and it took some time for the ripples of laughter to die down.

Bob raised his hand for silence. 'I can't promise free booze, but I can guarantee that having fun is what this pub is all about.' He gave a chuckle. 'And that's what makes it different from any other pub in the area. So just make sure you don't get them confused. "Any excuse for a knees-up" is our motto, because you must admit fun has been in rather short supply of late.'

Hilda had finally reached Lizzie and she leaned over

the counter. 'From where I'm standing, Bob Bennett looks like's never been short of having a bit of fun,' she said quietly, then she pursed her lips.

'I'm sure that's true,' Lizzie said with a grin.

'No, I didn't mean it like that,' Hilda said. 'Every time I look at him he seems to have his hand on someone's backside. And I'm just making sure it isn't mine.'

Lizzie raised her eyebrows.

'And he never gets within spitting distance of *you* that he isn't putting his arm round you and giving you a quick squeeze. Don't think I haven't noticed,' Hilda added wagging her finger at Lizzie.

Now Lizzie laughed. 'I can't say as I've noticed, Hilda, honestly, I've been that busy, but I'm sure he means no harm.'

'Maybe, maybe not,' Hilda said, 'though I'm not surprised tonight when you've got that really pretty frock on. It's far too nice for work. But I can tell you now I'll have something to say if he lays one finger on me.'

'I don't know how he's resisted that tonight, Hilda,' Lizzie said. Hilda turned to look at her sharply, not sure what to make of the remark. 'In fact, you'll have to look out for all the men. No, I mean it,' Lizzie said when Hilda protested. 'I've not seen you dressed up like that before and I've been wanting to tell you since you first came in, that you look lovely. I love the way you've brushed out your hair too,' Lizzie said. 'It's very in vogue, and it really suits you. It's good to see what's been hidden underneath your headscarf all this time. I can see I'll have to persuade you to leave off with your curlers more often.'

Hilda smiled coyly now. 'Ta very much.' She chuckled, her face suffused bright pink, and she had to turn her head away so that Lizzie wouldn't see her eyes glistening. 'That's the nicest thing anyone's ever said to me,' she said, her voice unsteady. 'Though it won't be me as wins the prize tonight.'

Bob's welcome speech was going down well, for everyone was smiling now and seemed in cheerful mood. Hilda kept hearing grunts of 'hear, hear' and saw nods of agreement all around as Bob continued speaking.

'So, are we ready for the fun and entertainment that's about to begin right here and right now?' Bob leaned forward. He cupped his hand behind one ear and waited until the crowd had shouted, 'Yes!'

'OK, then first things first,' Bob said. 'As you may have noticed, our staff have made a special effort to dress up for you tonight and don't they all look splendid?' He paused while a cheer went up and there was a round of applause. 'Well, we promised a prize for the best dressed and I'm sure you'll all agree that that prize must go to our terrific barmaid – Miss Lizzie Doyle! A round of applause ladies and gentlemen, please.'

Lizzie was surprised and pleased when her name was

called and there were approving shouts and wolf whistles from the crowd as Bob pulled her up onto the stage and then handed her a bottle of gin.

'Congratulations and well done to Lizzie,' Bob said, putting his arm round her shoulders and pulling her towards him in a flamboyant embrace. 'I'm sure I'm speaking for everyone here when I say that we look forward to seeing you dressed up every night,' he said, then he gave her a clumsy embrace and Lizzie was aware once more that she would need to keep her eye on him as he held on to her for several moments longer than was necessary while his hands slid down her dress to cup her backside and give it a pinch. She turned her head sharply when she realized he was going to kiss her, and his lips landed on her cheek but he recovered quickly and didn't let his smile drop. He patted Lizzie playfully. 'Now, please enjoy the rest of the evening,' Bob said. 'The first drink, as you all know, is on the house.'

'Been watering down the beer already?' some wag shouted and everyone laughed again, more loudly this time.

'I'll pretend I didn't hear that,' was Bob's response when he could make himself heard once more, and his tone was still jocular.

Hilda frowned. 'There's many a truth in jest, as my mother used to say, so I'll definitely be keeping an eye out for that one,' she muttered, though no one heard her for Bob was still talking.

'All I can say is that the Rovers Return must be deserted tonight,' Bob said with a broad grin. 'And that's how I hope it'll remain every night from now on. Remember, Saturday nights are cabaret nights and only the best will do for the Pride of Weatherfield. We'll be providing you with top-class singers and the funniest comics this side of the Pennines. And of course, at any time there could be the odd bit of magic thrown in.' As he said that, he turned over the top hat that he'd parked on the chair and shook it vigorously before showing it to the crowd. People leaned forward, straining to see what was inside, and they looked disappointed when they saw nothing more than a black lining. So a genuine gasp went up when Bob reached inside and, with nothing more than a flick of his wrist, began producing a seemingly endless stream of brightly coloured silk scarves. When the flow of fresh scarves had stopped and he had dropped them all on to the stage, he stooped to pick them up and began knotting them together, giving one end of the string to a member of the audience to hold and stretching out the whole string for everyone to see. He bowed slightly in acknowledgement of the spontaneous rumble of applause.

'Thank you, ladies and gents,' he said. 'Now – let the evening's entertainment begin!' He was about to make a grand gesture to herald the entrance of their first guest when there was a shout of, 'Three cheers for the Pride of Weatherfield!' and, with a chinking of glasses, a chorus of assorted voices bellowed, 'Hip, hip, hurray!' several times.

Bob looked delighted, then looked up at the clock on the wall. He took a moment to check that the microphone was working and then yelled, 'Now, will you please put your hands together in the traditional way, and give a warm welcome to our own Weatherfield nightingale, Miss Jenny Farrington!'

Lizzie was run off her feet for the rest of the evening once the show had begun. She was pulling pints, mostly for the men, and mixing port with lemon, and gin with tonic for most of the ladies once the singer had begun her act. She couldn't help thinking about the Rovers Return, and feeling sorry for the landlady of the pub that Bob saw as his main rival. Could there possibly be enough people in the neighbourhood to fill both pubs, she wondered, now that all the GIs had shipped out?

Lizzie knew Elsie Tanner often drank in the Rovers, but not tonight, she thought, seeing her neighbour making her way to the bar.

'My, don't you look posh,' Elsie said, peering over the counter to admire the full effect of Lizzie's dress. 'No wonder I heard him say you'd won the prize. That really is gorgeous, and the colour suits you. You're very talented, you know.'

'I didn't make it from scratch,' Lizzie protested.

'As good as, from what I saw. I can't believe it's the same old dress you showed me. I tell you something, you can make me one the next time I get married.'

Lizzie laughed.

'I'm serious,' Elsie said, 'but in the meantime I'll have a G & T when you've got a minute.' Elsie brandished her voucher. 'So who's in tonight to appreciate this work of art? Though I don't suppose you're familiar with enough of the locals to know who's who.'

'Afraid not.' Lizzie sighed. 'Though right now I'm too tired to notice anyone. I feel done in already. Don't tell anyone, but I'm not used to these kinds of hours. I've been run off my feet since I got here and the night's only halfway through!'

'I think it's busier than anyone thought it was going to be,' Elsie said. 'It's made quite an impact. Most of the Rovers seem to be here tonight. Here, this might help.' She pulled a packet of cigarettes from her handbag and offered one to Lizzie.

Lizzie shook her head. 'I'm sure it won't always be like this,' she said, 'but once word got out that we had a free round of drinks on offer it wasn't surprising the crowds came out.'

''ark at you with the we,' Elsie laughed. 'You've not been here five minutes.'

Lizzie blushed. 'I know, but I do feel right at home. Anyway, I'd rather be kept busy, no time to think.'

'The devil makes work for idle hands, eh?' Elsie said. 'Isn't that what they say?'

Lizzie felt the warmth rush to her cheeks. 'Oh, thanks very much!' she said and laughed.

'It's one of the favourite sayings of the Rovers' very own Ena Sharples,' Elsie said. 'She's the one I was telling you about who can bring two walls together any day of the week.'

'Is she here tonight?' Lizzie said. 'Maybe I'll get to see her in the flesh.'

Elsie looked around. 'She is indeed, with her two cronies as ever.'

'So, which one is she? Or can I guess?'

'Look over there and I'm sure you can tell me,' Elsie said and she pointed across the smoke-filled room. Lizzie's first gaze was drawn to a table where a young man was sitting alone, nursing a pint as he scanned the room. There was something about his face and she found it hard to look away. His dark hair was cut very short as though he was in the services, but what caught her attention was his fine moustache. For a moment he looked so familiar that Lizzie almost cried 'Joe!' and she made an involuntary movement towards him.

'Are you all right?' Elsie asked. 'You look like you've seen a ghost.'

'No, I'm fine,' Lizzie said. 'It was nothing, really.' She closed her eyes for a few moments and took some deep breaths. 'I'm sorry, I don't know what I was thinking.'

She forced her eyes open. 'Now, show me again, where's this Ena Sharples.'

Elsie pointed and this time Lizzie concentrated on searching for a table with three older women as she peered into the haze. They seemed to have placed themselves as far away as they could from the stage but Lizzie recognized Ena now from Elsie's description. She paused for a moment to steady her breathing.

'I'd say she's the one on that far table,' Lizzie said eventually. 'The woman with the hat and coat and the miserable face.' As she watched, the woman she'd decided must be Ena took off her hat, revealing a hairnet that completely covered her mousey-coloured hair. She had a glowering look on her face and she was sitting with her arms firmly folded across her ample chest.

'Spot on.' Elsie clapped her hands. 'That's our Ena, as usual with her two guardian angels, Minnie and Martha, though who looks after who there I'm not sure.'

'Do you think they might change their allegiance, then?' Lizzie said. 'Drinking in here from now on instead of the Rovers?'

'I don't really know,' Elsie said but she looked doubtful.

'And how about you?'

Elsie shrugged. 'We'll have to see about that, but I'm not sure it's really possible to change when you've been around as long as we all have. You know, if you support United you can't suddenly change your colours and become a City supporter. You're a red for life.'

'Spoken like a true fan, if I may say so,' a man's voice suddenly interjected and Lizzie looked up to find she was staring directly into the laughing eyes of the man she had momentarily mistaken for Joe. Close to, to her relief, he was nothing like Joe, though she had to admit he was good-looking and she was finding it difficult to ignore his warm, flirtatious smile.

'And which side do you come down on? It's Lizzie, I believe, isn't it?' he asked, not shifting his gaze from her face.

Lizzie nodded. 'Yes, it is,' she said, but then found for once she was lost for words. 'I can't say I'm much of a supporter of either of them,' she said at last, 'Mr . . .?'

'Steve Carter.' The man put his hand across the counter.

Lizzie shook it tentatively. 'I don't really know much about football.'

'But you can't live round here without declaring that you're on one side or the other,' Elsie said. 'You've got brothers, so you should know.'

'Yes, you're right,' Lizzie said. 'They do talk rather a lot about United if they talk of any team, so I suppose, if I'm honest, I lean that way a bit too.'

'Me, I blow whichever way the wind blows,' Elsie

said. 'How about you, Steve?' She turned to face him as she said this, lifting her eyebrows suggestively.

'I must admit, I'm a Reds' fan,' Steve said. His eyes flickered from Lizzie's face but only for a moment.

'Maybe when you're talking about which pub you'd choose to drink in, as we were,' Lizzie said, 'it's not quite so all-embracing. It doesn't have to be all or nothing, for life, does it? Not like it seems to be with football.'

Steve laughed. 'Probably not,' he said. 'I like to think people can be a little more flexible.'

'It might be more fun to share things out a bit when it comes to pubs.' Elsie grinned. 'Like, sometimes I might drink at the Rovers, sometimes here. Then there mightn't be so many fallings out.'

'Nothing to stop you going to both on the same night if you've a mind,' Steve laughed.

'Do you know?' Elsie pretended to think. 'I might even do that,' she said and her grin expanded into a personal smile that looked like she'd saved it just for him. 'So tell me, Steve, you're not from round here, are you? I don't reckon I've seen you in any of the locals. Have you ever been drinking in the Rovers Return?'

'Not yet,' Steve said. 'But as I'm thinking of moving into the area I'm sure I'll get to it eventually. I thought I'd try this one first as it was new.' He turned to look directly at Lizzie as he said this, but she was suddenly busy searching for a cloth to dry the glasses.

'Well, I normally go the Rovers,' Elsie said as if she hadn't noticed him addressing Lizzie. 'But I'm prepared to give this place a chance. I'll wait and see what else they have to offer.' She gave a wry laugh. 'I go to the Rovers more out of habit. It's not as though Annie Walker'd miss me. She's the landlady there,' she explained. 'She doesn't even like me. If anything, it's just the opposite. Let me tell you, she's given me a lot of grief over the years. When I first came to live in Coronation Street, I admit I was too young to be drinking legally but didn't she like to show me up, especially if I was with a bloke? It didn't matter what he ordered, she only let me drink lemonade. And she always seemed to be looking down her nose at me, like she thought she was too good to give the likes of me the time of day.' She gave an ironic laugh. 'She still does. It would serve her right if I were to switch my drinking habits and start coming here instead.'

'I'll be sure to try out the Rovers on your recommendation then,' Steve turned back to Elsie and laughed. Elsie flashed him another of her special smiles and said, 'I'll look forward to seeing you there.'

Steve grinned and turned away. 'And I'm sure I'll be back here again to see you, Lizzie,' he said, giving her the full beam of his smile. 'But for now, can you pull me another pint, please?'

By the time Bob had closed the bar and cashed up the till, Lizzie was hovering outside the kitchen, ready to go. She was feeling the effects of having been on her feet all evening and couldn't wait to get home.

'Well, that was a good day's work,' Bob said.

'Only it feels more like a day and a half,' Lizzie said. 'I wonder what the weather's like out there now? Everyone was coming in well bundled up, saying it was getting colder, so I hope it's not snowing.'

'Would you like me to see you home?' Bob said. 'Then it won't matter about the weather, I'll keep you safe and warm.' He reached out to put his arm round her waist.

'No, thanks,' Lizzie said. 'I'll be fine. I'm just tired, that's all.' She stepped away so that he ended up embracing the air.

'Bar work can be tough going,' he said as if nothing had happened.

'It's certainly that,' Lizzie said. 'So, I'll be off home now and I'll see you tomorrow.' She moved quickly towards the front entrance and was relieved that he didn't try to follow. She pulled open the doors and to her surprise found Hilda sheltering in the doorway.

'What's up with you?' Lizzie asked. 'I thought you'd long gone. Is anything wrong?'

'Nowt's wrong. I was waiting for you, that's all,' Hilda said. 'I hope you don't mind, but it had started to snow a bit and I know it's not far but it's a dark night and I thought you might like some company.'

Lizzie looked up at the black sky where the clouds had covered what was left of the moon.

'No, of course I don't mind. I'm glad to see you. But it's so cold you must be frozen.' Lizzie sank her hands deep into her coat pockets.

'It is a bit parky,' Hilda admitted and almost immediately linked arms and pulled Lizzie closer to her. 'Though I'm pleased to see the snow didn't stick. It's bad enough that it made the cobbles all slippery, so take care as you walk.'

'Can you believe it's the end of our first day, or should I say night, at the Pride?' Lizzie said.

'You were certainly rushed off your feet. I wonder if it will always be like that?'

'I hope not,' Lizzie said. 'I don't mind being busy in general but I felt as if I was stuck to the pumps all night.'

'That was a shame. You looked so bonny in that lovely dress,' Hilda said, 'but no one could see it. You hardly had time to show it off.'

Lizzie laughed. 'Maybe I'll get to wear it again another night. Just wait until I tell Ma I won the prize.'

'That's a great way to start a new job,' Hilda said. 'I don't reckon it'll feel the same when I start work first thing in the morning.' She sighed. 'I don't even want to think of what I might find.'

'I'm sorry I had no time to have a check round before I left,' Lizzie said. 'I did mean to. So I hope there won't be too much of a disgusting mess for you to clean up.'

Hilda's cackling laugh pierced the gloom. 'That's the first time I've had anyone worry about that!'

'Well, I've worked in schools so I know how unappetizing a cleaner's job can be,' Lizzie said with some feeling.

'Was you a teacher then?' Hilda sounded surprised. 'I always knew you were clever, much cleverer than me at any rate.'

'I went to a training college after I got my higher certificate, but I never finished,' Lizzie said.

'That's a shame. Why was that then?'

The question was straightforward enough but it caught Lizzie by surprise and for a moment she wasn't sure how to answer. 'Life got in the way, I suppose,' she said eventually. 'What with the war and – and all, th-things didn't work out quite as I'd planned.' She fumbled to find a handkerchief and wiped away the tears that were threatening to drip off the end of her nose. 'My da was killed and I needed to find a job quickly. Once his wages stopped coming in, I had to earn some money to help support my . . . my ma and . . .' She paused and bit her lip. '. . . And the boys.'

'I bet you could've earned much more as a teacher than a barmaid,' Hilda said.

'Of course, if I could have seen it through, but i-it didn't work out.' She was caught up for a moment in her memories. 'Maybe one day . . .'

'I'm right sorry,' Hilda said, her voice soft, and for the next few minutes they continued walking in silence.

'Ne'er mind, eh?' Hilda said eventually with a sigh, 'I don't suppose any of that will matter once you're wed. You'll be stopping at home to look after the babies.'

Lizzie looked surprised. 'Why? Will you be giving up work as soon as you're in the family way?'

'Well, once Stan finds a job, maybe I will, but we're not in the same class as you. Besides, it could take him a while,' Hilda said defensively. 'Though how on earth we'll go on once the kiddies start arriving, goodness only knows.'

'I suppose things have a way of working out.' Lizzie patted Hilda's arm.

'I suppose they do.' Hilda sighed. 'He's a good man, is my husband, despite what some folk say, and I know he'll do his best by me if he can. I do love him, you know.'

'I don't doubt it, Hilda,' Lizzie said.

'And I'm sure you'll find someone to love soon. Once the young men start coming back from the war.'

'Oh, but I don't want anyone,' Lizzie said quickly. 'I've had my chance and there won't be another one for me.'

Hilda drew in her breath. 'Don't say that. You don't know how you'll feel when—'

'Yes, I do,' Lizzie cut in. 'No one can replace Joe, I'm quite sure of that.'

Hilda hesitated before asking. 'Was Joe your young man?'

Lizzie nodded.

'You mean you was stepping out?'

'More than that. We were going to get married.'

'What happened to him?' Hilda said. 'If you don't mind me asking.'

'He was a pilot . . .' Lizzie took a deep breath. 'He – he got shot down. And I'll never find anyone like Joe; he was very, very special.' Lizzie's voice suddenly cracked.

'Oh, gosh! I'm sorry,' Hilda said. She stopped walking and turned to give Lizzie a sudden hug. 'I had no idea. But I'm sure you'll find someone else.'

Lizzie clung to her for a moment. 'No, I shan't,' she whispered.

'How can you be so certain?' Hilda asked, pulling away.

'Because I shan't be looking,' Lizzie said resolutely and she wiped her face with her handkerchief trying to wipe away the sudden smiling image of Steve Carter that flashed in front of her eyes.

Chapter 3

Spring 1945

Although they didn't know it at the time, by the end of March the residents of Weatherfield had seen the last of the V1 and V2 rockets that had done so much damage to people and property in England. The attacks had been random. A whining whistle followed by a short-lived silence then the shattering devastation of the giant bomb. It was never possible to predict when and where it would land, so that they became afraid to trust the silence. Now how could they believe they really had heard the last warning screeches of the air-raid sirens and the reassuring signals for the all clear? But by the middle of April, when no new explosions had been heard for several weeks, everyone began to hope that it was true, that they had seen the last of the flying bombs.

As spring officially arrived and the hours of daylight lengthened, so the mood of the residents of Weatherfield lifted and the weariness that had bogged them down for months was replaced by an atmosphere of cautious optimism. The news on the street was that the Germans were in retreat and the Nazis were floundering as the allies advanced, although it still took some time for the people of Weatherfield to believe that the war was actually about to end as the peace treaty had not yet been signed. But it was widely accepted that an official announcement would soon be forthcoming and there was a feeling of restlessness and suppressed excitement in the air as preparations began for the celebration of victory and there was much talk of street parties and the forthcoming bank holiday.

Annie Walker, spurred on by her husband's letters to think that he might be returning home soon, began to think about organizing a street party to celebrate VE day – Victory in Europe. It would be a local party where the Rovers Return would feature prominently. She had been disturbed by the successful appearance of the refurbished Pride of Weatherfield so close to her own doorstep and had been thinking about what she should do in order to hold on to her customers. After several sleepless nights she discussed her ideas with her trusted barmaid Gracie.

'If we were able to organize the biggest and best street

party ever seen in Weatherfield,' Annie said, 'it might encourage some of the locals who've been deserting us of late to come back to drink here again. We need to put the Rovers Return back once more at the heart of the community, where it belongs. What do you think, Gracie?'

'I think that sounds like an excellent idea,' Gracie said. 'And it would give you an excuse to go over to the Pride to tell them what we're planning and to find out what they're up to at the same time.'

Annie looked thoughtful, her brow furrowed as she absorbed Gracie's suggestion.

'Perhaps you could get some of our old regulars together into some kind of organizing committee,' Gracie said. 'That would make people feel more committed.'

Annie suddenly looked determined. 'You're right. The Pride might be enticing some of our customers away on a Saturday night with their second-rate cabaret acts, but I'm blowed if I'm going to let them seduce all our clientele permanently, like the Pied Piper. We can't have Jack coming home to find an empty pub, thinking we've no customers left, now can we?' She gave a sardonic laugh, though she knew it was really no laughing matter, not when she'd spent most of the war years working hard to prove how well she had learned to balance the job of running the pub single-handed, alongside her busy role as the mother of two young children.

Gracie's eyes lit up. 'We could put up notices about

the party in the bar and ask people to put them in their windows.' Annie laughed at her enthusiasm. 'That's the spirit – though of course the war hasn't officially ended yet.'

'No, but surely it soon will?' Gracie sounded anxious.

For a moment Annie had a dreamy smile on her face. 'Of course it will. And all the soldiers will come flooding home,' she said, 'eager to start their new life.'

'I know I for one can't wait to make a fresh start,' Gracie said with a sigh. 'It seems ages since Chuck and all the other GIs left for Europe. I can't wait to get off to America. As soon as Chuck sends for me, when he's posted back home I'll be off like a shot, believe you me.'

Annie had a wistful look as she glanced over to the barmaid she had come to love and trust. 'I know, my dear, though I so hate the thought of losing you, but all the more reason why we need to make this work. It will be doubling as a farewell party.'

'Will you be looking to find my replacement before I go,' Gracie asked, 'so that I'll have time to show the new girl the ropes? She could help us to organize the party too.'

'Actually my dear, I already have somebody in mind.' Annie's lips were taut but she forced them into a smile. 'Or should I say, Jack has. He's recommended I hire someone who has been serving with him who will apparently be coming home soon. He would be more of a bar manager.' She paused. 'It seems I am awaiting his call.'

'Well, that's a relief. I won't be leaving you in the lurch when Chuck sends for me,' Gracie said. 'And if Jack likes him then I'm sure he'll be fine.'

Annie nodded. 'An extra pair of hands is always helpful.' She smiled and patted Gracie's hand. 'Though it won't be easy for someone to fill your shoes, you know.'

The next morning Hilda was putting the finishing touches to the freshly whitened front step at the Pride when a smart-looking lady, all dressed up in her Sunday best, stopped by the front entrance. Hilda suddenly felt flustered, unsure about speaking to her, but she didn't have to worry because Annie Walker spoke to her, asking in clipped tones, 'Is Mr Bennett available? Could you tell him Mrs Walker from the Rovers Return would like a word with him?'

'Yes, of course,' was all Hilda could manage and, abandoning her cleaning equipment, she rushed inside to look for Bob.

'Mrs Walker!' Bob's voice boomed out as he stood by the door, arms akimbo. 'We meet at last. I've heard a lot about you. To what do I owe the honour?'

'I've come to welcome you to Weatherfield,' Annie said with a tight smile.

Bob gave a sardonic laugh. 'Well, isn't that nice and neighbourly? Maybe you'd better come in and sit down.'

He indicated a table in the public bar. 'Mrs Ogden, ask Lizzie if she can rustle up tea for two,' he said when they were both seated. He didn't look in Hilda's direction, for he was still eyeing Annie up and down. Hilda wasn't sure whether she should drop a curtsey like she'd seen maids do in the films, so she nodded her head before rushing off to the kitchen where Lizzie was preparing for the dinnertime opening. Hilda watched as Lizzie filled a small teapot from the permanently simmering cauldron then quickly piled a jug of milk and a bowl of sugar cubes onto a tray. Hilda was astonished when Lizzie added a few biscuits on a plate. 'Bob always insists on having some of these midmorning,' Lizzie said, 'so why shouldn't Mrs Walker have some as well?'

The two giggled and Hilda went off to serve the tray. Lizzie slipped into the bar and began busily wiping glasses behind the counter but she was careful to stand in a spot where she knew she couldn't be seen and she beckoned Hilda to join her.

When Hilda had left the tray, Bob leaned back and flung one arm carelessly across the back of the banquette where he was sitting opposite Annie. 'Now then,' he said, 'what do you *really* want?' His eyes narrowed and his tone was far from pleasant, but Annie chose to ignore it.

'I told you,' she said. 'It's a social call. I hope you're settling in well and managing to find enough customers.'

'Poof,' he said with a chuckle. 'That's not a problem! Trade couldn't be better.' Bob beamed. 'But surely you haven't come here to ask me that?'

'I presume you've reconnected with the old Tripe Dresser's clientele,' Annie continued in her most condescending tone as if he hadn't spoken. 'I always think it's good to have a core of loyal customers.'

'We've had a packed house every night. So much so I've been wondering whether there's going to be enough room for both of us in this neighbourhood.' He frowned suddenly and leaned forward, his hand to his mouth. 'Oh my goodness, is that what you've come to tell me? The competition's getting to you already?'

Annie stared at him scornfully while Bob merely spread his hands. 'Well, you know what they say. All's fair in love and war.' Annie bristled at that, though her smile didn't waver but Bob cut in before she could respond. 'How soon after peace is declared are you expecting your husband back?' he said. 'It must be so difficult juggling everything on your own.'

'No doubt he'll be home as soon as his services to his country are no longer required,' Annie said, her jaw stiff. 'But at the moment, as you must know, they still have unfinished business to see to out there and I'm sure you will understand that they can't shirk their duties, even when the war is finally over. Not that any of them would want to.' She gave a little laugh. 'But then, I take it you weren't actually called up into the fighting forces, were you? So maybe you aren't aware of how these things work.'

At that Bob stopped smiling, but Annie continued speaking. 'As I said, this is a courtesy call. I thought I would inform you of our intentions regarding VE day when it finally arrives.'

'Oh, that,' Bob said, with a disparaging wave of his hand. 'I'm doing my own thing, here.' Annie nevertheless went on to explain about the street party.

'Well, I have no such laudable intentions,' Bob said with a grin. 'So if the street wants a party, feel free to organize one.'

They glared at each other for a moment. 'However . . .' An unctuous smile spread across Bob's face. 'I might be able to do you a favour.'

'Oh?' Annie said.

'I could supply you with most of the food at a price you won't be able to get anywhere else.'

Annie stiffened, not sure what to make of the generous-sounding offer, not sure if she could trust him. She was aware that he had not taken his steely grey eyes off her face though she was unable to read his expression.

'I can assure you,' Bob said, 'you won't get a better deal anywhere in the county.'

Annie thought for a moment. 'I'll inform the organizing committee as they'll be responsible for the food,' she said. 'I'll tell them to contact you, but I doubt they'll need any of your help, they're a well-oiled machine.'

In her mind, Annie tried to square this statement with the thought of Elsie lounging around the bar at the Rovers with a fag in her mouth.

'Then I shall look forward to doing business with the esteemed ladies of Coronation Street,' Bob said. 'And perhaps, while we're talking business, I could offer the services of some of my working colleagues who specialize in security?'

'Security?' Annie was puzzled.

Bob shrugged. 'You never know when security guards might be needed these days, particularly when there's going to be large crowds and alcohol flowing – a heady mix.'

Annie's brows shot up. 'I don't know where you lived before, Mr Bennett,' she said, her voice dripping with scorn, 'but may I remind you that this is Coronation Street we're talking about, and I certainly don't anticipate the need for security guards at a Weatherfield street party.'

'Suit yourself,' Bob said. 'That will free them up to cover the special cabaret night we're planning for VE night, when we'll no doubt have another full house.' Bob had so far ignored the tea and now he leaned across the table and helped himself to a digestive biscuit from the plate. 'So, if that's everything, then you'll have to excuse me as I have some rather pressing business to attend to.' He stood up. 'No doubt our paths will cross again.'

*

Annie still felt cross about Bob Bennett's brusqueness as she sketched an outline of her visit to the Pride later that evening when she was alone with Gracie but she was determined to waste no time in putting together a list of regulars they might approach to become part of the organizing committee for the eventual VE street party.

'Security guards, indeed!' Annie snapped. 'Where does he think he's living?'

'All we have to do is involve Mrs Sharples and there'll be no need for any kind of security guards!' Gracie laughed and even Annie allowed a smile to play on her lips.

'Just as well, for I don't see how we could have a Coronation Street committee that didn't involve Ena Sharples, do you?' she said.

Gracie laughed again. 'Fat chance. And she'll no doubt want to include Minnie Caldwell and Martha Longhurst as well.'

'So, what about adding Ida Barlow?' Annie suggested. 'Not much gets past her and I think she'd be very conscientious.'

'And then there's Elsie Foyle from the corner shop. She should know about the catering side of things if anybody does,' Gracie said. 'Though I imagine that once the war is officially over, food will become more readily available.'

'I wouldn't bank on it,' Annie said. 'They've been

talking about the possibility of lots more things becoming scarce in the coming months, even after the war ends.'

'Then all the more reason to have Mrs Foyle. Hopefully, she'll have better access than most to whatever supplies are available.' Gracie laughed. 'And whether or not she decides to take up Bob Bennett's offer will be up to her.' She gave a mischievous grin. 'And what about Elsie Tanner?'

'What about her?' Annie swallowed hard, her jaw set firm.

'I know she's not your favourite person, but you've got to admit she is extremely resourceful and would be an asset to any such committee.'

'Is that what they call it?' Annie said, drawing her lips into a thin line, though she did grudgingly add Elsie's name to the list.

Steve Carter stood outside the Rovers Return, thinking how much better it would look with a fresh coat of paint. It was not what he had imagined when Jack Walker, who had served with him in the Fusiliers, talked about the local pub he ran with his wife in Weatherfield. Perhaps painting the outside was something he could offer to do almost immediately, something that would endear him to Mrs Walker in case Jack's recommendation wasn't enough.

Despite having walked a long way from the tram, he was early for his appointment, so he continued slowly up the street and back again checking out the neighbourhood. He was trying not to limp or show any sign of weakness, determined to ignore the dull ache that was plaguing him today in his injured leg. He took every opportunity to exercise his leg as he still marvelled at the fact that he could walk at all, the doctors in the battlefield hospital having told him he never would. On his return home from the front, he'd battled his way through a vigorous rehabilitation programme, determined to prove them wrong, and here he was, managing well enough, even though there were still dark days when the pain made it difficult for him to cope.

Jack had visited him in the field hospital on several occasions after the Jeep Steve had been driving had overturned, badly injuring his leg. When Steve had eventually heard he was being repatriated and invalided out of the army he could hardly believe his luck when Jack suggested he contact his wife Annie regarding a possible job in the pub they ran together.

'How can I ever repay you?' Steve asked.

'By working hard,' Jack said and chuckled. 'You'll be making life a bloomin' sight easier for me when I finally get out of this hellhole.'

'Let's hope that won't be too long. Sorry I'm leaving you behind to do the mopping up.'

'Never you mind that, now. You're only . . . how old are you, lad? Twenty-five, twenty-six?'

'Actually, I'm twenty-eight,' Steve corrected him.

'Still pretty young in my book,' Jack said, 'and thankfully still with your whole life ahead of you. All I'm doing is offering you a leg up, so to speak.' He grinned at his own wit. 'Look at it this way, you'll be ahead of the game in the job market if you get back to civvy street before the rest of us. So it's up to you to make the most of it.'

It hadn't taken much more persuading for Jack to convince him to try his luck at the Rovers and Steve was extremely grateful for the offer. He'd been thinking about his future while he was in hospital almost from the moment he'd come out of his coma and he was determined not to let his injury hold him back from the career he'd always wanted. Accepting Jack's offer would take him one step closer to his dream of one day tenanting a smart country pub.

As soon as he felt fit enough when his rehab programme was over, he telephoned Annie Walker to declare his interest and explain who he was. He was surprised at how posh her voice was – it sounded very far removed from Jack's down-to-earth accent. But he had to admit that, even during their brief conversation, she did sound every bit as Jack had hinted: a strong woman with a mind of her own.

Steve arrived back at the Rovers exactly on time for the interview she'd suggested and he paused outside for a moment to admire the large panes of frosted glass that had somehow survived the war. Just as the pub has survived the absence of its landlord, he thought in a fanciful moment. Surely it said something about the strength of the woman he'd come to see? There was no doubt she was some kind of a force to be reckoned with, even Jack had admitted that. Steve took a deep breath as he headed towards the door. Exactly what kind of force he was about to find out.

'I fully appreciate what Jack is saying,' Annie Walker said when they were finally seated in the back parlour and all the introductions and pleasantries were out of the way. She slipped some half-moon glasses onto the end of her nose and glanced back to Jack's letter in her hand. 'It's just like my husband to try to help someone out, but are you sure you're ready for all the heavy work? Because that is a large and integral part of the job.'

'I'm pretty well as fit as I ever was,' Steve said, crossing his fingers behind his back. 'And I'm still working on it, so I reckon I'm as ready as I can be to tackle whatever's needed.' Steve looked her straight in the eye as he said this, until eventually she looked away and he hoped that it was his eyes twinkling a little that had brought the slight smile to Annie's lips. 'After all, it was my leg that was damaged, not my arms,' he said, 'so I reckon I can still lift the odd barrel and the like.' Steve grinned, hoping she wouldn't ask him to demonstrate these skills right now as he was actually feeling the effects of his long walk.

'And do you really consider you're ready for the

managerial responsibilities this job entails? After all, you've been serving in the army for the last few years,' Annie said.

'As a corporal,' Steve pointed out. 'Which in itself involves taking on responsibilities.'

'But not as a high-flying officer, so at least you won't be after my job.' Annie gave a tinkling laugh. 'Though you will be used to taking orders.' Steve wanted to smile at the slightly patronizing way she said that and he hoped his face didn't give him away.

'And would you say, generally, that you have a good head for business?' Annie asked. 'I will, of course, still be in overall charge, but I need someone solid and dependable who can take care of all aspects of the day-to-day running of the place. I have two young children who need my attention as well as the pub, and until the Germans surrender and peace is declared, we have no idea when Jack is likely to be coming home.'

As if on cue the door suddenly burst open and a little boy ran into the room crying, 'Mummy, Mummy, who was that funny man with the limp who came hopping in?' He stopped when he saw Steve and stared up at his face before glancing down at his legs. The boy then drew back his foot as if to let loose a mighty kick at Steve but luckily Steve saw the sudden movement and caught the boy's leg before it could make contact. He held on to it while the boy could only hop in ever-decreasing circles. 'I bet I can make you hop much better than me,'

Steve whispered into the boy's ear. His voice was soft but steely and he continued to smile. He didn't want to say more as he was waiting for Annie to intervene.

'Tell him to stop!' the boy squealed, but Annie only made soothing noises. 'Oh Billy, you are such a one. I thought I told you to stay in the kitchen and look after Joanie? What will your father say? You know, he won't tolerate such behaviour when he comes home.'

'Then I don't want him ever to come home. I hate him!' Billy shouted. 'He's not going to tell *me* what to do.'

As if he suddenly realized he was still holding on to the leg of Jack's son, Steve stood up abruptly and as he did so he lifted the young boy off the ground.

'Put me down!' Billy screamed. Steve paid no heed at first, but when it became apparent Annie had nothing more to say, he eventually lowered him to the floor. As soon as he was standing upright, Billy aimed a kick again at Steve's legs which Steve was fortunately able to parry. Billy's jaw tightened as he turned away and he began to half run, half walk round the room with an exaggerated limp, shouting, 'I'm Mr Hoppy and I can hop better than you!' in a taunting voice. When he reached the door he turned and pulled out his tongue. Annie gasped, then Billy hopped off into the vestibule, leaving the door wide open behind him.

Annie shook her head and made a tutting sound as Billy disappeared, but then she got up to close the door and Steve could see she was smiling.

'What can you do with such a rascal?' she said with no attempt at an apology.

'Hope that he grows up to be a decent man like his father,' Steve offered diplomatically, making sure to maintain the smile on his lips, even though his leg had begun to throb in anticipation of what might have been.

'Now, where were we?' Annie said.

'Discussing my ranking, I think.' Steve handed her a sheet of paper, outlining his previous jobs. 'I'd say my work history speaks for itself,' he said. 'I think you'll find I can work at whatever level you require.'

'So, what would you say are the essentials for a good pub?' Annie asked as she glanced over the paper.

Steve was about to say, 'a pretty barmaid,' but he managed to check himself and said instead, 'A good pub should have contented staff. Someone behind the bar who has a sense of humour and a happy smile.' He gestured towards Annie with his hand as he said this. To his surprise she blushed as he held her gaze for a moment and he realized that was not the answer she'd been expecting. 'I've seen what looks like a new pub not very far from here,' Steve said quickly.

'Ah, yes, indeed,' Annie said, peering through the glasses that had slipped down her nose. 'That would be the Tripe Dresser's Arms, though I believe they have some fancy new name for it now, which I find not a little pretentious.'

'Well, as a newcomer to the area I'd certainly want

to check out the opposition.' He didn't want to tell her he'd already done that and that he intended to visit the Pride of Weatherfield again in the very near future in pursuit of the pretty barmaid in the green dress who did indeed have a sense of humour and a welcoming smile. Annie continued to probe with a further list of questions until there really seemed nothing left to ask. Finally, she stood up and Steve followed suit. He had assumed the interview was a formality so he was surprised when she said, 'I'd be happy for you to start tomorrow, but I'm afraid it would have to be cellar work only for the time being. I'm sure you understand that I'll have to follow up your references before I can make the bar manager's position official.'

'Yes, of course, I understand,' Steve said politely.' He didn't really, for he'd assumed the job was his, wasn't her husband's endorsement of him good enough? 'And how long do you think that might take?'

A flash of annoyance crossed her face. 'I shall get on to it as quickly as I'm able,' she said. She glanced towards the closed door. The sound of children squabbling was increasing. 'It's been very nice to meet you, thank you so much for coming, Mr Carter.' She put out her hand and Steve shook it. 'It's Steve, please,' he said. 'I look forward to working with you,' and he gave her what he hoped was a winning smile.

*

It was a week before Steve received notification that the manager's job was his should he still want it, and if his leg hadn't been playing up that morning he would have danced round his mother's kitchen with delight.

'At least that Mrs Walker knows a good thing when she sees one,' Mrs Carter said as he waved the letter in front of her.

'Only thing is, Mam,' Steve's face was suddenly serious as he sat down at the table, 'it means I'll be moving out of here again. You and dad have done so much to help me since I've been back, and you know I'm grateful, but I'm afraid it's too far for me to travel each day. I'll have to try and find some digs in Weatherfield, closer to the pub.'

'Don't worry, love. You don't have to make excuses. It's your life and you have to do what you have to do. It's not as though you haven't lived away before. You were never home much before the war. I'm just right proud you're not letting that nasty injury business get in your way,' she said, kissing the top of his sleeked-back hair. 'Just be sure to remember to visit us once in a while.'

'Didn't I always? At least once in a while.' Steve laughed.

'Maybe a little more often than you did before would be nice, and I promise not to ask what you get up to in between whiles, though I can guess.'

'Fair's fair. I'm not a kid. You know that.'

'You mean what I don't know can't hurt me, eh? Is that what you're saying?'

'Something like that.'

'Like I don't know what you get up to now that you're back on your feet!'

'Well, you don't, do you?'

'True enough. No more than I ever knew.' She sighed. 'And right embarrassing that could be. I lost count of the times a young lassie's mother would come up to me in the street saying how thrilled she was her young 'un were courting my lad. And me, I knew nowt about it so I couldn't say yay or nay.'

'Go on with you. You didn't really want to know all the ins and outs every time I went out with someone, now did you?'

'No, there were too many of them for me to keep track.' She gave a rueful smile. 'You were not like your sister. The only thing I can say is that at least none of them got up the duff. Not so far as I know, at any rate.'

Steve gave a loud guffaw. 'Oh, Mam, that's why I love you so much. You come right out with it. There's no beating about the bush with you, is there? And that's why I think it's far better that I live my own life. Can you imagine if I'd have told you about all the girls I've been out with over the years, not to mention those who I didn't go out with even though they said I did. You'd never have got a wink of sleep for worrying. So I'll do you a favour and this time I'll move far enough away so you can't bump into any young lassie's mother. Though I promise to tell you if I hit the jackpot.'

'What? You get wed?' Now his mother laughed with a throaty laugh that ended in a choking splutter. 'Never!'

'You know what they say, never say never. But for now how about lending me a few bob?'

'A few bob? You're only going as far as Weatherfield, aren't you?'

'Well, a few pennies then, so that I can get down to the telephone box and secure that job. I must let Mrs Walker know I'm fit and ready to start.' He went to the old jam jar that stood on the mantelpiece above the hearth and removed a shilling piece and some coppers, letting them jingle together as he dropped them into his trouser pocket. 'I promise to pay you back out of my first wage packet,' he said and he gave a little wave before crossing the room and banging the front door firmly shut behind him.

The following morning, when Steve arrived at the Rovers Return, ready to start in his new position, he was greeted at the door by a young girl who introduced herself as Gracie.

'I'm the current barmaid,' she said as she led the way. 'It's me you'll be replacing. Plus, plus, if I know Annie.' Gracie laughed.

'Plus, plus, plus,' Steve agreed, thinking of all the duties Annie Walker had outlined.

'Mrs Walker sends her apologies, by the way,' Gracie said, 'but she had to go up to little Billy's school to see his teacher.'

'Oh, I see,' Steve said, following her into the hallway he remembered from his interview. He hung up his coat on one of the hooks Gracie indicated.

'You'll get used to that.' She giggled. 'Between you and me, she's always being summoned to see Billy's teacher.'

'From what I've seen of him I'm not at all surprised,' Steve said. 'But don't tell Mrs Walker I said that.'

'Don't worry, I know exactly what you mean,' Gracie said, leading the way into the empty bar. 'Have you got kids?'

'Not that I know of,' Steve said without thinking.

To his relief, Gracie laughed.

'And I'm not married either,' he said.

'No girlfriend?'

'No one steady. I did have someone before the war that might have . . .' He waved his hand back and forth. 'Once I was called up we wrote for a bit, but then it fizzled out and since I'm back I've not really had time. Not that I'm ready to settle down or anything like that, but I wouldn't say no to having a nice someone on my arm, if you know what I mean.'

'Don't look at me,' Gracie said and giggled. 'I'm spoken for.'

'Shame,' Steve said. 'Though I remember now, Mrs Walker did say something about you going abroad.'

'I'll be sailing off to New York soon, to marry my sweetheart.' A light sparkled in her eyes. 'I really can't believe it.' She pinched her arm and laughed again. 'Chuck's parents are determined that I should be there to welcome him when he finally returns home so they've managed to wangle a passage for me and my mum on a transport ship. I've got to make sure I'm all ready because hopefully it will be sailing almost the moment the war ends.'

'I've heard a lot about GI brides,' Steve said, 'but I've never actually met one before.'

'Well, you have now. The Genuine Item, which is what I always tell people GI stands for. I'll be going to America as soon as the war's officially over and Chuck thinks it's safe for me to travel. He's actually sent me the money already so that I can book my passage.'

'He sounds like a smashing bloke. I wish you all the very best,' Steve said.

'Thank you.'

'It's a brave thing to do.'

'Brave or completely mad,' Gracie conceded. 'I never do things by halves.'

'It's something I'd love to do,' Steve said. 'Travel the world. You'd have thought I'd have had enough in the army but it's not the same. However, for the moment I'll stay put as I've got my eye on someone much closer to home.' He flicked his brow up and down suggestively.

'Sounds interesting. Am I allowed to know who?' Gracie said.

Steve half closed his eyes. 'I can't be giving away all my secrets, we've only just met,' he joked.

'C'mon,' she cajoled when he didn't reply. 'What's the harm? I'll keep your secret, I promise.'

'Well . . .' Steve wavered.

'This is a pretty small neighbourhood, you know. If she lives anywhere local I bet I can guess who she is.' She thought for a moment. 'Have you been down to the Pride of Weatherfield yet?'

Steve was startled.

'See!' Gracie sounded triumphant. 'I've got it in one, haven't I? Lizzie, they call her. Am I right?'

'Do you know her?' Steve asked in surprise.

'I've not met her but I've heard she's very pretty. She lives in Coronation Street with her family. They've not lived here long, so you might be in with a chance there.'

Steve frowned. 'Maybe, maybe not. It's a bit tricky, like.'

'Why's that? Did she take against you from the off? What did you say to upset her?'

Steve laughed. 'Nothing like that. She doesn't know me yet. I've only met her the once. She seemed friendly enough – though she was being nice to everyone; it was their opening night.'

'So I was right, you really are in with a chance,' Gracie said.

Doubt was in Steve's eyes and he shook his head. 'Could be, but you see, I've got this bad leg, on account of the war.'

'I'm sorry to hear that.'

'I'm learning to live with it, but it knocks your confidence a bit.'

'I can understand that. How did she react to it?'

'I don't think she saw it. Some days it's worse than others, you know how it is.'

Gracie grinned. 'Well, at least you're still good-looking from the neck up. If she's got anything about her she won't give a damn if you hop-along a bit.' As she said this, she nudged him gently in the ribs and her smile made him smile.

'It's just tough when nippers like this one make fun of you.' Steve sighed as he indicated a picture of Billy that was hanging on the wall. 'Kind of knocks you sideways for a bit till you can restock the armoury to fight back.'

'Bugger the nippers. What do they know? I can think of several round here who wouldn't care a jot,' Gracie said reassuringly.

'Let's hope Lizzie's one of them,' Steve said.

Gracie squeezed his arm. 'I hope so, for your sake. I'll be rooting for you. And you don't have to worry, I'll be gone soon, so your secret's safe with me.'

Gracie walked around the room switching on all the lights and taking down the towels that had covered the pumps overnight.

'Just imagine,' she said as she slid in behind the counter, 'Chuck and I met in this very place. For me, the Rovers Return is special, so make sure you treat it well.' She wagged her finger.

'Of course, ma'am.' Steve laughed and gave a mock bow. 'I wouldn't think to treat it any other way.'

'And be nice to Mrs Walker, because if she likes you she'll treat you well.' She lowered her voice even though there was clearly no one else about. 'She's really a very kind person and she does have a heart of gold, though I know she doesn't always come across that way.'

Suddenly there was a loud scream that seemed to come from a back room. It made Steve jump but Gracie just laughed. 'That means she's back,' Gracie said, 'and with young Billy in tow. He's a scamp and no mistake.' She shook her head. 'Make sure you don't stand any nonsense from him or he'll turn you inside out.'

'Don't I know it,' Steve said and they both laughed. Suddenly Gracie put out her hand. 'Look,' she said, 'I really do wish you the very best of luck and I hope you're as happy as I've been here.'

'And bon voyage to you, when the time comes,' Steve said, wondering just what he had let himself in for.

Chapter 4

It never took long for gossip to spread in Weatherfield and when the local grapevine buzzed with the whisper that a new young manager had been appointed at the Rovers, everyone was eager to see him and to give him the once-over. Stories about him quickly circulated, most of which weren't true, and there was much speculation about why he had been invalided out of the army.

'Happen I'll not be coming in here so often of an evening if what I've heard is right,' Lizzie's neighbour Elsie said with a knowing raise of her eyebrows as she leaned on the bar at the Pride with a gin and tonic. 'I believe there's summat really worth looking at in the Rovers.' She giggled.

'But then, any new young blood would light that

place up at the moment. The Rovers hasn't been the same since the Yanks deserted us.'

'Pardon me, but I thought you was spoken for?' Lizzie said with a laugh.

'In name only,' Elsie said. 'You know how I feel about my husband. Though maybe it's you who ought to be setting your cap at this one.'

Lizzie shrugged. 'I've told you before, I've no time for anything like that right now.'

'Not even if he's good-looking?' Elsie teased.

'Not even then.' Lizzie sounded bored.

'Funny, but you looked as if you could fancy the pants off him when you first clocked him,' Elsie said, studying her nails.

'What are you saying? I've met him already?' Lizzie reddened and looked puzzled. 'I don't recall . . .'

'Don't tell me you've forgotten the tall bloke with the 'tache who was in here on his own on Valentine's night? Steve Carter, I think he said his name was.'

Lizzie started, for she did indeed have a clear memory then of the dark-haired man with the neatly trimmed moustache she'd mistaken for Joe on the Pride's opening night and she was shocked to feel the hairs on the back of her neck stand to attention at the mere mention of his name now.

'I didn't think he was so good-looking,' Lizzie said trying to sound offhand. 'What's he got that any young man who drinks in here hasn't got?'

'Clark Gable's looks, for one,' Elsie said without hesitation, 'and you know how I feel about *him*.'

'Yes, I know all about that!' Lizzie laughed now.

'He said he planned to move into Weatherfield,' Elsie said, 'though he didn't say he had his eye on a job at the Rovers Return. Frankly, I was surprised to hear Annie Walker was prepared to hire someone – she always seems to want to do everything herself.'

'I suppose she had to get some help. Didn't I hear her barmaid is leaving for the States shortly?' Lizzie said.

Elsie nodded. 'Yes, Gracie will be off soon and I'm sorry you're not interested, Lizzie,' Elsie said, 'but it looks as if I'll be transferring my allegiance back to the Rovers for a while. This young man is certainly worthy of a second look and maybe even a third one. In my book, anyone who can survive an Annie Walker interrogation and come out in one piece is definitely worthy of a second glance.'

'If you ask me, from the sounds of it, he deserves nothing short of a medal,' Lizzie said, and she was glad she'd never gone for a job interview at the Rovers. It sounded like Bob was a pushover compared with Annie Walker.

'And I've heard he's got a motor car, would you believe?' Elsie said.

'Sounds like he's got everything.' Lizzie's eyes widened.

'Including a gammy leg,' Elsie said, 'but I'm sure we

can overlook that in the circumstances. There's only one thing for it, Lizzie,' Elsie said. 'You'll have to come up to the Rovers when you get a day off.'

Hilda was proud of Lizzie's friendship. She knew, first-hand, that not everyone in the neighbourhood felt so kindly towards her as Lizzie seemed to do, for she'd overheard neighbours gossiping: '*Lizzie's wasting her time with that half-wit . . . I can't imagine what the two of them can find to talk about.*' But she'd always found that Lizzie listened and from the first time they'd met, Hilda had thought Lizzie was not only kind but generous. Like today, when she had invited Hilda to come and visit them in Coronation Street.

'It's my night off,' Lizzie said, 'so why don't you come over this evening? We can have a good chin-wag.'

Hilda's first reaction had been to refuse politely. 'Oh no, I couldn't, thank you. I wouldn't want to be putting you to any trouble.'

'Don't be silly, it's no trouble. I'm only sorry I can't invite you for your tea,' Lizzie said, 'but I'm sure you can understand it's quite difficult making the food stretch as it is. The twins might only be seven years old but I swear they've got hollow legs. Even young Sammy never seems to be satisfied these days, he's growing so fast, and between them they drive my poor ma to distraction.'

Hilda smiled. 'They're healthy young lads, you don't have to apologize. I've got brothers too, you know.'

'But it does seem a shame for you to have to sit on your own night after night,' Lizzie said.

'I don't like to complain. There's them that's far worse off than me.' Hilda turned her head away, not wanting to look at Lizzie directly.

'It's quite the opposite in our house,' Lizzie said. 'I never seem to get a minute to myself.'

'It's just that I thought my Stan would have been demobulated by now cos there's been that much talk about the war ending. But not him.' Hilda sighed.

'Well, that settles it,' Lizzie said. 'Come any time you like, the kids go to bed early on school nights. It'll make a nice change for us to have someone else to talk to and, to be honest, you'd be doing me a favour.'

'How's that, then?' Hilda was surprised.

'Ma's always saying how much she likes talking to you and there may be something you can help us with. She's been getting into a bit of a lather lately, and it would be good for her to be able to tell you about it.'

Hilda could feel her face getting red and she had to look away. It had been a long time since anyone had said anything so nice to her. 'What's she getting so hot and bothered about, then? But whatever it is I'll be glad to help if I can,' she said.

'It's something one of the neighbours said when we first moved in,' Lizzie said. 'I laughed it off as a silly rumour, but I know my ma's been dwelling on it ever since.'

Hilda pursed her lips. 'Oh, there's always plenty of rumours in this neck of the woods.'

'It might sound far-fetched, but Elsie-from-next-door seemed to imply the house was haunted,' Lizzie said. When Hilda didn't react, Lizzie went on, 'I believe it stood empty for a while before we moved in and I've heard that folk round here thought that it was an unlucky house and that there was some kind of unhealthy aura about the place, so not surprisingly, Ma's got it into her head that there are bad spirits in the house and I can't convince her otherwise.'

'Hmm,' was all Hilda said.

'The problem is,' Lizzie went on, 'recently one or two strange things have been happening.'

'Like what?' Hilda was curious.

'Like weird noises that seem to be coming from overhead. But when I go upstairs to look, not only do they stop but there's nothing there to see. It's got to the stage where the boys no longer want to go out to the lav of a night. Even Seamus, who likes to think he's the tough guy of the family, says he finds it spooky. It might sound daft, but I don't know what to think.' Lizzie shook her head in frustration. 'I've tried to laugh it off and tell them they're imagining things but only the other night Ma and me were sitting downstairs when we both felt a sudden draught, as if a window had been opened. Of course, when I got up to check, the window was tight shut.'

'Well, it doesn't sound daft to me,' Hilda said, 'for

as I've told you before, I have a certain knowledge in these matters. Between you, me and the gatepost I've been told I've got "the gift", I'm a bit psychical.'

'I remember you saying that,' Lizzie said. 'Anyway, my ma's been telling anyone who'll listen that something bad must have happened to some of the folk who'd lived there in the past.'

Hilda rolled her eyes heavenward. 'Honestly, some people don't have the sense they were born with. She shouldn't be saying such things. Anyone with a ha'p'orth of sense knows that you have to tread carefully around any kinds of negative auras if you don't want to invite trouble.'

Lizzie gave a nervous laugh. 'The main thing I'm worried about is that my ma's in a very vulnerable state at the moment and now she's convinced bad things are going to happen to us all. I was hoping you could talk to her.'

'Hmm,' Hilda said and she folded her arms across her chest. Then, to Lizzie's surprise Hilda beamed. 'I can do more than that,' she said, her face glowing as she leaned towards Lizzie. 'I'll do a reading of her tea leaves. That should be able to put her mind at rest,' Hilda ended with a satisfied smile.

When Lizzie answered the door later that evening, she was surprised to see her friend was dressed up.

'Why, Hilda,' she cried, 'I've not seen you with your

hair combed out like that since the opening night at the Pride. It looks really pretty.'

Hilda blushed and patted the curls that bordered her face. 'I comb it up every night when I gets home from work,' Hilda admitted. 'Just in case . . . you know . . .' She suddenly looked coy and busied herself taking off the thin rain jacket that she wore summer and winter. She handed it to Lizzie.

Lizzie crinkled her forehead. 'No, I don't know. In case of what?'

Hilda's face was now bright pink. 'Well, in case my Stan turns up unexpected like. It's best to be prepared I always think. I do try to look nice for my husband.'

'Your Stan sounds like my husband.' Cora was standing by the small fire that flickered in the grate. 'A thoroughly nice gentleman, so it's only right you should want to please him. I do hope he gets home soon. Now, come and sit by me on the couch. I don't always hear so well these days.'

'Go on with you, Ma, making yourself old before your time,' Lizzie scoffed. 'What would the boys think? And talking of the boys, I haven't even had a chance to go up and say goodnight to Sammy yet.'

'He was already fast asleep when I left him not ten minutes since,' Cora said, 'so don't you go disturbing him. It took me ages to get him down tonight for some reason. Probably because he knew you were here.'

As if on cue, the sound of a baby's cry seemed to fill the whole house and Lizzie burst out laughing.

'I think he fooled you. I bet he wasn't really asleep,' Lizzie said, 'and he does like me to say goodnight to him,' she explained to Hilda, 'so why don't you go and sit down with my ma, and I'll be back in a tick.'

When Lizzie came downstairs again, Hilda and Cora were each clutching a small glass filled with what looked like water and, as Lizzie had hoped, they were chatting away as if they were old friends.

'I hope you don't mind but I opened that bottle of gin you won on Valentines. Sorry we've nothing to go with it, but I've poured one for you. A small one, mind,' Cora said, 'we've got to make it last.' Lizzie was about to say that if Cora kept on topping up the bottle with water from the tap like she'd seen her doing to the sherry they treated themselves to at Christmas, they would have no trouble making it last, but she decided that would be unkind.

'Why don't you put the kettle on before you sit down, Lizzie, love,' Cora said. 'We need to mash the tea so's we can get started. I'm dying to hear what Hilda's got to say. And while we're waiting, maybe you could top up Hilda's glass, they are only small.'

'Ooh, how many's that?' Hilda's eyes grew wide.

'Who's counting?' Cora said, and Hilda giggled.

'But there's work to be done,' Hilda said, proffering her glass, 'so I can't afford to get squiffy.'

'I do hope the leaves or whatever it is they put in those so-called tea packets nowadays will be as reliable as real tea leaves. Do you think it will make a difference to your reading, Hilda?' Cora asked.

Hilda waved her hand and for a moment looked dangerously close to toppling off the couch, but Cora managed to prop her up in time.

Hilda hiccupped and apologized. 'No, I'm sure it won't,' she said. She gave a little cough. 'Now then, let me just refresh my memory on a few points. This house is number nine, isn't it?'

'That right,' Cora answered. 'Nine Coronation Street.' For a moment she looked anxious. 'Are you saying that nine is an unlucky number?'

Hilda shook her head. 'No, not generally speaking. Though it's always possible . . . but let's not jump ahead.'

'What do you mean?' Cora couldn't let it go. 'How would it be unlucky?'

'Like maybe it was meant to be a six so it's "turning our life upside down",' Lizzie said.

A bloom rose on Hilda's cheeks as she wagged a finger in Lizzie's direction. 'I do hope you're not mocking, Lizzie Doyle, because I'm being perfectly serious.'

'No, I'm not mocking, Hilda,' Lizzie said, 'I'm trying to understand.'

Hilda set her mouth firmly in a thin line and addressed her next question to Cora. 'So, what do you know about the previous tenants?'

Cora shrugged. 'Nothing. And none of the neighbours have told us much either.'

'I believe there hadn't been anyone living here for a while before we came,' Lizzie said.

'Aha!' Hilda said. 'That might well be the problem.'

'What kind of a problem?' Cora looked concerned.

'When a house has been left empty for a time sprites . . .' Hilda shook her head and tried again. 'I mean spir-its,' she said slowly. 'Spir-its,' she said again, 'can come to live in it.'

'Oh dear.' Cora looked crestfallen.

'That doesn't necessarily mean that they're bad-luck omens,' Hilda said hastily. 'They might just be restless spirits looking for somewhere to settle. Of course, they might not have had any original connection to the house at all, in which case they might need some persuading to show themselves.'

'Is that difficult?' Cora asked.

Hilda tried to reassure her. 'Hopefully I'll be able to encourage them to appear when the time comes. Though getting rid of them may not be so easy. It may be more a matter of persuading them to move on. But first things first. We need to get a reading of the teacups. Once we can see exactly what they have to tell us we can start thinking about the next step.'

Lizzie had mixed feelings about where all this might be leading, but she forced herself not to show her concerns; after all, she had encouraged Hilda in the first place, and Cora seemed to be listening attentively. At that moment the kettle began to whistle and Lizzie went to mash the all-important tea.

Later, as they drained their cups, Hilda looked worried that there might not be sufficient leaves left at the bottom of the cup for her to do a proper reading.

'It does look more like sawdust than proper tea leaves, I'm afraid,' Lizzie apologized. 'It may not matter too much, I'm just trying to get a handle on what I'm seeing,' Hilda said as she peered intently into Cora's cup. 'The remains do seem to have clumped into some kind of pattern that may yet be perfectly usable.' She rotated the cup for a full turn, her eyebrows raised in hope, and continued to puzzle in silence for several minutes, scratching her head as she tried to make sense of what she saw. But if she hoped to get a definitive answer, it seemed she was going to be disappointed. She peered into all three cups in case she'd been looking for a message in the wrong place, but after considerable anguish and much cup turning, Hilda decided that the powdery remains told her nothing of any interest.

She took a deep breath and shook her head. 'I'm afraid it's going to take a proper meeting with the spirits to give us the answers we need,' she said.

Lizzie didn't know whether to be glad or sorry when Hilda made the announcement and she wasn't sure what to say, but Cora was eager to go ahead as soon as possible.

'I think that's what we should do then,' Cora said. 'We've come so far and now we've really got to find out what's going on before anything nasty happens, don't you agree, Lizzie?' Cora turned to her, eager and expectant.

'The thing is, I'm not so sure . . .' Hilda began. 'I've never actually done . . .' She looked at Cora's face and suddenly she brightened. 'But I'm sure we'll manage somehow,' she added hurriedly. 'So why don't we hold a proper one of them meetings – what do you call it?'

'You mean a séance?' Lizzie asked hesitantly.

'That's the one,' Hilda said. 'We can do it between the three of us.'

'Ooh!' Cora sounded excited. 'I know we shouldn't be dabbling in such things but I'm ready to do anything if it will sort this thing out.'

'Then I'll have a word with my friend who knows about such matters and we'll see what we can do,' Hilda said.

It was several days later before they could get together and on the appointed evening Hilda arrived at number nine on time. 'This is it, The Ouija board,' she said brandishing a small wooden board as Lizzie opened the door, and she went in and put it down on the table.

'What do all them markings mean?' Cora was curious as she peered at it. 'Do you understand what it says, Hilda?'

Hilda cleared her throat. 'My friend said it might be best not to bother with all of those picture things as it's my first time. She said to concentrate on the letters and numbers that are around the edges for now, and maybe use the words yes and no, which are over there.' She pointed. 'Otherwise it might get too complicated.'

'I can see that.' Lizzie frowned, not knowing what to make of the strange-looking symbols that seemed to have been burned into the wood.

'So, why don't we sit down and join hands,' Hilda said, trying to remember her friend's instructions.

They sat for some time, hands spread across the board, then Hilda, with her eyes closed, began to ask questions, waiting anxiously to see what words might be spelt out by movements of the board. But try as she might to will it to happen, the board didn't move, and the tension between the three of them mounted.

'Oh, dear, I must be doing something wrong,' Hilda said eventually, her voice trembling as her eyes filled. 'It doesn't seem to be working.'

They all sat back from the table.

'No, I'm afraid it doesn't,' Lizzie said folding her arms across her chest, her mouth set in a firm line.

'I think what we could all do with now is a strong cup of tea,' Cora said and she pushed her chair back and went to put the kettle on to heat.

'Never mind tea,' Lizzie said, trying not to show her

frustration. 'How about seeing what's left in the gin bottle? I somehow think that's the only kind of spirits we're going to be in touch with tonight.'

The last thing Steve imagined he would be doing when he had taken on the job at the Rovers was listening to a bunch of women squabbling about a street party as Annie Walker seemed to expect him to do. So it was with some relief that he welcomed Elsie Tanner into the snug to join the inaccurately-named organizing committee. When she sashayed in with an exaggerated swivel of her hips it was like a breath of fresh air, and her breezy, 'So sorry I'm late,' with no kind of explanation seemed to cut through all the nonsense about bunting and tables and chairs that they'd spent the first half hour of the meeting fighting over.

Steve caught an overwhelmingly seductive waft of perfume as Elsie went by and couldn't prevent a smile as her eyes twinkled at him and she pouted her amazingly reddened lips in his direction. A heady cocktail. It was enough to make him believe the stories he had heard about what she'd got up to when the GIs were in town. This was quite some lass. Very much like those on his long list of previous girlfriends, but not like . . . He stopped, for this time he knew there was competition from an unexpected source. He had a sudden vision of Lizzie Doyle's fresh face, her smooth skin mostly devoid of make-up, her innocent expression. He'd known instinctively as soon as he saw her that she was in a different class. What would he give to be down at the Pride right now?

Elsie carefully crossed her legs as she sat down opposite Steve, and Ena Sharples didn't look very pleased as Elsie set her gin and tonic down on the beer mat in front of her. 'What are you doing here?' Ena scowled. 'This is a private meeting. Nowt to do with you.'

'I think you'll find it has everything to do with me, because I'm in charge of the food for this here party,' Elsie said. 'Elsie Foyle has passed it on to me.' She leaned back in her chair and lit a cigarette, deliberately puffing the smoke in Ena's direction. 'No food, no party, wouldn't you agree?'

'Oh, aye?' Ena looked doubtful. 'So where will all this food be coming from?' she sneered.

The two women glared at each other and Ena added scornfully, 'I mean, we all know about Elsie Foyle and what goes on under her counter when she thinks no one's looking. But where are you going to magic up enough food for the whole street? Answer me that. Got secret supplies that we don't know about?'

'You don't need to worry your hairnetted head about such things, Mrs Sharples,' Elsie Tanner said, 'I have my sources and we already have it all in hand. I can assure you we'll be negotiating the best deal in town.'

'Who's this "we", all of a sudden?' Ena picked up on the word.

'Me and Steve,' Elsie said and flashed him a grin.

Steve, surprised by the sound of his name, looked up in time to see the cheeky grin morph into her most alluring smile and there was no mistaking the triumphant glint that lit up her eyes.

Steve gradually settled in at the Rovers though he was aware of Annie Walker hovering in the background, a constant presence, monitoring his every move. That was why, on his first night off, he wasted no time in getting away for a few hours and going down to the Pride, where he hoped his memories of Lizzie's good looks and welcoming smile would be as he remembered.

It was not as busy in the Pride as the first time he had been there, though it was more crowded than the Rovers had been the previous night. He recognized one or two Rovers' customers among the drinkers at the bar, but he couldn't put names to them, even though they obviously recognized him.

The layout of the pub looked the same as it had on his first visit, like the kind of bar he'd seen many times in films, and as he walked through the saloon-style doors he was aware, once again, that the atmosphere was very different from the Rovers. The air of stale tobacco was blended with cigar smoke, something he hadn't come across before in a northern pub. There wasn't actual sawdust on the stone-tiled floor, nor were there any spittoons, but he wouldn't have been surprised if some young man had fired off a couple of rounds from a gun in a holster at his hip. He swivelled his head, his gaze taking in the whole room, and only stopped when he reached Lizzie at the pumps pulling a pint. The curls of her fair hair framed her heart-shaped face and he was delighted to see she was just as pretty as he'd remembered. He hovered by the door for a few moments, once more taking in the china-like paleness of her flawless complexion and her million-dollar smile. Then, as he approached the bar, he cleared his throat and she looked up. For a moment she looked startled, then there was a hint of recognition and her face softened.

'I see you're not in your prize-winning frock,' Steve said. 'Pity, the green suited you. It matched your eyes.' He thought to tease her further but her cheeks had already blushed crimson as she gave a shy laugh.

'What can I get you?' she asked politely.

'A pint of your best bitter, please,' he said. Her eyes made contact with his momentarily but then she looked quickly away.

'I'm saving that dress for a special occasion,' she said.

'Maybe I can help to create one of those. How would you like to go out for a drink on your next night off? You could wear it then.'

'No, thanks. I'll save it for something really special,' she said.

Steve clutched at his heart. 'Oh dear, you've cut me to the quick. Have you got a better offer?'

'I've got other commitments,' she said.

'You've got a boyfriend?'

'No,' she said, but didn't elaborate.

'Then you must let me know when your next special occasion is going to be so I can be here to witness it,' he said. 'I'm free as a bird.'

'Don't hold your breath,' Lizzie said. And this time she had the good grace to grin as she turned away to serve another customer.

Steve didn't move away in the hope that Lizzie might return and they could continue the conversation, minimal though it had been, and by the time he was ready for a refill his persistence had paid off for the crowd had cleared from the floor and he was the only one left at the counter.

'I've got a job up the road since we last met,' he said as she handed him the glass. 'At the Rovers Return.'

She gave a noncommital nod. 'I've not been there,' she said, 'but we get quite a few of your customers in here. How do you like it there?'

'It's fine. How about you, are you settling in here?'

She shrugged. 'It's a job.' And the expression on her face didn't invite further inquiry.

'Have you lived in this part of Weatherfield long?' he asked.

'Not long,' she said. 'How about you?'

'I've just moved into digs in Charles Street. They're not brilliant but they'll do till I find something better. At least it's handy for the Rovers.'

There were several moments of awkward silence as he watched her tidying up and rehanging all the glasses and for once Steve didn't know what to say. He wanted to know all about her and it wasn't like him to be stuck for small talk, but he was used to girls coming on to him, rather than him wondering what he might say that wouldn't drive her to the other end of the bar again.

'How do you get on with your boss?' Lizzie asked unexpectedly. 'I've heard she can be quite difficult.'

'Who told you that? Elsie Tanner?'

Lizzie looked sheepish.

'That was because Mrs Walker gave me a ticking off the other day that everyone in the bar could hear. She wasn't happy that I'd let the cleaner go before her official time was up. She'd promised she'd make it up some other time. But Mrs Walker seemed to think she'd be cheated out of that extra half hour in the long run and she told me in no uncertain terms that I was too lax.'

'What did you do?'

'I made sure the cleaner gave back the half hour within the next couple of days and made a point of telling Mrs Walker it was happening because I had to save face.'

'And did Mrs Walker say anything?'

'Of course not. She had to save face too. She thinks I'm muscling in, but I'm not – I'm just doing my job and I'm used to taking charge.'

'She likes being in charge too! But I suppose it's not been easy for her – I believe her husband's been away a long time,' Lizzie said, 'and the war's not over yet.'

'Whose side are you on?' Steve protested. 'She can be very frustrating at times, though I'm learning to adapt.'

'I know what you mean,' Lizzie said. She looked as if she was about to say something more but at that moment a large man blustered his way in from the kitchen at the back, a fat cigar clenched between his teeth.

'How are things going out here, Lizzie?' the man said. 'Are you coping on your own?'

'Yes, thanks. I'm fine, Bob,' Steve heard her reply and his attention was drawn to him. Seeing him close to like this for the first time he realized there was something familiar about his large blubbery face – and not just because he'd seen him on stage on opening night. He was clean-shaven and for some reason Steve could see him with a moustache. As Steve was trying to pinpoint where he might have seen him before, he noticed the man's banana-like fingers slide across Lizzie's slender shoulders and down her back to smooth the soft fabric of her dress over the cheeks of her bottom. He saw Lizzie tense as he did that and, as the man tried to give her a clumsy sort of squeeze, Steve couldn't help but notice that her jaw clenched and she shied away.

'Everything all right, sir?' the man asked Steve

directly, as though nothing had happened. 'I'm Bob Bennett, the landlord here.' He put out his hand but showed no signs of recognizing Steve.

'All's fine, thanks,' Steve responded automatically. 'In fact,' he said, 'I'm glad to meet you.' He shook Bob's hand. 'I'm Steve Carter, the new manager at the Rovers Return.' Bob pumped his hand vigorously, the name obviously meaning nothing to him.

'Delighted to meet you, Steve. Please call me Bob – and by the way, that pint's on the house.'

'Thanks very much.' Steve nodded, still trying to work out where he might have seen Bob before.

'Mrs Walker must have been very glad to secure your services. A woman needs to have a man about the place, I always say,' Bob said and he took a long draw from the cigar before expelling a couple of smoke rings into the already fuggy atmosphere. 'Lots for you to be getting on with over there, I don't doubt.' He gave a deep-throated chuckle and leaned forward across the counter. 'I couldn't help noticing that a fresh lick of paint wouldn't go amiss for starters. And I might be able to put a few tins of nice gloss paint your way – if you play your cards right. For a good price, if you know what I mean.'

There was something about the way he said those last few words that triggered a memory for Steve, but before he could recall the details a bell sounded in one of the back rooms and Bob's face suddenly switched from jovial to businesslike.

'Don't worry Lizzie, I'll deal with that,' he said, patting her bottom one more time. 'Lovely to meet you, Steve. We must have a proper chat sometime.' And without another word he disappeared as abruptly as he'd arrived.

Almost immediately images began whirling in Steve's head of another time and a different place. He was in a pub in Blackpool, a place where he'd worked briefly, soon after leaving school. Suddenly it all came flooding back. Only the Pride's landlord hadn't been called Bob Bennett then. His name in those days had been Dave Elliott and he'd been notorious for fencing stolen goods.

Steve turned his attention back to Lizzie, but she was busy cleaning tables and collecting the remaining dead glasses. Now was not the time to continue their earlier conversation; he would have to drop in again soon.

He downed his pint and called out to tell her that he was leaving and said, 'Pop up the road to the Rovers when you have a night off.' But Lizzie didn't answer nor did she acknowledge him as he gave her a wave of his hand before slipping out of the pub.

He crossed the poorly-lit lane leading to the Pride's back yard and automatically glanced in both directions. At the end of the short alleyway two figures seemed to be in deep discussion. One had the coat collar of his donkey jacket turned up so that it was impossible to see his face but Steve was certain from the bulky outline of his figure that it was Bob Bennett. The other was a scrawny-looking character with long hair who was dressed in clothes that didn't seem to fit. As Steve watched, Bob poked the other man in the shoulder, following him as he backed away. Steve could hear raised voices, though he couldn't make out the words and he pulled back into the shadow of the wall. As he watched, he saw what looked like a wad of notes change hands in return for a heavy, coarse hessian bag. So, Bob Bennett or Dave Elliott or whatever he was called now was still up to his old tricks, Steve thought, and he stood without moving wondering what he should do. Should he tell the police, or would they once again be unable to find any incriminating evidence? For now, it was too late for him to do anything because the two men parted almost immediately. The larger man returned to the pub while the skinny one hurried down to the other end of the alley and disappeared into the night.

Chapter 5

It was not until the beginning of May that there was a formal declaration ending the hostilities in Europe. On the evening of 7 May Lizzie was on duty at the Pride. The radio was on at low volume in one corner of the bar because the news was expected at any minute, but no one seemed to be paying it any particular attention. Then suddenly someone shouted for quiet. The BBC were interrupting their scheduled radio programmes for a newsflash. A complete hush fell over the room and immediately a rather sombre-sounding voice came over the airwaves announcing to the nation that the war in Europe was indeed over. Instantly, the whole bar erupted with a giant cheer that drowned out the remainder of the news bulletin.

Lizzie was as relieved and delighted as anyone in the bar that night to think that there would be no more bombs and no more sirens, and she couldn't help smiling at the very thought. She could at last begin to think about the new world Tommy, Seamus, and little Sammy would be growing up in, something she had once feared might not be possible. But her joy was edged with sadness, for she had already lost the two most important men in her life and no peace treaty now could bring them back. She swiped away the tears she felt forming before anyone could see them and she was relieved to hear Hilda's voice trilling above the din, for her friend always managed to make her smile. To Lizzie's surprise, Hilda looked like she was dressed ready for going out, in a pretty cotton frock and with her hair combed out into sausage curls.

'I wanted to make sure you'd heard the news,' Hilda said. 'I can hardly remember what peace feels like.' Her giggle was lost in the hubbub.

'I thought the bank holiday wasn't until tomorrow?' Lizzie said. 'But you look as if you're ready to party now.'

'I am,' Hilda said. 'Everyone seems to be buzzing and the streets are already crowded with people, so I thought maybe we should start celebrating too.'

'That sounds like a great idea!' Lizzie said. 'Bob said I can get off early tonight.'

'Ooh,' Hilda said, rubbing her hands together. 'I was

thinking maybe we could go into town, though I hear Mr Churchill's going to speak to everybody on the radio.'

'Yes, but that's not until tomorrow so there's nothing to stop us having fun today,' Lizzie said.

'Maybe we should have a quick drink before we go?' Hilda said.

'Why not?' Lizzie said. 'I've some tips left in the pot.' And she poured two port and lemons without waiting to be asked.

'Just think, no more rationing,' Hilda said, lifting her glass in a toast.

'Oh, I don't know about that,' Lizzie said but Hilda was softly humming an unrecognizable tune and seemed to be in a world of her own.

'You do realize that means my Stan will be coming home any day now,' Hilda said proudly, as if her husband had been personally responsible for ending the fighting. 'He can't be a prisoner of war if there is no more war, now can he?' She chuckled.

'No, Hilda, he can't,' Lizzic said, grinning at her friend's logic.

'They'll have to let him go now so that he can be demobulated,' Hilda said.

That made Lizzie smile. Hilda could always be relied on to say something that would make her want to laugh. 'I'm sure you're right, but don't pin your hopes on it happening soon. There's bound to be a lot of POWs to be released and it will probably take some time to get through all the paperwork. You know what the army's like.'

'Why's that then?' Hilda said. 'Cos it took them no time at all to get him listed and sent off to Italy, so why can't they be as quick now in sending him home?'

'That's because there was a war on then.' Lizzie sighed. 'It's amazing how they can shift themselves when they want to.'

'I'm sorry your dad won't be coming home,' Hilda said suddenly. She put a tentative hand out to pat Lizzie's arm. 'And your young man.' She paused. 'I know you don't like to talk about it, but I want you to know I do understand. A GI, wasn't he?'

'Canadian airman.' Lizzie was never able to say the words without her voice cracking as it did now, though she did her best to disguise it as she tried to smile. She took a deep breath. 'But that doesn't mean I can't be happy for you, Hilda, and the thought of you getting your husband back.' She glanced up at the clock. 'Finish your drink and then we can walk down the road, see who's about and what's going on.'

'That would be nice. Though there's already that many people out there we might not be able to walk far. It's heaving just like it was wakes week.'

'Then we'll have to take our chances,' Lizzie said.

'Why don't we start off by popping into the Rovers,' Hilda said. 'You've always said you wanted to see what it's like.'

'What, like go on a pub crawl? You sound as if you intend getting drunk,' Lizzie said with a laugh.

'That's as may be,' Hilda said, then she leaned over the counter and added in a confidential whisper, 'but I was actually thinking we could take a deck at the new manager I've heard so much about.'

'Steve Carter? Oh, but I've already met him,' Lizzie said. Hilda looked surprised. 'Aren't you the quiet one? When were that, then?'

'He was there at our opening night, only he hadn't got the job yet then. But he's popped into the Pride since. Came to introduce himself to Bob, I think.'

'More likely spying for the Rovers,' Hilda said.

'No more than we would be if we went there now.'

'So, what did you think? Do you think he's dishy?' Hilda was excited.

Lizzie shrugged, not wanting to admit that she thought he was very good-looking. 'He's pleasant enough I suppose.'

The inside of the Rovers was much as Lizzie might have expected from what she had seen of the outside, although it was darker than she'd imagined. The wood panelling and the paintwork were dark and the lighting was dim despite the fact that the blackout curtains had been removed, and the heavy fug of smoke and beer fumes that hung in the air was oppressive. At least the booths were brightened up by the deep crimson upholstery of the seat covers. It matched the velvety material of the stools and chairs that stood round the little tables. It was more crowded than she'd been led to believe of late, particularly given how many people were out on the streets, and as they pushed their way through to the bar Lizzie was surprised how many faces she recognized, having served them at the Pride.

They'd hardly got inside the door than Lizzie felt Hilda's elbow in her ribs. 'He is a bit of all right, isn't he?' she said in an embarrassingly loud whisper. 'Oh, but I'll have to leave you to it. I've got to go to the lav.'

Suddenly alone, Lizzie looked round the well-filled room and was pleased when Elsie Tanner caught her eye. She was propping up the bar and called to her. 'Lizzie! What are you doing in here? Come on over and let me get you a drink to celebrate the wonderful news. I don't know about you, but my night's only just getting going.'

Lizzie didn't believe that, for Elsie already had that faraway look she'd seen before when she'd had one too many. Besides, she'd already caught the blast of gin on Elsie's breath.

'Hey, Mr Barman!' Elsie called to the young man Lizzie recognized behind the counter. Steve Carter had a tea towel in his hand and was polishing some freshly washed glasses. Lizzie felt a strange frisson as he treated her to a beaming smile and she had to look away. 'Can we get some service over here?' Elsie said. 'Give my young friend whatever she wants to drink. We've got lots to celebrate tonight.'

Steve looked up at Elsie's shout and stopped what he was doing.

'You remember your rival from the Pride of Weatherfield,' Elsie said. 'No doubt she's checking out the opposition, so you'll have to be on your best behaviour.'

'Of course I remember.' Steve smiled again and nodded in Lizzie's direction, and this time there was no avoiding his gaze. 'Nice to see you again,' he said.

Lizzie was aware of the intensity of Steve's gaze though she tried hard not to meet his eyes. From this angle she could see why he had reminded her of Joe, for he had the same strongly chiselled jaw, a similarly styled moustache, and he combed back his thickly Brylcreemed hair in the same way, highlighting his high forehead.

'What can I get you?' she heard him ask. Suddenly she felt hot and confused, trying to remember why she had come there.

'Nothing, thanks. I don't want anything.' She turned to her neighbour. 'Thanks anyway, Elsie,' she said, 'but I won't be stopping long. I can't, not right now . . . I–I just wanted to . . .'

'Never mind, you can take a raincheck.' Elsie giggled. 'Isn't that what the Americans always say?'

Lizzie bit her lip, for that was what Joe used to say as well. She looked up, aware that Steve was still staring at her though she couldn't look directly at him.

'Are you sure I can't persuade you to stop and have one drink at least, to celebrate?' he said, hanging up the glass over the bar. 'After all it's not every day the war ends. And I owe you a drink, so you really must let me show you that the Rovers is every bit as hospitable as the Pride.' His voice was persuasive.

'Thanks, Mr Car—'

'Steve,' he quickly corrected.

'Steve,' she said with a sudden diffidence. 'Maybe some other time.'

'I'll hold you to that,' he said. 'But you must promise not to leave it too long or you might find me down at the Pride again.'

'Oh!' Lizzie didn't know how to respond.

'So how about you promise to come on your next day off?'

'Maybe,' Lizzie said, and she lowered her eyes as she turned back to Elsie. 'Thanks for the offer, but we're not staying,' she said. 'I'll come again another night to have a drink with you, Elsie, but right now we're going to join in the celebrations.'

'Where are you off to, then?' Elsie asked.

'Everyone else seems to be heading into Manchester,' Lizzie said. 'I reckon that's where we should go an' all.

And looking at the crowds already out there I think we should get started.'

'I'm ready when you are,' Hilda said cheerily as she came back wiping her wet hands on her thin raincoat. She looped her arm through Lizzie's. 'I'm sticking with you,' she said. Lizzie hesitated for a second, then pulled Hilda away from the counter.

Lizzie watched as Elsie grabbed the arm of the young man in uniform who'd been drinking quietly beside her. 'We're going to celebrate by having a nice quiet night in, aren't we, chuck?' She gazed up into his face.

For a moment he looked bemused but then he smiled broadly and nodded. 'Sounds good to me. It's Elsie, isn't it?' he said. He gave her an exaggerated wink and Elsie chortled.

'Be seeing you, then Else,' Lizzie said, and with a wave of her hand in the general direction of the bar she turned quickly and left the pub.

'Well, you've certainly made a hit there with that young man,' Hilda said and she raised her eyebrows knowingly as they stepped outside. 'The way that Steve was looking at you, I don't know why you didn't want to stop for a bit.' She turned as if to go back. 'There's still time to change your mind.'

Lizzie shook her head and Hilda sighed. 'I could have fancied him myself if I didn't already have my Stan.'

Lizzie raised her eyebrows and smiled. 'Shall we head towards Manchester and see how far we get?' she said and they set off in the direction of the main road, picking up the crowds the further they went. Suddenly Lizzie felt the coarse material of army-issue khaki rub against her bare shoulder and looked up to see a soldier's face peering down at her. He was trying to wrap his other arm around Hilda at the same time. 'Now where are you two fair ladies off to tonight?' He slurred his words. 'Because wherever it is, I'm sure you could do with an escort.'

'No, we couldn't, thank you very much.' Lizzie shook his arm off irritably but with such unexpected force that he lost his footing and slipped on the cobbles. Lizzie grabbed hold of Hilda, brushing his other arm away from her friend to ensure he didn't pull her down with him. 'We need nothing of the sort. What we need is to be left alone,' Lizzie shouted over her shoulder, although Hilda seemed a little reluctant to follow as Lizzie tried to pull her away.

The two linked arms and walked away as quickly as they could. As they made their way through Weatherfield, Lizzie was amazed to find how many merrymakers were already on the streets, making it difficult in some places to walk. Everyone seemed to be caught up in the excitement and there were feelings of madness and euphoria all around them. Lights were on in all the houses and children of all ages were running up and down the streets while the adults were spontaneously dancing and singing on the busy pavements as if they never wanted to stop.

'It doesn't look like anyone will get much sleep tonight,' Lizzie said.

Hilda gave a chuckle. 'But it is quite exciting, isn't it? I've never seen anything like it.'

They had come to the large open space people called the Field when Lizzie suddenly stopped and cried out, 'Oh my goodness, will you look at that.'

'What's the matter?' Hilda asked in alarm.

'I haven't seen one of them in a long while,' Lizzie said in amazement. She was staring at the bonfire that was burning brightly on the normally deserted recreation area.

'Oh, that! I thought there was a problem. I've seen lots of bonfires, much bigger than that one, on Guy Fawkes' night when we were kids. We used to ask for a penny for the Guy when what we wanted really was to cadge some money to buy liquorice and ha'penny chews.' Hilda giggled.

'Yes, we did that too,' Lizzie said. 'And we'd roast spuds in the fire. At least, my dad did; we weren't allowed anywhere near.' Lizzie's eyes filled as she remembered better times when the twins had been the babies in the family and her father had still been alive. 'But I've not seen any kind of fire like that since before the war.'

'Well, we couldn't show any lights when there was all those bombers flying overhead, could we?' Hilda said with a shudder. 'One flash of light and we'd have

119

had one of them warders after us like we was the crinimals, not the Jerries.'

Lizzie laughed as a rocket flew up over her head, scattering a shower of coloured sparks in its wake. 'Yes, those ARPs were a bit like jail warders, weren't they? Keeping us prisoners in the dark the whole time. It's great to see people having so much fun. Though I'm amazed that the little ones don't seem to be afraid of the bangers. Me, I jump every time one goes off.'

'Here, I'll have one of them,' Hilda suddenly called out to a young boy who was running past her, waving a handful of sparklers. He stopped and handed her one. 'Her'yah, Missus,' he said, a cheeky grin on his face. 'It'll cost you a ha'penny, though.'

Hilda's face fell.

'Here, I've got some change, but you'll have to settle for half that, I'm afraid,' Lizzie said. She fished in her skirt pocket and produced a farthing that she handed over to the boy.

'Ta, Missus, be glad I'm feeling generous,' he said as he gave Lizzie a sparkler too. 'But I'll tell you summat for nothing . . .' He turned to Lizzie, a serious look on his face. 'Did you know we just won the war?' Suddenly a huge smile lit up his face and he began to cackle loudly as he ran off.

Hilda was almost squealing with childlike delight as she jigged about, whirling the firework round and round in front of her. 'I've not had one of these since I was a nipper,' she shouted to Lizzie, though it was getting harder to hear her above the screams and shouts of the over-excited children who were now dancing round the fire. Sparks flew as she continued to whizz the stick of the firework round and her face lit up as if she was a child too. Then suddenly her face changed and her voice sounded fearful as she cried out, 'Help! It's going to burn my fingers! What do I do with it now?'

'You must be holding it too far up. Chuck it on the fire,' Lizzie said, but Hilda panicked, and without looking where she was throwing it, tossed the still glowing remains into a nearby box that looked to be full of rubbish.

'You've not burnt yourself, have you? Where did it go?' Lizzie was concerned.

'No, I got rid of it into that box in good time, thank goodness, so no harm done.' Hilda sounded relieved.

Suddenly there was a whirring and a whooshing noise, followed by a series of loud bangs and there were rainbows of sparks flying everywhere and explosions of light accompanied by the sounds of people screaming, 'It's a bomb!'; 'The Germans are back!'; 'What's happened to the sirens?' while others shouted, 'Get down!' 'Get out of the way!' as parents threw their children to the ground and tried their best to shelter them with their bodies.

Lizzie grabbed hold of Hilda and did the same thing. She forced herself to lie quite still, trying to calm her friend until there was a momentary silence when she dared to look up, but all she was in time to see were the brightly coloured flashes dying away, leaving thin trails of smoke. Lizzie was still breathing hard and her body was trembling, but she sat up and looked around before gingerly standing up when there were no more bangs or flashes. She heard several small children crying.

'Have the bombs stopped now, Daddy? Will the planes be coming back?' a little boy wanted to know, between sobs. 'I want to go home!'

'It wasn't a bomb,' Lizzie heard his father say in an authoritative voice. 'There weren't any planes and there are none now.' She looked up into the clear sky and then at the man who was staring down at a charred patch of grass. He disturbed the ashes of a burnt-out box with the toe of his shoe. 'It's all right, son,' he said. 'It looks like some bloody idiot dropped a sparkler into our fireworks' box and set the whole bloody lot off at once.' He picked up what was left of the sparkler's wand and regarded it ruefully. At that the little boy peered into the remains of the box and began to wail. 'They've all gone! All our fireworks have gone,' he cried, and it was then that Lizzie realized that it must have been Catherine wheels and bangers and rockets that had exploded all around them, not flying bombs.

Then a woman's voice joined in the mêlée. 'Has anyone been hurt?' she shouted, and she started running around the Field. No one answered, but one by one other people stood up, unharmed, and went to check on their own boxes of fireworks. Several came over to survey the box that had been so thoroughly destroyed.

'It's an absolute miracle, is all I can say.' The woman came back. 'I can hardly believe it, but I don't think anyone's been hurt.'

'Thank God for that,' the man said, 'though I don't know how. Did you see which stupid bugger did it?' He looked at the other families as if expecting to find the culprit just by looking.

The woman shook her head.

'Lucky for him I didn't see who it was,' the man said, 'because if it was just a prank it was not funny. I tell you, if I ever find out!' He clenched both hands into fists. 'They cost almost a week's wages, them fireworks did. They were meant to last all night, not be snuffed out in five minutes.'

Lizzie helped Hilda to her feet and they backed away from the light of the fire. 'What . . .' Hilda began, looking bewildered. She didn't seem to know what had happened. Lizzie put her finger to her lips. She had seen the anger on the man's face and didn't want to wait to hear more. She took hold of Hilda's arm and indicated they should leave. Without another word they walked quickly away from the Field and within minutes were lost in the crowds that were still thronging the main road that led into town.

They walked in silence for a while, Hilda bemused

at first, Lizzie not really wanting to discuss the unfortunate incident.

'I should have made a wish,' Hilda said, 'what with all those rockets going off like that.'

Lizzie frowned. 'A wish? What for?'

'It's what we always did, my brothers and me, when we was kids. We'd go down to see the fireworks in the park and we'd take a milk bottle to stand the rockets in. Once the paper was lit and they flew off we'd make a wish. Do you think it's too late to do it now? I could still make at least one wish for all them rockets, couldn't I?' She stopped walking and closed her eyes for a moment while her lips were moving silently.

'What did you wish for?' Lizzie asked when they started walking again.

'I can't tell you that or it won't come true,' Hilda said, raising her eyebrows.

'That's what my ma used to say when I'd blow out the candles on my birthday cake,' Lizzie said. 'Make a wish but you mustn't tell.'

'I'd just like to have my Stan back so that we can live happily ever after,' Hilda said after a few moments, disregarding her own maxim. 'Like they do in the films. How about you? What would you wish for?'

Lizzie, caught unawares by the question, had to press her lips tightly together to stop them trembling. All she could do was to shake her head.

Hilda's hand flew to her own mouth. 'Oh, I'm so

sorry,' she said, 'I didn't mean to pry. I wasn't thinking . . .'

'It's all right,' Lizzie managed to say, though she couldn't look at her friend. 'But I'm not sure I'd wish for anything. Wishing only seems to bring me bad luck.' She sighed. 'None of my dreams ever seem to come true . . .' And she walked on, leaving Hilda to trot briskly behind her in order to catch up.

'I wonder what my Stan is doing right now,' Hilda said as she came alongside. 'Packing up ready to come home, I shouldn't wonder.' She squeezed Lizzie's arm as she smiled. 'P'raps he really will be home soon.'

Their pace slowed as they continued to wander idly through Weatherfield. They had come to streets full of terraces of larger, older houses and the crowds were beginning to thin. It was getting dark when, without warning, Lizzie stumbled, getting her legs entangled in what looked like a pile of old clothes that had been left out on the pavement at the top of one of the driveways. She grabbed hold of Hilda's arm to stop herself falling over and managed to regain her balance.

'What the hell was that?' she said. She peered more closely at the bale without wanting to touch it but it was impossible to see what it was. To her astonishment, Hilda gave the bundle a hefty kick. Then she stood on it and gave a little jump.

'Well, I can tell you one thing it isn't,' Hilda said. 'It's not my Stan.'

That made Lizzie laugh out loud. 'What are you talking about? And what are you doing? I can see clearly now that it's just a bundle of old clothes. Why on earth should you imagine it could be Stan?'

'Because that's how him and me met, that's why,' Hilda said, and Lizzie couldn't help but stare at her friend. 'I've not told you the story, have I?' Hilda asked.

Lizzie shook her head. 'Wasn't he in the army when you met?'

'He was. The war had already started but he hadn't yet been sent overseas. Turned out he was on leave, waiting to go off to somewhere fancy. "Somewhere warm",' he said. I think he was hoping to get some time in the sun.'

'I always assumed you'd had a romantic meeting, though I don't know why,' Lizzie said.

Hilda smiled, a dreamy look on her face. 'Oh, but it was. Dead romantic,' she said. She looked almost coy now and Lizzie was surprised to see the pink spots high on Hilda's cheeks suddenly deepen.

'I never told Stan, but I'd actually gone to the pictures with someone else that night,' she said. 'He was a soldier too.' She thought for a moment. 'I can't even remember his name! I know we'd been to the cinema to see Clark Gable – he's my special favourite, you know – though I can't remember the name of the film he was in. Any road, afterwards this soldier was walking me back, only it were very dark, of course. No lights anywhere and

126

not many folk out on the street. Something to do with Corfu, they said, though I was never quite sure what they meant cos my brother said Corfu was in Greece.'

Lizzie's natural reaction would have been to shudder at the memory of the curfew Hilda was struggling to describe, but Hilda's version made her want to laugh. Nevertheless, Lizzie said, 'I don't like to think back to those dark days even though they weren't so long ago.'

Hilda nodded agreement. 'But I remember it was particlar dark that night,' she said. 'The soldier kept wittering on all the time but I wasn't really listening cos all I could hear in my head was Clark Gable's voice.' She sighed. 'I do like him.'

'So do I,' Lizzie said, 'though not as much as my neighbour. She's so crazy about him she's papered her walls with his pictures.'

'Ooh, I don't think Stan would like that.' Hilda giggled.

'No, probably not. I'm not sure I like it either. So, what happened then?'

'Well, the next thing I know I'm falling over. Tripping on a bundle just like that one and like you I thought it was a heap of old clothes.' She pointed. 'But then it moved. And when I looked closer I could see this face peering out at me. All I saw at first was a very red nose and some kind of bushy moustache.' A dreamy look came over Hilda's face as she relived that moment. 'At first I really did think it was Clark Gable and I almost swooned. My soldier friend thought it was just some old tramp so he went mad with me when he saw me almost fainting away. Anyway, this bundle did manage to stand up after a fashion. I must admit you could smell the alcohol fumes a mile away, and when I got closer I could see it wasn't Clark after all. It were just another soldier who was drunk as a lord.'

Lizzie couldn't help laughing at that as she pictured the scene but she quickly stopped for she could see Hilda had once again been swept up by what she saw as the romance of it all and she didn't want to spoil things as her friend relived her special moment.

'My soldier friend wasn't very pleased and he told me to leave the old bundle of rags where I'd found him. "Let him sleep it off and make his own way home when he's good and ready," he said. But I felt sorry for him. How could I not when he looked so like my idol?' Hilda's face took on a lovelorn look, though her preoccupied smile was soon replaced by a look of pride. 'Stan told me later that he'd just won a drinking competition at a pub somewhere,' Hilda said, beaming. 'Of course, by this time the soldier fella had scarpered, so I offered to see Stan back to his digs, him not being so steady on his feet and that.'

'How long did you know him before you got married?' Lizzie asked.

'Six days,' Hilda said proudly. 'And as he was in the

army I went to live with his mother for a bit but – but that didn't work out.'

Lizzie was about to ask why but she was distracted by a rumbling sound in the distance. 'Do you think that might be thunder?' she said. 'I do hope there's not going to be a storm.'

Hilda shrugged. 'Then we'll have to get wet.'

'You're right. No point in turning back, we'd get wet either way. So where did you go and live, then?' she asked, not wanting to interrupt Hilda's story.

'I managed to find us some rooms to rent on Charles Street, where I am now. But we didn't actually live there together because he was sent abroad soon after we was wed.' She hesitated, then she said, 'I got my brother to send him a note to tell him where I was, but he's not a great one for writing, is my Stan.' Then she chuckled. 'And that's a good job, because neither am I.'

Lizzie had no idea how far they had gone or how they would get home but the numbers on the streets had picked up again as they continued to follow the steady stream of people heading towards town, and they stopped only when a crowd of singers or dancers blocked the pavement. She was beginning to feel a little weary but didn't want to be the first to suggest that they turned back because Hilda seemed happy and was showing no signs of flagging. 'What did Stan do before he went into the army?' Lizzie asked. 'Do you think he'll be able to find a job when he comes home?'

'He drives one of them great big pantechnicals, so I expect he'll be away lots. Leave me to look after the kids.'

Lizzie stopped and stared at her. 'You're not? You can't be!' she said staring down at Hilda's slender waistline.

'No, no, not yet!' Hilda looked wide-eyed at the thought. 'Though I did think I might be when we were first wed.' She hesitated. 'Leastways, I told his mother I was. That's why she took pity on me and asked me to go and live with her. You should have seen her face when she found out I wasn't.' She gave an ironic laugh at the memory. 'Threw me out of the house, she did. Wouldn't talk to me no more. It was a shame, really; it was so much easier living with her but I've not seen her since.'

Lizzie could see a tear trickling down Hilda's cheek and was about to say something but Hilda said, a sob in her voice, 'It was only a little fib so that she'd be nice to me.'

Lizzie took hold of her friend's hand and gave it a squeeze. Hilda smiled up at her and then took out a pocket handkerchief from her handbag and blew her nose loudly. 'I don't know why I told you that. I've never told anyone else before.'

'Then I'm glad you did and I promise I won't tell a living soul,' Lizzie said. She was rewarded with a watery smile.

Hilda wiped her eyes. 'Was you and Joe . . . you know, like . . . going to get wed?' she asked softly.

Lizzie caught her breath at the unexpected question, but at that moment the rumbling that had remained in the distance for some time suddenly got louder so that it drowned out her answer as an army truck trundled by, bumping and rattling over the uneven cobbled street. The back flap of the truck had been tied back, revealing two benches of soldiers mostly in their shirt-sleeves. As the truck slowly overtook the walkers, the men were leaning out and waving, calling to the young women among the crowd on the street to come and join them.

'Give you a lift into town, girls!' one of them called. 'Come and join us and we'll give you a good time.'

'We can show you where all the action is because we're going to dance the night away,' called another and he pantomimed holding someone close and dancing.

'Once in a lifetime opportunity!' Others joined in the shouting as the truck slowed almost to a stop. The men then began to lean out of the back, extending their arms and trying to catch hold of girls who were standing nearby. Some backed away but several in the crowd had no hesitation in taking up the soldiers' invitation. Within minutes, half a dozen of them had been hoisted into the truck, squealing and giggling as they were offered seats on the benches while the soldiers continued to hang out of the back gathering up more takers.

Hilda looked at Lizzie. 'We could at least hitch a ride into town,' she said. 'My feet are killing me.' And before Lizzie had time to think about it, she watched as Hilda was lifted off her feet and hoisted into the truck.

'Come on, Lizzie, give him your hand,' Hilda called down as the truck began to pick up speed again.

'Yes, Lizzie,' the nearest soldier said, leaning down towards her, 'give me your hand before it's too late. You don't want to miss this ride, there might not be another one.'

Lizzie had no time to think and before she could change her mind she allowed him to lift her into the air and drop her unceremoniously onto a bench inside the truck.

Lizzie was hazy on the details about what happened after that. She had a memory of being helped to climb out of the truck somewhat inelegantly after someone had shouted, 'We're here!' though no one had bothered to explain where 'here' was. Then she and Hilda and all the others who had hitched a ride were escorted by the soldiers into a dimly lit dance hall that was already packed with people. A large, mirrored glitterball hanging from the ceiling caught the beam from a spotlight and eerily highlighted different couples as it slowly spun round.

As they inched their way inside, Lizzie was aware only of the pandemonium. The boom of the musicians' instruments, together with the singing and shouting of the jubilant audience who all wanted to join in, combined to create a level of noise the like of which she had never heard before and she had to jam her hands over her ears until she acclimatized to the din. Any kind of conversation was impossible. The loudness of the music was not something she enjoyed, nor was the heat that rose from the herd of dancers who were practically rubbing together shoulder to shoulder on the dance floor and she tried to indicate to Hilda that she would prefer to remain outside. But her friend was pulling her along and urging her to go in so that Lizzie felt trapped. It didn't take long before a young soldier pushed a pint of shandy into her hand and then tried to entice her onto a few square inches of space on the dance floor. She welcomed the drink but used it as an excuse to resist the invitation to dance, indicating she was happy to stand and watch the others. Hilda had somehow found some space to start swaying her hips and when a young man stepped in to partner her friend, Lizzie was surprised that she seemed to know all the steps.

Lizzie didn't remember much about the rest of the night, other than being plied with alcohol, most of which she managed to avoid. She watched from the sidelines as Hilda danced wildly and drank steadily. Lizzie had some memory of fending off a particularly persistent young soldier who kept trying to drape his arms round her but the next thing she knew she and Hilda were both being dropped off at the end of

Coronation Street from the back of an early-morning milk cart. The smell of hay and manure mingled in her nostrils as the milkman paused long enough for them to slide down gingerly onto the cobbles and she watched as the horse contentedly chomped its way through the contents of its nosebag as it ambled onwards through the sleepy Weatherfield streets.

'Thank goodness Bob's given us the time off to go to the street parties,' Lizzie said as she and Hilda prepared to part company. 'At least I've got a few hours to recover from last night first.'

'I wish I did, but I've got to do my early morning shift, worst luck,' Hilda moaned.

'Yuk, but imagine what state the place would be in if you didn't?' Lizzie said, rubbing her hands over her eyes as if to shut out the vision.

'Never mind the place, what state will I be in? I'll certainly not be fit for any party. My head hurts already at the very thought,' Hilda said.

'Oh, but you must go to a street party. VE Day's a once in a lifetime event and you'll regret it if you miss out,' Lizzie said. 'I tell you what, if you don't feel like going to the Charles Street party on your own, why don't you come and join us on Coronation Street? I'm sure that's going to be a lot of fun. What do you think?'

'Ta very much,' Hilda said, and her face suddenly brightened. 'If I'm awake enough that could be nice, though I haven't got anything to bring.'

'Don't worry about that. I've made enough cakes to be able to count you into number nine's contribution,' Lizzie said, 'though I'll check with my friend Elsie to see if they need anything extra, as she's in charge of food.'

'That's really very kind, thanks Lizzie,' Hilda said, her voice suddenly quaking. 'So hopefully I'll see you later.'

'Never mind hopefully, you must come,' Lizzie insisted and she gave a little wave as she turned towards home.

Chapter 6

Steve was up early on the morning of VE day but he wasn't the first to be up and out on Coronation Street. Ena Sharples was already supervising a group of men who were doing their best to place an assortment of tables and chairs in a straight line down the middle of the street. Steve was amused as they tried to ensure everything was standing as steadily as possible on the uneven surface. It had rained overnight so the cobbles were more slippery than usual underfoot but thankfully, now the air was crisp and clear, it looked as if it might develop into a bright morning and perhaps even a warm and sunny afternoon which was when the Prime Minister was going to speak on the radio to the nation.

The scene made Steve smile. Ena Sharples was in her

element, barking out orders, shouting at her helpers, unaware that Steve was watching.

Ida Barlow had already begun to distribute the yards of brightly coloured triangles she'd so carefully stitched together. She'd persuaded her husband Frank to help out, and Kenneth, her older son, had inveigled some of his schoolmates to join them, so that by the time Steve arrived most of the lampposts and telegraph poles had already been festooned with the celebratory bunting.

'It all looks very festive,' Steve said. Ida beamed and offered him a large red, white and blue hat. 'I ended up with loads more stuff than I thought,' Ida said. 'It was shipped down from the loft rooms of the old mill. So rather than let it go to waste I made it up into hats. Here, let me crown you King for the Day.' She giggled as she handed Steve the large stove pipe hat and he dutifully placed it on his head. He doffed it in Ena's direction. 'You could be selling these,' Steve said, and Ida laughed though Ena gave him a withering look.

Elsie Tanner hadn't yet made an appearance but he found her helpers beavering away inside the Rovers' kitchen. 'If we bring stuff out too early the kids will make off with it before you can say Bob's your uncle and Sally's my aunt,' they told him.

Steve left them to it and went for a walk up and down the road, checking everyone else's progress. Most of the furniture was now in place and the tables had been covered with brightly coloured tablecloths and large sheets of material.

When he got to the furthest point he paused, for his leg was beginning to ache and he didn't want to make it any worse. He looked up, realizing that at this corner of the street he was within sight of the Pride and he wondered if he might catch a glimpse of Lizzie later. He remembered she lived in Coronation Street, and as the Pride wasn't doing anything special during the day, he wondered if she might be coming to the party. He pictured her face, thought of seeing the sparkle in her blue-green eyes and couldn't conceal a smile. As he walked across to the Rovers, his leg was no longer feeling quite so sore and he almost had a spring in his step.

Lizzie answered the door when Hilda knocked at number nine later that morning. 'I hope I'm in good time,' Hilda said, her voice almost too quiet for anyone else to hear. Her eyes were pink-rimmed and she was wearing a headscarf, although without the usual curlers, and she was rubbing her forehead ruefully.

'How much do you charge to haunt a house?' Lizzie said and she couldn't help laughing. 'I have to say you do look a bit rough, Hilda.'

Hilda frowned. 'I can't look any more rough than I feel,' Hilda said. 'My head feels like . . . well, let's just say I might not be the best of company today.'

Lizzie laughed again. 'I'm sorry, but you were drinking rather a lot last night, I did try to tell you.'

'Would you mind not speaking so loud,' Hilda grumbled.

'Never you mind,' Lizzie said. 'I bet half the world feels the same, and who can blame them? Maybe you should pop round to the Rovers first. You know what they say about the hair of the dog and all that.'

Hilda drew in her breath sharply. 'Please, I don't even want to think about supping right now – and will you stop moving about so quickly. The only thing I want to do is to go back to bed, so I'll just sit quietly in the living room if you don't mind and you can pretend I'm not here.' She sat down and, folding her arms onto the table, closed her eyes and rested her head.

By the time the Doyle family emerged onto the street, the neighbours had started to gather together and were laying out their party contributions on the long tables. The front door of number eleven was not locked, so Lizzie knocked and shouted, 'Anyone home? It's only Lizzie from next door,' and she walked in without waiting for an answer. She had only stepped into the hallway when a tall, dark, Mediterranean-looking young man brushed past her, nearly knocking her over in his haste to get out of the front door. At the same time Elsie called from the kitchen, 'Come in, love, and don't mind Antonio.'

'I am in,' Lizzie said, 'and who the heck is An—'

Then she stopped in amazement for Elsie was almost hidden behind a huge stack of individual savoury pies. 'I came to see if you needed a hand,' Lizzie said and laughed. 'And I can see without looking that you do. Where on earth did you get all those? They've not come from your ration coupons, that's for sure!' She took a closer look. 'If I had to take a guess, I'd say they looked a lot like the pork pies Bob sometimes buys in at the Pride.'

Elsie put her finger to her lips. 'I've promised I wouldn't tell. Bob's been extremely generous, though he doesn't want anyone to know. He's got it into his head that Annie Walker wouldn't be very pleased if she knew what kind of a deal he gave me.'

'Gave you?'

'Yes. I had to go to talk to him on my own in the end, Steve couldn't come.'

'She won't hear about it from me.' Lizzie giggled, making a zipping motion across her lips. 'Want me to give you a hand carrying them out?'

'Nah, you're all right,' Elsie said. 'Steve will be here in a minute. Him and me'll shift them in no time.' At that moment Lizzie's mother put her head round the door and she was clutching baby Sammy to her chest. 'This is the kind of party I like,' Cora said. 'On the doorstep of my own home. Ooh.' She stared at the pies on the table. 'They sure look good enough to eat.' She went to get a closer look.

'Ma, why don't we go outside and grab us somewhere to sit?' Lizzie said. 'We don't want Seamus and Tommy coming in here and seeing this lot ahead of time.'

'Good idea,' Cora said, although the boys were already in Elsie's hallway, but she shooed them outside quickly and earmarked enough chairs so that they could all sit within a few feet of their own front door. The twins looked uncomfortable, dressed in their Sunday best, and they sat down unwillingly in the seats Cora indicated, kicking their feet back and forth. Cora shot them a look that almost seemed to pin them to their chairs, then she too sat down, folding the baby into her lap.

'Thank goodness I don't have to carry our Sammy very far,' Cora said, 'because he's getting to be quite a heavy lump these days, aren't you, my little plum pudding?'

'Don't speak to him like that,' Lizzie said crossly. 'He understands everything you say now, and before you know it he'll be repeating the words and you won't be able to stop him. Do you want him to grow up not knowing whether he's a child or an afters? Here, give him to me.' She held out her arms and the baby readily reached towards her. 'Who's gorgeous?' she cooed. 'You are, aren't you, Sammy, my love?' She took him in her arms and nuzzled her nose into the creases around his neck before sitting down and bouncing him on her knee.

'It's not every day I get the opportunity to take my

favourite little one to a party like this, now is it?' she said, indulging his gurgles of pleasure with more bouncing. 'They're not babies for long. I'll be working later so I have to make the most of every chance I get to be with him or he'll be all grown up before you know it.'

'Are you working this afternoon too, Hilda,' Cora said. 'Or is it just my poor daughter having to work on VE day?'

Hilda frowned as she took a seat. She had just woken up and still looked bleary-eyed. 'I've already done my stint for the day, thank goodness, so I'll not be working again today, thank you very much.' She closed her eyes and took a deep breath. 'And it wasn't very nice work either, if you catch my drift, the morning after a night like that one.'

'Don't you knock it, Hilda,' Lizzie said. 'At least you've got a steady job. That's how we have to look at it, working in a bar where the hours are antisocial.'

'It's not just the hours. Sometimes the work is anti . . .' Hilda flapped her hands in the air, 'It's anti whatever you said. But it does pay the rent, right enough.' She sighed. 'Only thing is, if it's a heavy night again in the bar tonight the place could be in an even worse state come tomorrow morning.'

Crowds of people were now beginning to fill the street so Steve was surprised when he managed to spot Lizzie in the mêlée. She was with a group he assumed to be her family and they were sitting outside number nine.

He would have liked to have had the opportunity to talk to Lizzie before things began to get hectic, to get to know more about her, but she seemed to be busy with the family and she hadn't seen him. Maybe he would have a chance to catch up with her later. Besides, it would soon be time to eat and he'd promised to give Elsie a hand transporting the food.

There were gasps of approval followed by applause as plates piled high with sausage rolls and pork pies began to appear and people quickly identified their favourite sandwiches among the corned beef, Spam, paste, and dripping fillings that were on offer. There was a surprising number of cakes and biscuits too, given all the shortages, and they seemed to have been made from the most unusual lists of ingredients. The dishes and plates piled high with food were quickly distributed throughout the street and soon the tables were groaning under the sheer weight of it all. Glasses were raised for a toast as the people of Coronation Street looked hungrily at the vast quantity of food. There was more to eat than any one of them had seen for many years and Steve felt a certain amount of pride that, in spite of all the acrimonious meetings, they had ultimately produced an incredible spread.

The crowning glory, however, was the trifle that filled a huge glass bowl and everyone wanted to sample it to see what it was actually made of. Before anyone could touch even a sandwich, however, Steve thought he had better make an announcement.

'I'm sorry to say it's not mine,' he said, with a laugh pointing to the trifle. 'I wouldn't know where to begin making such a thing. Let's say it was a team effort. But you can all get to try it if . . .' The rest of his words were drowned out by the sudden pounding of feet and the sound of smashing crockery. Everyone turned and stared open-mouthed in the direction of the noise in time to see a snaking procession of children tearing through the street at great speed. They took everyone by surprise as they wove in and out of the adults who were standing or sitting together in small groups. The youngsters were hanging on to each other with one hand while with the other they grabbed as much food off the tables as they could as they flew by, stuffing it into their mouths. They didn't seem to care who they pushed out of the way or how much crockery and furniture went crashing to the ground in the process.

It took several moments for everyone to realize what was happening and, by the time they did, the last of the line had made their smash and grab and, screaming with laughter, they were running away down the alleyways between the houses where somehow they melted into the side streets beyond Coronation Street. It had been almost impossible to identify individual children as they had all zoomed by so quickly and only one or two parents who thought they had spotted their own child attempted to make chase.

Steve stood rooted to the spot. He was certain that he recognized Billy Walker in amongst the leading group, although he didn't want to say anything in case he was mistaken, but it seemed plain that Annie Walker thought so too as she made a half-hearted attempt to run after her son, shouting threats about what his father would do to him when he came home.

'Fancy that! The son of our lady of the Rovers,' someone said unkindly as Annie gave chase.

'I'm not surprised,' said another in disgust, 'he's totally out of control, that child, and will be, I reckon, till his father comes home.'

'A good leathering, that's what that one needs,' someone suggested. 'Then he'd soon learn how to behave.'

Lizzie clung on tightly to Sammy, glad she didn't recognize any of the culprits. She looked across at Tom and Seamus who looked innocent and confused and she felt relieved that, for once, neither of her brothers were in any way involved in the mischief. As the runners had raced by, out of the corner of her eye Lizzie had caught sight of Seamus shifting in his seat, as though considering whether to join in the excitement.

'No you don't, young man,' she'd cried grabbing hold of his braces. 'I don't know where you think you're going but it's not with them!' And she'd yanked him back, holding him firmly down on the chair with one hand while she struggled to contain a squirming Sammy in the other. Tommy had been slower off the mark and didn't actually move out of his chair so a glaring look and a sharp, 'Don't you dare,' from Lizzie had managed to stop him in his tracks.

'What's going on?' Cora looked bemused.

'I'm not sure, Ma, but whatever it is it's nothing that concerns our two, thank goodness, is it, boys?' Both boys shook their heads, though they refused to look at her.

People were getting up now and shooting off in all directions, desperate to find out whether their child had been involved. Lizzie saw the relief on Elsie Tanner's face as she caught hold of Dennis and Linda halfway down the street. Ida Barlow too smiled gratefully as she was able to draw Kenneth and David down into the chairs beside her. But the same couldn't be said for Annie Walker who looked angry as she trudged back up the street from the fruitless pursuit of her son. She pulled her shoulders back and there was a resolute expression on her face as she came back to the Rovers, doing her best to sidestep the jagged shards of glass, china and pottery that carpeted the cobbles, though there was a flash of dismay as she contemplated the pile of ruined food. For a few moments it looked as if the whole party was about to disintegrate, and no one was quite sure what to do but Steve hastily piled together some wooden pallets to form a platform and Annie grabbed hold of a megaphone and stood up to address the crowd. 'Ladies and gentlemen!' Her voice was surprisingly strong. 'I really don't know what just happened, I'm as shocked as you are,' she said. 'But we're lucky enough to have two of our very own neighbourhood policemen here with us today and they're already on the case. I'm sure we'll all give them our utmost cooperation.'

All eyes turned to look at the familiar faces of the two local bobbies who were standing on the spot where, not ten minutes before, they'd been trying to guess the number of marbles in a large glass jar. Now they had removed their faintly ridiculous Union Jack fancy-dress hats and stood, feet firmly planted, note-pads in hand, already interviewing people about what they had seen.

'But can I just say that we didn't let the enemy bombs subdue our spirit,' Annie went on, 'so we certainly aren't going to let something like this spoil our day. The party has barely got going but there's loads more food in the kitchen that we'll be bringing out in a minute and, more importantly, there's plenty of beer.' A huge cheer went up. 'There's also lots more entertainment in store so you can all stay and enjoy yourselves.' There was another loud cheer. 'So please, tuck in and have fun.'

Several people applauded as Annie stepped down, Cora Doyle among them. 'I thought she handled that very well, didn't you?' Cora said. 'I know I wouldn't have liked to have been in her shoes.'

'How about you, Lizzie?' Hilda said. 'Would you like to be in her shoes if it meant you could be working with Steve Carter?'

'What on earth does that mean?' Lizzie said.

'I can see that you fancy him,' Hilda said. 'Plain as day.'

'No, I do not!' Lizzie was adamant but Hilda just laughed. 'Well, he's got an eye out for you. I've seen the way he looks at you, it's very romantic.' Hilda fluttered her eyes, dramatically. 'In fact, he's barely had you out of his sight all morning. Don't tell me you haven't noticed?'

'Oh, Hilda, you do love to exaggerate. He's done nothing of the sort,' Lizzie said, and she knew she was blushing. 'Now help me to get this table on its feet again.'

Hilda didn't move. 'You can mock. But you mark my words,' she said, and she gave Lizzie the benefit of her elbow. 'Anyone could see he was disappointed not to be able to buy you a drink the other night, so my advice would be for you to get in there quick, before anyone else gets their mitts on him.'

'If I didn't know you better, Hilda Ogden, I'd say it was you who fancied him,' Lizzie scolded. Hilda lifted her nose in the air. 'I hardly need someone like him when I've got my Stan,' she said. Then she sighed. 'I wonder what kind of celebration he'll be having today. I bet it won't be owt like this.'

'There's a lot of folk missing out on a celebration like this,' Cora suddenly said, her voice wistful.

'But on the bright side, Stan'll be home soon, I'm sure,' Lizzie said. She patted Hilda's arm and glanced up as she spoke. Steve was looking across the tables in her direction and he was smiling at her. He started to walk towards them – she felt a sudden warmth rush once more to her cheeks and had to resist the urge to run away. 'Here, let me help you with that,' he said grabbing hold of the other end of the table Lizzie was struggling to get upright. 'Are you and your family all right? I presume those three little boys who were with you before are your brothers?'

Lizzie nodded. 'And this is my mother.' She indicated Cora. 'And we're fine, thank you.'

'It was a bit of a thing, though,' Cora said, 'coming out of the blue like that. How did it get started, I wonder?'

'From the murmurings I've heard . . .' Steve looked over to where the policemen were still painstakingly taking notes. 'People seem to be saying it's the work of a neighbouring gang, some kind of a group of troublemakers who are not unknown to the police, whipping up the younger ones.'

'But why would they want to stir things up like that? It's almost as if someone deliberately wanted to sabotage Mrs Walker's party,' Lizzie said. 'Any theories?'

Steve bent to pick up some leaflets that were fluttering on the ground. 'Have you seen these?' he said. They were advertising the evening's cabaret show at the Pride and they had a white flash across the shiny red paper inviting everyone to enjoy a free glass of punch at the Pride that afternoon at a time when the Rovers' street party should have been in full swing. 'That wasn't what was agreed, I'm sure,' Steve said. 'The Pride's trying to muscle in on the Rovers' day.'

'Bob certainly didn't ask me or Pat, the other barmaid, to work this afternoon, so I wonder what he's playing at,' Lizzie said.

'Perhaps he's up to no good.' Steve said.

Lizzie thought for a moment. 'I can believe that.'

'Why, Lizzie, have you seen something going on at the Pride?'

She nodded, hesitating to say anything more at first for she didn't want to be disloyal, but eventually she said, 'I've seen him talking to some men in the yard. A very unsavoury lot. The kind of men that made me wonder how he could seriously consider being involved with them,' she went on. 'Goods and money have definitely changed hands, I've seen it myself.' And she told him about some of the mean-looking characters she'd seen hanging around the yard at the Pride and how they'd filled her with fear when they'd tried to approach her. 'You don't think Bob could have been responsible in any way for all this?' Lizzie shivered as she gestured up the street. But before Steve could reply, a familiar and cantankerous voice broke into their conversation.

'What about the breakages, that's what I'd like to know?' Ena Sharples demanded as she tapped Steve on the shoulder. 'Who's going to pay for them, can you tell me that?'

'They were some of my best plates as got smashed,' Minnie Caldwell added in her high-pitched whine as she came to join them.

'Never mind that,' Ena snapped at her, 'you should have known better than to put out your best china in the street. I'm more worried about my broken chairs.'

'But they didn't belong to you in the first place, you only brought them up from the mission, Ena.' Minnie sounded indignant now.

'That's hardly the point, is it?' Ena argued. 'It was down to those hooligans that they got broken, but that doesn't help me any as we don't even know who half of them were. But if that Billy Walker was involved, then I'm telling you—'

'Come, come, Ena,' Steve spoke up. 'We need to be reasonable here and not bandy about names when we've got no proof of anything. Besides which, you're talking about a child. And if you start making unfounded accusations you'll get us all into trouble.'

'I still need to know who's going to pick up the bill.' Ena was insistent. 'And if it's Annie Walker . . .'

As if on cue, at the mention of her name Annie Walker appeared, directing the drinkers carrying out the piano from the bar and into the street, where everyone would be able to hear it, but before she could stop her Ena Sharples sat down on the music stool and started belting out her repertoire of hymns. She didn't seem to care that only a few people were politely singing along. It was a relief to everyone when one of the neighbours suddenly appeared with an accordion, while one of his companions pulled a harmonica from his pocket and they struck up some modern dance tunes. It wasn't long before several couples had cleared a space and begun to dance. This brought Elsie Foyle from the Rovers' kitchen and she began to sing along with the musicians. With such competition, Ena was forced to abandon her attempts at 'Jerusalem' and the twenty-third psalm and she grudgingly allowed Elsie Foyle to replace her at the keyboard. Elsie had a powerful singing voice and she knew how to make the most of it as she had once been on the stage, so others were encouraged to join in and, before long, everyone was singing and dancing to Vera Lynn and Judy Garland favourites.

'Perhaps we should be setting an example,' Steve said as the tempo picked up, and he stepped in front of Lizzie and held out his arms as if ready to dance. When she didn't respond immediately, he grasped her hand while at the same time placing his other hand in the centre of her back. It was the lightest of touches, but it still felt like a bolt of electricity to Lizzie and momentarily she stiffened. She hadn't been held in this way for so long. Before she could say no she was in Steve's arms, moving with him in time to the music.

'Is your leg giving you gyp, moving like this?' Lizzie had to raise her voice to be heard over the music.

'Is it that obvious?' Steve said.

'Sorry, I didn't intend to pry and I understand if you don't want to talk about it,' Lizzie said.

'I suppose it's not something I can easily keep secret, even if I wanted to.'

'I'm afraid not, but that was rather clumsy of me, blurting it out like that.'

'I'm glad you did, for I honestly don't know how long I can last jigging about on it like this. But my physical therapist keeps telling me exercise is good for me.' He laughed.

Lizzie had begun to relax and was astonished at how much she was enjoying dancing with him, but after a few numbers he pulled up. 'I'm really sorry, I hope you don't mind if we sit down. I've proved I can do it, but it's been a long day,' Steve said, and Lizzie could see that he was trying not to wince as he led them back to the chairs.

'At least the day hasn't been a total disaster,' Lizzie said, 'even though someone was obviously trying to make it so. I think you did well to save it after the way things looked this morning.'

'Weatherfielders are obviously made of tough stuff,' Steve said. 'It's been fun.' He glanced at his watch. 'But right now it's time to listen to Winston Churchill's address. Coming to join us?' he asked. 'We've got the radio set up in the Rovers and I could buy you that drink that I owe you.' He smiled and raised his eyebrows by way of invitation. Lizzie suddenly felt flustered and had to look away. Then she shook her head. 'Thanks, but I'd best be getting off home to help my ma with the baby,' she said. 'I've left her to it for long enough on her own, cheerio.' And without further ado she turned and walked quickly away.

Lizzie woke the next morning to hear one of the twins crying, an unusual sound in the Doyle household where normally the boys hated to be seen as 'soft girls' and were only anxious to show off how big and brave they were. She was about to throw off the covers, wondering what could be wrong, but as she tried to lift her head from the pillow she felt a blinding flash of pain across her eyes. It only took a few seconds for her to realize that if she tried to move, not only would she be sick, but she wouldn't make it to the midden in time. She called out to her mother that she needed a bucket or a bowl quickly, but she got no response and by this time she realized the other twin had joined in the cacophony and that baby Sammy too was wailing piti-fully and calling for her. She took a deep breath, trying to stave off the inevitable for as long as possible and closed her eyes, uncertain what to do, then she heard someone murmur her name.

'Lizzie! I'm not well,' Cora's voice whispered. 'Can you go and see to the boys?'

'No.' Lizzie was aware that her own voice was barely above a whisper. She would have preferred to shake her head rather than talk but the slightest movement threatened to unleash the unpredictable contents of her stomach. Then Cora retched and Lizzie heard the swiftly retreating patter of her mother's feet as she padded down the wooden stairs and when the back door banged shut she swallowed hard and lifted herself up from the bed in her own attempt to flee downstairs to the kitchen sink before it was too late. She paused at the boys' bedroom only long enough to register their distress, but at that moment there was nothing she could do about it.

It wasn't until the afternoon that some kind of order was restored. There was a knock at the front door and a white-faced Elsie Tanner let herself into the living room calling softly, 'Anyone home? Is everything all right here?'

Lizzie was sitting at the kitchen table by this time, wrapped in her outdoor coat while the only warm night-dress she possessed was soaking in the kitchen sink. 'There's only me up and about so far, Elsie,' Lizzie said, sipping water from a cup. 'And I wouldn't say I was either up or getting about much.' She gave a wry laugh. 'So, on the whole no, things are not all right. We're all poorly, me, the boys, the baby and Ma.' She looked at Elsie and frowned. 'And you as well, by the looks of you.'

'Me and everyone else apparently. I've been throwing up all night. It must have been something we've ate. And it seems to have affected almost everyone in the street. Not that there's much we can do about it mind, except wait it out.'

'No, there's not much anyone can do.' Lizzie sighed. 'But I will have to find a way to get a message to Bob.' She put a hand to her brow which felt warmer than usual. 'I couldn't possibly go in to work today. I can't stand for more than two minutes at a time.'

'You don't have to worry about letting Bob know,' Elsie said. 'I'm feeling a bit better now so I should be able to pop down to the Pride to tell him, a bit later on. If not, I can get our Linda to do it. I don't know why, but she seems to be all right. Got the constitution of an ox that one.'

'I'm glad to hear someone's OK. It's taken ages for Ma and me to sort out everyone here. Ma's crawled back into bed not half an hour since, and I presume she's sleeping but I couldn't face the idea of lying down.' Lizzie put her head in her hands and closed her eyes. When she opened them again Elsie had gone and Cora had taken her place at the table. 'I wonder if Hilda's all right?' Lizzie said. 'She was with us most of yesterday.'

'Then I'd take bets she's not,' Cora said.

'Oh dear, I'll have to try and get in touch with her. I worry about her living on her own,' Lizzie said.

'She's got a landlady, hasn't she?' Cora said. 'Hopefully she'll do the right thing if Hilda's sick.'

'Do you think any of the folk in the neighbouring streets might have been affected?' Lizzie said.

'I've no idea and I'm not about to do a door-to-door poll to find out,' Cora quipped.

Lizzie started to laugh and as a result had to rush out of the back door.

'Sorry about that,' she said when she came back. She sat down gingerly by the table again and buttoned up her coat in an effort to stop shivering.

It was some time later when Elsie reappeared and this time she came in without knocking. 'Just wanted to let you know I got your message through to Bob and it does seem that loads of people were affected.' Elsie sat down and drummed her fingers on the table. 'I've had a thought,' she said.

'Congratulations! Is that a first?' Lizzie attempted humour though she didn't really feel like laughing.

'Cheeky monkey! I'm talking about where all this might have started,' Elsie said.

'Well?' Lizzie was curious.

'It could well have been them pork pies.' Her lips were drawn into a thin line.

'And where . . .?' Lizzie said, but she knew the answer

without asking. The pies had come from the Pride.

'I did wonder why Bob offered me such a great deal, but he said not to ask questions.' Elsie drew in a deep breath and wagged her finger at Lizzie. 'And I shan't be telling that to no one else but you.'

'The funny thing is they tasted all right to me,' Lizzie said.

'And I didn't hear anyone complaining when they were busy stuffing their faces, did you?' Elsie was scornful.

'Definitely not,' Lizzie said.

'But we'll hear them now. No doubt they'll take great delight in telling us how much they've suffered. And they'll be quick to point the finger, you mark my words.'

'Do you think Bob knew there could be a problem?' Lizzie asked. She didn't want to believe that he would have offered Elsie bad stock knowingly. 'It wouldn't do his reputation much good . . .' She paused. But it wouldn't matter, because he had sworn Elsie to secrecy as to where they'd come from so it would be the Rovers who got the blame.

Elsie shook her head. 'Only he knew why he was being so generous.'

'But you can hardly accuse him,' Lizzie said.

'No? Just watch me,' Elsie said.

The next day Steve was on his own serving behind the Rovers' bar and he had to put on a brave front. Gracie had gone to New York on a transport ship arranged by Chuck's parents so that she would be there in good time to greet her fiancé when he was eventually sent home from Europe, and Annie Walker was upstairs tending to Billy who had been very sick. Steve was upset when he found out how the party had ended for most of the Coronation Street residents, but he wasn't sure what he could do. No one had accused him or Annie directly but they had been sounding off about Elsie Tanner and he knew that the Rovers had to bear the brunt of the blame. He hadn't had time to eat anything at the party, so to his relief he'd been spared the distressing symptoms. But fingers were naturally being pointed in the direction of the Rovers, and in particular at Elsie, and people wanted answers.

'Not the best party I've ever been to.' Ena Sharples' voice was the loudest in the bar as usual as she waited impatiently for her bottle of milk stout. 'First that gang of hooligans trying to spoil everything, then the next day everyone going down like ninepins with upset stomachs. If you ask me, that was down to them blooming sandwich fillings. I never did trust them jars of paste. They might call them fancy names, but you never know what they really put into them.'

'I think it was those wretched cake concoctions,' Ida Barlow said, cautiously sipping her pint of lager. 'Did you go in for one of them competitions to name the ingredients?' she asked Ena.

Ena shook her head. 'I didn't waste my time on such nonsense.'

'Aye, well I thought I knew the answers but it turned out I was way off the mark. And when I found out what they'd really put into them I was sorry I'd eaten them. You couldn't call them real cakes.'

'Well, I don't know about the sandwiches or the cakes, as far as I'm concerned it was the meat that was rotten.' Minnie Caldwell's voice sounded strong and determined for once.

'You mean them sausage roll thingies and the supposed pork pies?' Ena said, scornfully. 'I doubt there was much meat in any of them.'

'It still could have been off, though,' Minnie said.

'I never did trust Elsie Tanner further than I could throw her. What she knows about food could go on the back of a postage stamp,' Ena said. 'It's all her fault, as far as I'm concerned. She knows nowt about catering but I bet she's not above a bit of black-marketing on the side.'

Ena cleared her throat. 'Never put your faith in a Grimshaw, I've always said. I don't imagine too much catering went on in the slum where she was dragged up.'

Steve had his own theories about the cause of the problem as he listened to all the comments. But he knew that trying to expose the real culprit and provide some kind of proof, would not be an easy task.

Steve had to wait until the next day for Annie to be available once more to serve in the bar before he was able to take an hour off to venture over to the Pride. But he was anxious to see if he could shed any light on Elsie's supplier.

The Pride was busy and as he scanned the bar through the hazy atmosphere he was disappointed to find not only that Bob was nowhere to be seen but that there was only one barmaid on duty and it was not Lizzie. Pat Evans was rushing from one side of the bar to the other and it took some time for Steve to get served. 'What can I get you? I'm really sorry about the delay,' she eventually apologised and he was glad she didn't seem to know who he was.

'Is Lizzie not here?' Steve asked, although he already knew the answer.

'I believe she's still poorly,' Pat said, 'but hopefully she'll be back tomorrow. Any message? Want to leave your name?'

Steve shook his head and picked up his pint. In a quieter corner of the room he'd spotted several Rovers' customers deep in conversation and as he moved away from the counter they beckoned to him to join them.

'We don't usually see you in here,' Albert Tatlock said. 'Busman's holiday?'

Steve laughed. 'Believe it or not, I fancied a change.'

'Fancied the barmaid more like!' Albert chuckled. 'Only she's not here, as you can see. Not that I've owt against Pat, nice enough girl even if she is married, but that Lizzie is in a different class. She's a bit of all right.

Pity she's gone down with the sickness bug that seems to have caught everyone on the hop.'

'A bad end to the day,' Steve said.

'From where I was standing it didn't start off too well either,' Frank Barlow said. 'What on earth was all that about?'

Steve shook his head. 'Not really sure. Unfortunately, everyone seems to have a different version of events,' he said.

'It seemed plain enough to me that it was that bunch of scalliwags that hang around the back yard here of a night,' Frank said. 'They riled up the younger kids to get them to cause mayhem. They told them to grab as much food as possible and tip everything upside down. I think the idea was to mess things up and make it look as bad as possible for the Rovers.'

'Well, they certainly succeeded in that,' Albert said.

'But the idea must have come from someone at the top,' Frank said.

'It doesn't take a great brain to work out who that is,' Albert muttered. 'From what I heard it was Bob himself who paid the older lads to get things going.'

'Hey!' Steve warned. 'We've got to be careful before bandying about accusations we can't prove.'

'They might not stand up in a court of law, but I'd put my money on it. And as to the food business, that were all Elsie Tanner's fault.' Albert sounded unequivocal in his indictment.

'You can't say things like that,' Steve protested, 'not without definite proof. Besides, Elsie was hardly to blame. She was just doing what she'd been asked to do. It wasn't her fault if she was given damaged goods.'

'It's what folk are saying hereabouts,' Albert said with a shrug.

'To be fair, it's not clear what the cause was,' Steve said. 'And it won't be so easy to find out.'

A shadow suddenly fell on his pint and Steve looked up to see Bob Bennett standing over him.

'Sorry to hear that the Rovers' party didn't go exactly to plan,' Bob said, emphasising the word Rovers as he folded his arms across his broad chest. He shook his head. 'It nearly didn't get going at all from what I heard. All them unruly kids. They can be quite a problem.'

'You could say that.' Steve had to take a deep breath to hang on to his temper.

'What was it? Some kind of gang warfare?' Bob said, but Steve didn't answer.

'And then everyone getting sick as a result of your food.' Bob had a grin on his face.

'I would hardly say it was our food seeing as most of it came from outside sources,' Steve said pointedly, 'like a pile of pork pies.' Steve stared directly at Bob as he said this but Bob's smile didn't flicker. 'Whichever way you look at it, nobody bargained for finishing off a great day with food poisoning,' Steve said.

Now Bob's eyes narrowed and he leaned over so low that Steve could smell whisky on his breath. 'I don't know what you're implying, mate, but you know very well you haven't a cat in hell's chance of pinning down the cause of that sickness, so I'd be very careful before I made any accusations if I were you.'

'And if I were you I'd be very careful not to make any sudden moves without looking over your shoulder,' Steve said. 'For if I find out you had anything to do with this you will be sorry that you were ever born.'

Bob straightened up. 'Whichever way, the poor buggers missed out on a great show here that night.'

'But you got your comeuppance. You lost half of your customers. It's only a shame the sickness got to your workers as well,' Steve said, looking over to the bar.

'You mean Lizzie?' Bob said. 'Yes, I'm afraid it did.' He stared down at Steve for so long Steve was beginning to wonder if he had at last remembered him from all those years ago. But then Bob grinned and turned away. 'I'll tell her you were asking after her when she gets back to work, shall I?'

Chapter 7

It was a few days before Lizzie was fit enough to return to work, and she and Hilda immediately planned a trip to the pictures for her first afternoon off.

'I hoped you'd be fit again before the film came off,' Hilda said eagerly, 'only I so want to see *Blithe Spirit* and it's showing at the Roxy this week. I hope you fancy it?'

'I fancy anything that gets me out of the house,' Lizzie said. 'These last few days have been hell, so I'll be glad to see any film and *Blithe Spirit* is as good as any.'

'I do love the way Rex Harrison talks, don't you?' Hilda said. 'He always sounds so posh. "What did you jolly well say you were called again?"' Hilda's imitation of Rex Harrison, speaking as if she had a mouthful of plums, made Lizzie laugh and she was reminded of it again when she heard him speaking in the film. But before the main feature they had to sit patiently through the B-film, a rerun of a Sherlock Holmes mystery they had both seen some weeks previously, and after the interval there was an extended Pathé newsreel about the VE celebrations that managed to capture the atmosphere of excitement and release that had pervaded the whole country on that day.

'I'm enjoying VE day much more the second time around,' Lizzie whispered to Hilda, licking the ice cream she'd bought during the interval as scenes from different street parties up and down the country appeared, showing people singing and dancing and obviously having a good time.

'At least none of them suffered like we did from hooligans and food poisoning,' Hilda giggled. 'For me, the best part of VE day was the night before, if you know what I mean,' she said and she concentrated on unwrapping her own ice cream as the pictures panned to St Paul's Cathedral and Buckingham Palace. 'Do you know,' Hilda said, 'the King's not bad looking when he's in his full naval togs, is he? Mind you, I like any kind of uniform. I love Princess Elizabeth in hers. Whatever it is.'

'It's the ATS,' Lizzie said. 'The Auxiliary Territorial Service.'

'Sounds like the Girl Guides.'

'It's a bit more grown-up than that,' Lizzie said.

Hilda sighed. 'I think I should have gone in for something with a uniform, instead of having to wear a pinny all the time. I bet it would have suited me, don't you think?'

Lizzie looked at her, eyebrows raised. 'Fancy driving an ambulance, do you?'

'I might.' Hilda thought for a few moments. 'I wonder how it feels to be a princess.'

'Well, they obviously don't always like it much. They couldn't wait to slope off on their own,' Lizzie said.

'I know, fancy disappearing into the crowd like that, inmosquito.'

Lizzie couldn't help laughing. 'I think you mean incognito, Hilda,' and even in the darkened gloom of the cinema she could see her friend's face go as pink as her neck scarf.

'Course I did,' Hilda said with a chuckle, 'but like I say, just fancy the two of them buzzing off into the crowd like that. Anything could have happened to them.'

'Fortunately for them no one noticed,' Lizzie said. 'I suppose I can understand them wanting to experience a bit of the excitement of real life without anyone knowing who they were.'

'Then how come I don't find real life so exciting? No one ever knows who I am.' Hilda looked puzzled.

Lizzie batted her arm playfully. 'You daft ha'p'orth. You do say some of the funniest things.'

Almost immediately the picture changed to show a close-up of Winston Churchill and all Hilda could say was, 'Blimey, is he really that fat?'

Lizzie smiled but she couldn't speak for she felt a sudden lump in her throat, thinking about the part the Prime Minister had played in bringing the war to an end. She thought of the soldiers who would be coming home, and of those that wouldn't, and had to swipe at the tears that had gathered in the corners of her eyes. As the newsreel drew to a close there were long-distance shots of the crowd outside the royal palace and the audience in the cinema began to sing gustily, 'For he's a jolly good fellow,' ending with a spontaneous round of applause. But Lizzie could only sniff noisily into her handkerchief. She was relieved when the main feature began almost immediately and the opening scenes of the film actually made her laugh out loud. By the end of the film, however, she and Hilda were both laughing and crying at the same time.

'Eh, that were good, weren't it?' Hilda said, as they came out into the foyer. 'Even if it was sad at the end.'

'At least Madame Arcati was funny – she made me laugh when she kept trying to get to the ghosts through Daphne.'

'Do you know,' said Hilda, 'she got me thinking, did

Madame Arcati, and I reckon that's what we should do. I don't know why I didn't think of it before.'

'What are you talking about Hilda?'

'Does your ma still hear them noises in the roof?'

Lizzie nodded. 'I'm afraid so, why?'

'Well, I know the tea leaves didn't work when we tried to find out what was going on, and . . .'

'Neither did the Ouija board,' Lizzie said, suddenly realizing what Hilda was referring to. 'Are you thinking we should have another go at getting through to the spirits?'

'Exactly. Maybe we could make contact with them in a different way, like Madame Arcati did. We could conjure up our own Daphne to talk directly to whatever spirits are in the house.'

Lizzie's heart sank as Hilda was getting excited now. 'Has your ma seen any polter – poltice thingies flying around? Like in the film when the ghost moved the flowers and all you could see was this vase floating cross the room?'

'A poltergeist? I don't really believe . . .' Lizzie began. But it didn't matter for she could see that Hilda was already getting carried away. 'I know that it's got to be more than rats running around in the eaves, we do hear all kinds of different noises but I've never considered it might be a poltergeist,' she said. She didn't really believe in ghosts and she wasn't sure how many more of Hilda's clumsy attempts she could cope with.

'Do you think your ma would let me try out some of Madame Arcati's tricks of the trade?' Hilda said, unable to disguise the excitement in her voice.

'I suppose I can always ask her,' Lizzie said slowly, 'but for now we'd best step on it and be getting home before she sends out a search party.'

They linked arms and were passing along the queue of people waiting to go in to the next showing of the film when Lizzie was forced to step off the kerb and into the road as a car was driving by. She felt someone grab hold of her arm and pull her back onto the pavement.

'Watch out, or you'll get knocked over!' a male voice said sharply.

Lizzie was about to protest that he was gripping her arm too tightly and for a moment, with his hat almost covering his eyes, she wasn't sure who he was. Then she recognized his neatly trimmed moustache and his flashing smile and felt the colour rushing to her cheeks.

'Why, if it isn't Lizzie from the Pride,' Steve Carter said. He touched the brim of his hat and pushed it back on his forehead so that his eyes stared directly into hers. 'I trust this means you've fully recovered?'

'Yes, thanks.' Lizzie could feel her cheeks burning. 'But how did you know I was ill?' she asked, surprised.

'I dropped into the Pride the day after the party,' Steve said. 'And fortunately for you, somehow I keep popping up, for here I am again today, only this time

I was saving your life.' He grinned, then asked in a more serious tone, 'Are you sure you're OK?'

'Yes, thanks, I'm fine, really.' As he let go of her arm, somehow the tips of their fingers touched and Lizzie felt a blush rise from deep within her neck. She was aware of his scrutiny and wanted to look away but she felt rooted to the spot.

'Is the film worth seeing?' Steve asked, though from the way his gaze continued to be fixed on her face Lizzie wasn't convinced it was the film he was interested in.

'We enjoyed it, didn't we, Lizzie?' Hilda said quickly. 'It's got real ghosts in it.'

'We both wanted to see Rex Harrison and thought the film looked like fun,' Lizzie said. 'I felt I needed a laugh after being ill,' she added, trying not to look at Steve.

'It's a shame I didn't know; we could have gone together,' he said. 'But I tell you what. Why don't I drop in at the Pride on my way home and we can compare notes? A man living together with his two wives, one of whom is dead? I'm sure we'll have lots to talk about.'

Lizzie looked at him, aware that his eyes had never left her face. She wasn't usually stuck for words, but aware that Hilda was looking on with interest, she felt flustered and didn't know what to say. There was a mischievous, teasing look in Steve's eyes and she wasn't sure whether or not to take him seriously. Then he smiled, and her legs suddenly felt unsteady.

'So how would you like to go with me to see that new film, *Brief Encounter*?' Steve said. 'It's opening at the Gaiety in town at the weekend. Not a ghost in sight apparently, just falling in love at the train station with engine smoke in their eyes. I bet that's just up your street.'

'I don't think . . .' Lizzie began.

'I promise we won't go in the back row, if that's what's stopping you,' Steve said. He held both his hands up, palms out, an innocent look in his eyes. 'We can go in the one and sixes if you like, best seats in the house.' He paused. 'Go on,' he said suggestively, lowering his voice so that she had to strain to hear him. 'We can still have a lot of fun.'

He was certainly persuasive and for a moment Lizzie didn't know what to say. She felt trapped by his gaze and found it difficult to look away, the power of his attraction drawing her like a magnet; just like she'd felt when she'd first met Joe. But this time it was different; this time she knew she didn't dare respond.

'I rather think we might have the same taste in films,' Steve said, his voice chatty and matter-of-fact again. 'I bet we're both hopeless romantics.' He put both his hands over his heart, a pleading look on his face. 'Think of what you'd be missing. C'mon, what do you say? Sunday night? I could pick you up around six.'

He looked at her so eagerly a ripple of excitement made her whole body tingle and Lizzie wanted to say yes. But right now she was weighted down by a secret that was almost too heavy for her to bear and she knew she had to say no.

'I'm afraid I won't be able to go,' she said at last, 'but thanks all the same. I have to help out with the baby,' she added by way of explanation when she saw his disappointed expression.

'Well, you know where to find me, if you change your mind,' he said.

'Sure,' she said though she was not able to look at him. 'But right now we need to be getting home. My mother worries,' she said and she made a point of linking arms with Hilda.

'I'll see you later, at the Pride, then,' Steve said and he touched the brim of his hat, tilting it forwards again as she walked away.

Lizzie kept her own face forward, fighting the urge to look back. This was the way it had to be. As she battled against her feelings, common sense told her it could only end in tears.

It was late when Steve arrived at the Pride and Lizzie was about to call for last orders. She had spent so much of the evening wondering if she had indeed scared him off or if he would prove to be a man of his word, that she wasn't sure how she felt when he eventually appeared. He took his hat off and immediately his eyes caught hers. His face lit up with a smile. 'Good to see you again,' he said. 'Been busy?'

'So, so,' Lizzie said.

'I bet you've missed me – you have, I can tell.' His eyes twinkled.

Lizzie raised her brow. 'What can I get you?' she said. 'You've timed it well.'

The pub was almost empty with only a few stragglers remaining and Lizzie was already clearing up. Hilda had dropped by earlier, bubbling with the news she'd received from an official source: Stan would be coming home very soon. She'd told as many people as possible, and then gone home 'to wait for him'.

Steve stood by the counter with his glass of bitter and Lizzie wanted to laugh when his first sip resulted in the white head of the freshly pulled pint sticking to his moustache like snowflakes. Without her saying a word he wiped the excess off with his finger.

'That better?' he said, his eyes flashing flirtatiously. Lizzie smiled coyly then looked away.

'So, did you enjoy the film?' she said after a few moments' silence.

Steve laughed. 'It was great if you believe in ghosts,' he said, 'which I imagine your friend Hilda does. But it's not a film to be taken too seriously.' His eyes crinkled with laughter.

'It was a fine bit of nonsense to lift the spirits, shall

we say?' Lizzie said, and she was gratified when he grinned at her pun.

'It was certainly a film to make you think twice before stepping off the kerb without looking, wouldn't you say?' There was something about the way Steve regarded her quizzically that made Lizzie catch her breath. 'And I, for one, am very glad I managed to stop my favourite barmaid from becoming a ghost this afternoon,' he said.

Lizzie looked behind her.

'No,' Steve said, raising his glass. 'I do mean you.'

'And I was very grateful,' Lizzie said with a nod, not wanting to look at him. She was about to walk away but he beckoned her back.

'Talking of which,' he said, 'I'd hate to think of you vanishing in any way before your time. So maybe you'd allow me to walk you home tonight?'

'Why?' she asked without thinking.

'Because I'm here and because – well, I don't know why, but it seems particularly dark and spooky out there.'

Lizzie couldn't help laughing. 'You've obviously been reading too many ghost stories. I have to walk home every night and it's always dark and spooky, or maybe you hadn't noticed?' she teased. 'And anyway, I thought you said you didn't believe in ghosts.'

'I don't, though I was worried you might.'

'Just because you don't believe in them doesn't mean they don't exist,' she said.

Steve hesitated for a moment, then burst out laughing. 'I'm sure that's right! And if you let me accompany you it would give me a little more time to be able to make sense of what you've just said.'

Lizzie found herself responding to his laughter and was surprised to find that she liked the idea of him seeing her home, though she didn't want to admit it. 'It will only give us a few minutes more,' she said lightly, 'as I live just around the corner on Coronation Street.'

'A few minutes it shall be then,' Steve said, and he downed most of his pint as Lizzie came out from behind the counter and began collecting the dead glasses. 'I like to watch other people working,' Steve said. 'I'll wait here while you lock up.'

'Thankfully, that's one thing I don't have to worry about,' Lizzie said. 'Bob lives on the premises so he usually does the honours.'

At that moment Bob appeared from the scullery behind the bar. He didn't seem to notice Steve or any of the other remaining stragglers; he had obviously come looking for Lizzie. As she went back behind the bar Bob stepped in front of her and, reaching out, he put both of his large hands on her shoulders making a playful attempt at massage. But his enormous bulk made the whole manoeuvre look menacing.

Steve was impressed with the way Lizzie tried to

sidestep out of his way as soon as she saw him and pre-empt him touching her, but she was carrying several glasses in each hand and found it impossible to slip out of his grasp entirely. Steve, suddenly alert, realized Bob still wasn't aware of his presence and he didn't want to make a move that might be mistaken for an attack. The landlord was too large a man for it to be possible to spring a surprise and Steve was concerned about the damage Bob could do in retaliation. So Steve cleared his throat to announce his presence. Bob looked up. But the big man merely grinned in acknowledgement and didn't change his course. He held on to Lizzie for several moments, kneading her shoulders before giving her what looked like a firm, if over-zealous, pat on the bottom that steered her in the direction of the kitchen.

Steve didn't know whether to refer to the incident as he and Lizzie slowly walked together along Rosamund Street so he was relieved when Lizzie brought the matter up.

'You don't have to worry about me, you know,' she said. 'It's amazing what you learn when you work in a place like that. I'll admit I was a bit green when I started but I think I've got the measure of the likes of Bob Bennett by now.'

Steve glanced at her face as they passed under a street light and he was surprised to see her very determined look as she clenched her jaw and made a fist of both her hands.

'I'm very pleased to hear that,' he said, then paused, wondering if he should say more. 'It's just that Bob is more than just a local pub landlord, you know,' he said eventually. 'The thing is, I've actually come across him before.'

'Really?' Lizzie sounded surprised. 'Where was that, then?'

Steve hesitated and before he had a chance to reply Lizzie stopped walking and he realized they had already turned the corner into Coronation Street and reached number nine.

'This is where I get off,' Lizzie said. 'I told you it was no more than a stone's throw. But you can't leave the story there, you must tell me more.'

Steve looked up at the house. A light was on in the front bedroom, shining clearly through the curtainless window. 'Perhaps I'll save that story for another time.' She looked disappointed. 'That is, if you'll allow there to be another time?' he said.

'Thanks very much for walking me home,' Lizzie said.

'It was my pleasure,' Steve said. 'And I'd be happy to do it again, any time.'

He was disconcerted when she didn't respond so he said, 'Can I at least pick you up at the Pride on my night off next week? Same kind of time?'

It took several moments for her respond. 'Thank you,' she said, finally, 'that would be nice. But I'd better go in now; Ma likes to see me safely indoors before she goes to bed.'

'I'll say goodnight then.' Steve put out his hand, and felt the warmth of her hand as his fingers closed around hers. 'All I will say now is that Bob's a canny customer and you should always be on your guard. There's more to him than meets the eye.'

Lizzie didn't want to admit how much Steve's remarks had disturbed her, though she'd tried to pass them off as nothing. But he had looked so serious when he had warned her about Bob that later she began to wonder if she might have underestimated her boss's level of cunning. She'd believed she was beginning to understand how to handle him and to parry his unwanted advances, but Steve had sewn seeds of doubt. She obviously still had a lot to learn. Not that she had ever really trusted Bob, not since the first time she'd seen money and goods being traded in the yard between him and various rough-and-ready characters. Mystery packages would suddenly appear and it was commonplace for her to catch Bob passing money secretively to the delivery drivers, money that she could tell would never be recorded in any business's books.

Only the other day she'd seen Bob slip rolled-up paper notes into the hands of the suspicious-looking youths who'd taken to hanging around the place since the street party. They would huddle together over a fag and a joke and if she attempted to approach them they would stop whatever they were doing, yell rude and abusive names at her, then they'd race off in different directions, shrieking with laughter. She had to admit they scared her, but she tried not to think about them and did her best to avoid them. She certainly didn't talk about them to anyone other than Hilda.

'If anyone started pawing me I'd just bash them with my handbag where it hurts,' Hilda said when she confided in her friend. 'Then they'd soon learn not to be so free with their mitts.' She pursed her lips and looked so fierce that Lizzie had to laugh.

'Oh, Hilda! That look alone is enough to put anyone off,' Lizzie said. 'Maybe I should try that. But if I took your advice and clobbered Bob I'd most likely lose my job and you know I can't afford that.'

The following evening Pat went home early as it hadn't been a particularly busy night, and Lizzie had already covered over the pumps and washed all the glasses as there was only a couple of minutes to closing time when some rowdy last-minute customers barged in, demanding another drink, and now they stubbornly refused to leave. They were a mixed bunch, though generally older than the usual gang. Rough-looking by any standards, they were a large enough group to intimidate anyone, let alone a solitary barmaid in a deserted bar. They were wearing what looked almost like a uniform of navy-blue donkey jackets with scruffy, tattered trousers. Several of the grey-haired men had so much facial hair she could see nothing but the steely glint in their eyes, and one fresh-faced young boy didn't look old enough to shave, let alone drink.

She had seen them before in the Pride, occasionally. They usually arrived much earlier in the evening and left long before closing time when there were still plenty of people about, although the way they looked at her always sent a shiver down Lizzie's spine. Normally she left Bob to serve them, but this time they had come in so late, already much the worse for wear, and their behaviour from the moment they arrived made Lizzie feel afraid that she was alone. As soon as the last of the regulars had gone, she went into the kitchen area to call for Bob to help her, but to her horror she found him sprawled out in the armchair in the back parlour, snoring, with a half-empty bottle of whisky on the table in front of him.

'I – I need some help in the bar . . .' She leaned forward and shook his shoulder, though she was uncertain whether he was really in a state to help anyone. 'There's a group of men demanding another round and I don't know what to do,' she said when he eventually opened his eyes and peered at her. 'I've told them that I've already called time and the bar's closed.'

'What men are those?' Bob asked.

'I don't know any of their names, but they've been

here before and you always serve them,' Lizzy said. 'Two of the older ones have tattoos and long grey beards,' she said, unwilling to describe them as the ruffians they obviously were.

'Oh, them. You don't have to be scared by any of them,' Bob said with a dismissive wave of his hand. 'They're harmless enough. Just tell them to push off.' He let out a loud belch. 'Surely you don't need me to come and do it for you?'

'I'd rather you did, please,' Lizzie said, but then she was alarmed to see the cumbersome way he got out of the chair and lurched towards her.

'You don't have to be scared of them,' he said again, 'though I don't advise meeting them up an alley on a dark night,' he added with a chuckle. 'Come with me and I'll introduce you.' And he suddenly leaned towards her and grabbed her by the shoulders before she could twist away. He propelled her forwards into the public bar where several of the men were banging their empty glasses on the table as they chanted, 'We want a drink,' over and over. The oldest-looking one with long greasy hair and a grey beard was behind the counter investigating how to operate the pumps.

'What's going on in here, gents?' Bob shouted above the din. 'Are you intim-interim-intim-timating my lovely Lizzie? Why, she's trembling at the very sight of you. Now that's not a very nice way to behave, is it?' To Lizzie's horror he began to stroke her arm and the back of her neck, then his hand wandered inside the V-neck of her jumper. She gave a noticeable shudder that Bob ignored and tried to knock his hand aside. 'See, there's nowt to be afraid of, is there?' he said, his voice lower now and more husky. Lizzie felt revolted.

Lizzie pulled her arm away, not caring that she grazed the skin and spun out of his grasp before he had a chance to realize what she was doing. She needed to get out of the pub and get right away. It wasn't until she was outside and heard the click of the door closing after her that she remembered she had left her coat behind. But that didn't matter. At least she had managed to grab her handbag before she fled and she clung to it now, breathing hard. She hadn't even been aware that she was crying until she heard footsteps echoing on the empty pavement and she looked up to see the hazy outline of a figure coming towards her. Then she felt the wetness on her cheeks for the first time and heard the rasp in her throat. Someone called her name and, confused and terrified that Bob had followed her out of the pub, Lizzie broke into a run. She didn't realize that that meant the figure coming towards her would be upon her faster and when she felt her arm being grabbed she swung round and punched out at the face.

'Lizzie, stop! Please. It's me, Steve,' a voice shouted, and she hesitated long enough to see that it was true. 'Steve? Oh my goodness, I'm so sorry.' Even in the dim street lighting she could see that one of his eyes was blood-streaked and watering. 'You'll have a shiner there by morning. I really am sorry,' she said and, without thinking, reached out to touch his reddening cheek.

She gasped as she made contact and, realizing what she was doing, she quickly pulled her hand away, flapping it wildly in the air. Steve grasped both of her hands by the wrists, holding them together in front of her. 'Lizzie, calm down. Tell me what's happened. You look terrified. Like you've actually seen a ghost.'

'Oh, Steve, am I glad to see you!' She began to cry again and in between sobs told him the whole sorry tale. As she was talking, Steve took off his jacket and, gently putting it across her shoulders, pulled her towards him to stop her shivering.

Cora was still up when they reached the house.

'I was just getting ready for bed so I'm a bit of a sorry sight,' she said, slipping on her coat. 'I wasn't expecting visitors,' she went on as Steve stepped into the house first. Then she gasped. 'But what's happened to your eye?'

'It's a long story,' he said as he helped Lizzie into the hallway.

'I'm fine, Ma, don't fuss,' Lizzie said before Cora could say anything. 'I think Steve came off worse.' She grinned. 'But I tell you, I could murder a cup of tea.'

She led the way into the kitchen where Cora moved to put some water on the boil. 'A really strong cup of tea is what you need, my gal, with a pile of sugar and a drop of brandy to go in it. But as we've neither of those, I'm afraid a shot of gin will have to do. I'm making one for you as well, Steve,' Cora said, 'so sit yourself down.' She tended to the tea, all the while shaking her head as Lizzie revealed the events of the night. 'How will you ever be able to go back there to work? I'd be worried stiff whether you were safe or not,' she said anxiously as she placed a steaming cup in front of Lizzie.

'Don't be silly, of course I'll go back. I can't afford not to. I'll just give Bob time to sober up first, that's all.' Lizzie spoke with a bravado she didn't feel but she knew she had to for her mother's sake. But then Steve said, 'There'll be no need to worry on that score, Mrs Doyle. Because I shall be collecting Lizzie from work and walking her home every night from now on.'

Lizzie opened her mouth to protest but Steve said quickly. 'And I won't take no for an answer.'

Chapter 8

Summer 1945

After all the excitement that had surrounded the end of the war and the thrilling prospect that the world had changed, for most of the residents of Coronation Street life after VE day settled back into old familiar patterns and the euphoria of victory wore off much sooner than anyone might have expected.

'I thought we were all going to have such a bright future, but look at us now, we're in exactly the same place,' Cora moaned to Elsie Tanner one particularly warm evening as the two were sharing a cigarette sitting on the front doorstep.

'I know what you mean,' Elsie said. 'There's really not much to get excited about, is there?'

189

'I do my best for the kids,' Cora said, 'but it's not easy on my own and there's no fun in it.' She hesitated and gave a short laugh. 'Listen to me complaining to you, when you're in exactly the same boat!'

'The only difference is that I never want that bugger Arnold back under my roof under any circumstances.' She gave a throaty chuckle.

Cora sighed. 'Life's as tough now as ever it was before the war.'

'True enough,' said Elsie, 'and I can't help thinking that after all we've been through, we deserve better.'

'I'll tell you something for nothing,' Cora said. 'All this rationing doesn't help the situation. You'd have thought they could have stopped it by now, but I think it's getting worse.'

Elsie agreed. 'It seems to me that every time I go into the corner shop something else is missing from the shelves with no notion of when we might be seeing it again. Honestly, sometimes I can even forget that the war's actually over.'

'I feel like I've nothing to look forward to any more,' Cora said.

'Just more bloody misery on the horizon,' Elsie said glumly.

'I'm not that old,' Cora said, 'and yet I feel washed-up already. What kind of a world are we creating for our kids to inherit?' She took a long drag on the cigarette before passing it back to Elsie.

The two sat in silence for a few minutes then Cora said, 'I thank God I've got Lizzie's wages coming in, such as they are, but by the end of the week it's still hard to make ends meet.' She sighed. 'I'd love to get some new clothes for myself, but I've no idea how I'm going to manage that. Not when I've the kids to see to first. I've been pretty good about making do and mending, even if I do say so myself, but I honestly don't think there's much more I can do to this lot.' Cora looked down ruefully at her well-darned jumper and put her hands over the patch in her skirt where she'd used embroidery stitches to cover up the areas that were becoming threadbare. Elsie didn't say anything, but Cora didn't expect her to, for her neighbour did have the reputation for being better off than most. There were always boxes of chocolates, bottles of booze or extra pairs of nylon stockings in Elsie's house, and rumours were rife about where they came from. Recently Lizzie had said she'd even seen Elsie wearing a rather splendid brooch that looked as though it might be the real thing.

'I suppose Mr Churchill did warn us that things weren't going to change overnight,' Elsie said at last, 'but how long are we expected to wait?'

Cora stubbed out the cigarette and ground the filtered end into the pavement with the heel of her shoe where the rubber had worn away completely. She sighed. 'I suppose it did take Hitler six years to bring us down to rock bottom, so it'll probably take at least that long for us to build back up again.'

'Job's comforter!' Elsie gave a rueful laugh.

'Well, I can't be dealing with the world's problems when I've got enough of my own.'

'Something new?' Elsie asked. 'What's happened? You'd best tell us. You know what they say about a problem shared.'

Cora sighed. 'It's not new I'm afraid. It's the same old business with the house,' she said. 'The noises have started up again at night, the sounds of scratching and dragging.'

'Oh dear,' Elsie said. 'So is it haunted? Are there restless spirits flying all over the place?'

'Who knows? But one of Lizzie's friends has offered to try to do something about it.'

'Not more tea leaves or another Ouija board?' Elsie said, her voice scornful, 'Lizzie told me about those.'

'I know nothing ever came of the business with the tea leaves, or that board thing,' Cora said, 'but she's offered to try something different. Her and our Lizzie went to the pictures the other day so she wants to try calling up the restless spirits like they did in the film.'

'That one with Rex Harrison?'

'That's the one. I know it might sound a bit far-fetched but I'm willing to give it a try because I'm honestly at my wits' end.'

'I can see that and I'm right sorry, but are you really

sure about letting that daft-sounding ha'p'orth loose? I don't know her myself but isn't she supposed to be a bit cracked?'

'I'm not entirely happy about it, if I'm honest,' Cora said. 'But it's got so bad that it can't do any harm for her to have a go at confronting the spirits or whatever they are.' She paused. 'I don't really believe in them, but we've got to find out what's making all that racket, because it's really driving us all slowly round the bend.'

'So what are you going to do?'

'If she wants to come and hold a different kind of séance or something. then I'm prepared to give her another chance.'

Elsie rolled her eyes.

'Well, it's got to be better than nothing,' Cora said, 'it can't do any harm, can it?'

'What does your Lizzie say?' Elsie said.

'She's always tried to be tolerant because after all, it is her friend and she doesn't want to upset her, but I'm not sure how she'll feel about giving it another go. And I can tell you I'm not looking forward to telling Lizzie that that's what's going to happen.'

'Have you actually told Hilda she can go ahead?'

Lizzie was angry when Cora did finally tell her of her intentions and lost no time in making her feelings known.

'There's no point in flying off the handle with me,

young lady,' Cora said, 'because we agreed something had to be done and I'm afraid I invited Hilda to . . .' she flapped her arms in the air impatiently, '. . . to do whatever she has to do to bring up the spirits and make them go away.'

'I thought we were still discussing the matter?' Lizzie said. 'I didn't realize you'd actually said yes when I was trying my best not to respond to her until we'd had a chance to consider things.'

'I'm sorry if you don't approve, Lizzie love, but let's face it, we don't really know where to turn and Hilda kindly offered.'

Lizzie exhaled noisily.

'Well, something had to be done because the noises are not going away. If anything, they're getting worse. You've heard what goes on of a night sometimes. The boys are spooked out of their heads, and so am I and we can't carry on pretending there's nothing wrong.'

'But Ma, Hilda of all people!' Lizzie said. 'You know what she's like.'

'I do and despite her faults I'm very fond of her . . .' Cora said.

Lizzie threw her hands up in frustration. 'So am I but the only problem is I don't honestly believe she knows what on earth she's doing, it's all silly ideas in her head, can't you see that?'

'Well . . .'

'I know she likes to think she's "got the gift" but

you can't have forgotten that dreadful evening with the tea leaves, or even worse the night she brought that Ouija board. She was hopeless,' Lizzie said.

'No, I grant you those were both unfortunate non-events,' Cora conceded. 'But it didn't help that the tea was more like floor sweepings than anything that had once grown naturally in the sunshine.'

'So? What's changed? She'll never know one end of a Ouija board from another.'

'That's not entirely fair. Hilda has been learning, asking people's advice. Besides, she said she wasn't going to use the board again so maybe it will be better this time.'

'Well, don't expect me to be there is all I can say,' Lizzie said.

'Why on earth not? It's our house we're talking about. You can't desert me!'

'It doesn't matter how hard you try to dress it up it's all stuff and nonsense as far as I'm concerned. I don't believe in ghosts and friend or no friend, I can't go along with it any more.'

'If you don't believe in ghosts then you won't be frightened by whatever happens. But you *must* come because, to be honest, I'm a bit afraid of what she might find.'

Lizzie rolled her eyes heavenwards. 'Honestly, Ma, sometimes your logic is as weird as Hilda's. No wonder you two get along so well.'

Cora ignored the remark. 'It's not as though I'm asking her to conjure up your da's ghost, or spirit, or what have you; or Joe's, for that matter. Neither of them ever lived here, so I don't expect it's anything to do with them. No, I'm sure whoever it is who's wandering about the place has been around since long before our time. Don't forget the house stood empty for a while before we moved in and already had a reputation by the time we arrived.'

Lizzie let out an explosive breath but Cora took no notice.

'All I want,' Cora said, 'is for Hilda to find out what or who keeps making all that racket in the roof timbers. We've all heard it, so you know I'm not making it up.'

'And then what?' Lizzie was almost sneering. 'What's she going to do if she finds something?'

Cora shrugged. 'I'm sure Hilda will know what to do.'

Lizzie let out an exasperated sigh. 'Who else are you inviting to this – this *charade*?' She couldn't bear to say the real word.

'No one! I'm counting on you, my darling, for support,' Cora pleaded.

Lizzie frowned.

'And one thing I will promise you,' Cora said, 'if it's not successful, then I'll ask Father Keeley if he can help. I believe priests can sometimes do an exorcism or something like that. So maybe he'd be able to do the trick if Hilda can't.'

Lizzie raised her eyebrows. It was the first time Cora had hinted at doing anything quite so drastic and she realized how deeply her mother had been affected.

'But Hilda seems so keen to help,' Cora said, brightening. 'So I thought it only fair to offer her the opportunity first.'

Cora wanted to wait until the boys were in bed before letting Hilda begin the proceedings. But they were trying to delay their usual bedtime routine, curious to know what was going to happen and Lizzie was finding it difficult to shoo them to bed.

'Do you know what time it is?' she challenged them. 'You're never normally up this late. You're in bed long before I get home from work.'

'But you're not at work tonight,' Seamus said mischievously.

'Now stop trying to be clever and get off to bed the both of you. How do you think you're going to get up in the morning for school?'

'Who cares about that? We want to see what Hilda's doing,' Tommy said.

'Oh, go on, please, please can we?' Seamus pleaded. 'Then I can talk about it in show and tell tomorrow.'

'No, you definitely cannot. And if you wake up our Sammy with all your shenanigans then I'll be really cross,' Lizzie said. 'Get on with you!' And she pushed the twins out of the kitchen. 'Now, get up them stairs before I get Ma to take her slipper to your backsides.' She followed closely behind them so that they couldn't turn tail and come back down. She'd left Hilda setting up the chairs round the card table they'd borrowed for the session while Cora was putting some water up to heat so that they could have a cup of tea when they'd finished.

'Are you sure you know who has to sit where, Hilda?' Cora couldn't disguise the uncertainty in her voice.

'Yes, of course I do. I'm sorting things out so that it can all go smoothly,' Hilda said, and she sat down for a moment and closed her eyes. 'I'm just getting into the mood. It's important to create the right atmosphere so that the spirits will feel comfortable about making themselves known.'

Cora raised her eyebrows but didn't say anything more.

By the time Lizzie came back downstairs, having had to resettle the baby who had suddenly woken up, full of mischief and wanting to play, Hilda and Cora had taken their seats round the small table. 'This chair is for you, Lizzie,' Cora said, patting one of the wooden seats. Lizzie reluctantly sat down.

'Should we turn the light off?' Cora said. 'Isn't that what they always do in films? We don't want any bright lights putting the spirits off, do we, Hilda?'

Hilda sucked her lips back against her teeth so that they formed a thin line and gave a curt nod of her head. Lizzie noticed that she was wearing a faint dusting of face powder that slightly lightened her skin and she looked almost prim in her freshly washed and ironed cotton dress, with her hair uncovered and tightly curled. Hilda was the only one who had closed her eyes while Lizzie and Cora were staring at her, not knowing what to expect. There was an almost unnatural silence in the room, broken only by scratching sounds overhead and something that could almost have been the scuffing of feet. The sounds were real and the reverberations louder than usual in the silence so Lizzie was sure the others must have heard them too, though neither of them flickered so much as an eyelid. Lizzie tensed and saw Cora close her eyes so she lowered her lids a fraction too. Despite her scepticism she hardly dared to breathe.

'Now then, ladies, if we're ready?' Hilda's voice sounded softer than usual. She had opened her eyes and Lizzie saw her spend a few moments checking out each each of them as she looked across the table before splaying out her fingers. Hilda tilted her chin upwards as she spoke, as though gauging the pressure of the atmosphere. 'If you'd both be so kind as to put your hands on the table and spread the fingers of each hand until they connect with the fingers of the person next to you . . .'

Lizzie felt the touch of Cora's and Hilda's fingertips and found it strangely reassuring, though it seemed to bear many similarities to their efforts with the Ouija board. When they were all connected as Hilda had instructed, and Lizzie and Cora had their eyes closed, Lizzie found she was tingling and she jumped when Hilda spoke again.

'Is there anybody there? Is there anybody there?' Hilda's voice took on the same beseeching tone Madam Arcati had employed in the film and she swayed a little as she called out again.

Lizzie could hear Cora's deep intake of breath beside her and was tempted to turn her head and open her eyes fully to look at her. She half expected a vase to go flying across the room and her arms twitched ready to catch it, but through the slits of her eyelids she could see that Hilda was frowning so sternly that Lizzie didn't dare to move an inch. Instead, she watched Hilda close her eyes and begin to breathe deeply.

At that moment there was a loud banging noise. Hilda's eyes flew open and all three women jumped in surprise.

'Oh, my goodness!' Cora said. 'What was that? The spirits can't have come so quickly, can they?'

'Don't be so daft, Ma!' Lizzie said. 'It's someone knocking on the front door.'

'But who on earth can it be at this time of night? We're not expecting anyone, are we?'

'Maybe it's one of the neighbours wanting to join us. You know how folk round here can never bear the thought that something exciting might be going on in the street without wanting to muscle in,' Lizzie said and she laughed.

'Maybe it's one of them who is the bad spirit that's been haunting this house,' Cora said and Hilda momentarily glowered at her.

'Well, at least it can't be the ARP wardens complaining about the blackout,' Cora said. She giggled and Lizzie realized how grateful she was that the tension in the room had been broken. She stood up and brushed out the creases in her skirt in an effort to steady her hands, not wanting to admit that even though they hadn't really started she'd begun to feel uneasy. 'I suppose there's only one way to find out,' she said, and she marched with more confidence than she felt to the front door.

Two men filled the doorway. Lizzie didn't know them though she had seen them both at the Pride, but she rather thought they were also regulars at the Rovers. 'What are you doing here when it's almost bedtime, frightening people half to death?' she said sharply.'

'My name's Ron Bakewell,' the taller one said, touching the peak of his cap as they jostled for position on the red stone step. 'And this here is my mate Eddie.'

'Sorry to bother you at this late hour, Miss, but we have reason to believe a Mrs Ogden might be here.' His voice was gruff and he sounded anything but sorry.

At the mention of her name Hilda got up with a dazed look and started towards the front door. 'What's up? Did someone call me?' she said in her poshest voice as her hand went automatically to pat down her curls.

'Mrs Hilda Ogden? Our Phyllis' friend what cleans at the Pride?' This time Ron didn't touch his cap.

Hilda preened for a moment. She wasn't sure Phyllis would call her a friend exactly but she was more than willing to accept the description. 'Aye, the very same,' she said. 'I'm Hilda.'

'What can we do for you gentlemen?' Lizzie asked. 'P'raps you'd best come in.'

'We was at the Pride earlier and Bob Bennett thought you might be here so we've come to tell you that we've just made a delivery to your home.' Ron spoke up first. 'We had to dump it on your front doorstep. So you might want to be going home to deal with it.'

'In your own time, like,' Eddie chipped in.

Hilda frowned for a moment not understanding. 'A delivery? I'm not expecting anything!' She looked puzzled.

'I think Bob said it had come all the way from Italy,' Ron said. 'Leastways, he seemed to think it might belong to you.'

Hilda's hand flew to her mouth. 'Italy, did you say? What kind of delivery are you talking about? You don't mean . . .?'

Ron nodded. 'I believe that's just what I do mean, only I'd best warn you, he's a bit the worse for wear.'

'Seems like nothing's changed,' Hilda said half

laughing, half crying, suddenly not sure what to do next.

'How long has he been here in Weatherfield?' Lizzie asked.

'Long enough to get into the kind of state where we had to hold him up because he could hardly stand up,' Ron said. 'As you say, nowt's changed.'

Hilda was flustered. She grabbed her coat from where she had flung it carelessly over the bannister when she'd first arrived. 'I didn't even know he was due today,' she said. 'He's kept saying he would be here soon and that he'd let me know. But where's he been all day?'

'I can't speak for the whole day, but he's been down at the Pride for most of this evening at least,' Ron said. 'His bags are still there. We thought he could fetch them hisself once he's slept it off.'

'You mean he's been there all night, supping with you lot, while I was sat here, working?' Hilda suddenly sounded angry.

'Until he'd had a skinful and Bob refused to serve him,' Eddie said. 'And when he got a bit abusive, Bob thought it was time for him to leave.'

'So he gave us the address and we offered to see him safely off the premises,' Ron said. 'For old time's sake. If you'd like we could see you home an' all.'

'That's very kind of you, I'm sure,' Hilda said, 'but I'll be quite all right, thank you very much. From the sound of it Stan's not going anywhere, so I reckon he'll still be there whatever time I get home.' Hilda sighed. She turned to Cora who had joined them at the front door.

'I'm sorry to rush off like this, Cora, when we hadn't finished. But I'm sure you understand that I couldn't go back right now, not now that the connection's been broken. I hope you don't mind, but I'm sure we can rearrange it for another day.' She gestured towards the table. 'I'm convinced there's at least one troubled soul lingering somewhere in this house. I could feel it, but I'd need some time to reconnect so that we could sort things out.' She shrugged her shoulders. 'However, it seems that right now I've some rather more pressing business to attend to.'

Chapter 9

Hilda's feet were killing her but she set off walking as fast as she could. She'd dressed up specially for the occasion. It made her feel like she was really 'working'. But she would never have put on her best high heels that she'd found in the Sally Army shop if she'd have known she was going to have to walk home in such a hurry. They were a size too small and she couldn't do much more than teeter.

She'd felt cross when she'd first heard Ron and Eddie's story; to think that Stan had spent so much time in the pub! But when she turned into Charles Street she suddenly forgot all about her anger; she forgot about her uncomfortable shoes too, for all she could think about was seeing Stan. She actually wanted to laugh when saw what looked like a bundle of old clothes on the doorstep, remembering the other occasion when she had mistaken her husband for a pile of rags. The only difference this time was that the pile was dressed in what she now recognized as a demob suit. As she approached, she wasn't surprised to see the bundle move, but what she wasn't prepared for was the two bloodshot eyes that appeared over the top of the dark jacket. They were set deep into the darkly tanned face that was mostly covered by the stubbly beginnings of a black beard. She frowned. Surely the face was far too thin to be that of her husband? For a few moments her feelings softened. But when he spoke she was in no doubt that it was him and she stiffened up again. 'Give us a couple of quid, chuck. I owe it to one of the men down at the pub,' he said.

'You've been back five minutes and you've been borrowing money already?' Hilda snapped, almost forgetting that this moment of reunion was supposed to be joyful. But then she became aware of the furrowed depth of his mud-coloured brow, and what she could see of his cheeks was well-wrinkled too. He looked years older and she wondered what hardships he might have been through since she had seen him last.

'What's up, our Hilda, aren't you glad to see me after all this time?' he said.

In that moment Hilda's anger evaporated and her

face creased into smiles as she held out her arms. 'Course I am, chuck. Come here, yer daft lump.' She leaned over to help him stand up, and ignoring the ripeness of the smell that emanated in waves, she wrapped him in a huge hug.

'What am I going to do with you?' she asked as she held him away from her at arm's length to look at him properly, but she didn't really expect an answer.

'Need me to help you up the front step?' she asked. 'I'm sure I could most likely manage it. You don't look to be half the size you was when I last set eyes on you.'

'No, thanks, you're all right,' Stan said. 'I'm sure I can do it on my own.' But he didn't stop her when she put her arm round him and tried to hold him upright as he was swaying unsteadily.

Hilda was searching for the key to the front door when, without warning, he burst into song. Then he stopped and just as suddenly began to cry. 'Oh, I'm so glad to see you, our Hilda, my love,' he said. 'You've no idea. There were times when I didn't believe it would ever actually happen. I can't tell you how pleased I am to see the back of that bloody war.'

'Did they starve you in the prison camp, chuck?' Hilda's voice was full of concern as she realized how thin his arms were.

'Na, let's not talk about that, eh,' he said. 'Tell me, what's for tea?'

'Tea, at this hour?' Hilda laughed.

'Why not? I can't remember when I last ate and I'm hungry.'

'But I've got nowt but bread and dripping in the cupboard, I'm afraid. I've nothing put by. I didn't know you'd be coming home tonight, now did I?'

Stan stared at her in disbelief. 'But the war's over, woman. You've got to have more than bread and bloody dripping. Even in the camp we got more than bread and bloody dripping.'

Hilda drew in a breath. 'The war may be over, but I can assure you rationing ain't, not in England.' She poked him with her index finger.

'You're kidding me.' Stan looked disbelieving. 'I thought I'd be coming back to steak and chips.'

'In your dreams,' Hilda said. 'And don't you go thinking we've had it easy while you've been gone because we haven't. Life's been blooming tough here, I can tell you.' Then she softened her tone. 'Tell you what, I'll go first thing tomorrow and see what I can get from the butcher.' She was pleased to see his face light up. 'I'll go see if he's any bones so that I can make you some special thick soup. Or he might be able to spare some bits of offal I could make into a nice stew.'

Stan pulled a face. 'Sounds almost as bad as the bloody camp.'

Hilda ignored his comment. 'Right now I think a good night's sleep is what you need most – though if I could get up some hot water, a bath wouldn't come amiss,' she muttered. She tried to propel him forwards so that he could make his own way as best he could up the steep stairs to the two rooms they rented on the first floor. She all but pushed Stan inside and dragged his feet over the threshold and then went to hang her coat on one of the hooks behind the door. By the time she turned back into the room he had somehow fallen across the couch and was snoring loudly.

Lizzie didn't see much of her friend over the next few days, for Hilda was keen to get home from work as soon as her early morning cleaning session was over.

'Sorry I can't stop for a chat,' she said on the first morning after Stan arrived, 'but I've got to get to the shops before they sell out of everything. I need to see if I can pick up summat tasty at the butchers. He's not had a decent meal in years, poor love, so I've promised to cook him something special tonight.' She grinned and lowered her eyes. 'It'll just be the two of us, like.' She blushed then and giggled.

'Nothing wrong with that!' Lizzie said. 'After all, it's been a long time.' She suddenly felt her throat tighten as she said that, thinking the same was true for her as well. Now that all the soldiers were being demobbed and were drifting back, she wondered how many more times she would be confronted by the stark reality that her young man was never going to return.

One thing that made it more difficult for her to bear

was that since the unsettling incident at the Pride, Steve had kept his promise and had come to pick her up every night after work to see her safely home. But as she walked beside him she dared not get too close, for she was conscious of the secret that was hers to bear and which would always come between them; and when his eyes smiled flirtatiously at her and he tried to grasp her hand, she was careful not to touch or encourage him in any way, even when she longed to respond. She knew she must never lead him on to think there could ever be anything more than a polite friendship between them and she could only dream about what might have been.

After the dreadful fracas at the Pride, the terrifying gang had not appeared again inside the pub, at least not during opening hours when Lizzie was there, and Bob had not made any reference to them either. But the threat of meeting them again was constantly on her mind, so that when she caught sight of some of them in the yard, passing what looked like money in exchange for large boxes and well-filled bags, she almost fell in her haste to keep out of sight and couldn't wait to tell Steve when he came for her that night. She had to admit it was comforting to find him waiting for her at the end of the day. It was only a short walk home and she began to enjoy his company. He was funny and seemed to be able to put a smile on her face even though they talked mostly about work and the vagaries of the day. Sometimes he would suggest taking what he called 'the long route home' and they would walk away from the Pride in the opposite direction and amble through the narrow Weatherfield streets, making a large loop through the terraces before finishing at number nine. Lizzie found he was a good listener, a trait she had always valued, and she even found herself telling him about Joe. She told him how courteous and considerate Joe had been, always insisting that Canadians were more like British people in their manners, not 'brassy and loud' which was how he described the Yanks. Joe had been proud of his British heritage and the fact that not too many years previously his ancestors had set forth from Scottish shores seeking pastures new and trying to improve their lot. They had spent several disastrous weeks at sea, until they had finally sailed up the St Lawrence Seaway and disembarked at Montreal. There they had been horrified by the freezing winter temperatures that greeted them and the extraordinary amount of snow that was banked up by every roadside in the city. They were also disappointed to find people speaking French rather than English and feeling intimidated they had soon moved on, trekking across the country for many long months, not stopping until they had finally arrived in Vancouver. From there they realized they could go no further west. 'It sounded like such a beautiful city the way Joe described it with its backdrop of mountains,' Lizzie told Steve one night.

'Apparently it's locked in between the Rocky Mountains and the Pacific Ocean and the weather is more like England. He promised to take me there one day to meet his family and show me the amazing sights,' she said, stopping for a moment as her voice became unsteady. 'But it turned out that was only a pipedream.'

When the weather was fine they would continue their conversation outside Lizzie's house, often without any awareness of the time. Almost without realizing, Lizzie caught herself thinking about him during the day, anticipating what they might talk about that night on their stroll home. Steve was usually at the front door of the Pride before her, and on the odd occasion when he was late he was full of apologies. Then, one night he arrived red-faced and out of breath, the limp that he usually worked so hard to disguise now impossible to hide.

'The old war wound stopping you running like you used to?' Lizzie said without thinking. She had said it light-heartedly and had meant it as a joke but the look that flashed across his face indicated he didn't see it that way. He'd never talked about his war experiences and she regretted having drawn attention to the very thing he'd taken such pains to ignore.

'Something like that,' he said, his voice gruff, and unconsciously he massaged the top of his leg as he stared down at the pavement. Lizzie turned towards Coronation Street to take the shortest route to her house and they didn't speak until they reached number nine, when he offered a curt, 'See you tomorrow!' and left.

'Did he say he wanted nothing more to do with you?' Cora asked as she and Lizzie prepared for bed and her daughter told her what had happened. Lizzie shook her head.

'Well, there you are then. He was obviously feeling out of sorts before he came.' Cora chuckled. 'To be sure, you've not done any lasting damage to your friendship.'

'I should have been more sensitive. I hurt his feelings,' Lizzie said.

'If you ask me, you hurt his feelings all the time by keeping him at arm's length. Why you won't give him a chance to get any closer beats me. He's obviously sweet on you,' Cora said.

'Oh Ma, you know perfectly well why not. I can't let him be "sweet on me" as you so delicately put it. It wouldn't be fair.'

'Not letting him get to know you is what's not fair. I've told you that before, particularly when you seem to have so much to say to each other. You can't stop another person's feelings. I think you worry far too much. You should be going out together and enjoying yourself, not worrying that he might be getting to know you,' Cora said. 'It doesn't mean he's going to ask you to marry him.'

Lizzie took a deep breath; she had heard it all before, but Cora hadn't finished.

'And why do you have to keep him standing out on the doorstep every night if you've got so much to talk about? Why don't you invite him in? I tell you what,' she added before Lizzie could say anything, 'why not ask him to come for his tea one day, on his day off?'

'What makes you think he'd want to come here for a meal?' Lizzie said.

'You mean apart from fancying you?' Cora ducked as Lizzie threw a pillow at her. 'He's a long way from home, for one, so he might well appreciate a spot of home cooking. There's nothing wrong with us being neighbourly and saying thank you for being so good to you.'

'But I'd hate him to get the wrong idea.' Lizzie frowned.

'It's far too late for that,' Cora scoffed. 'I'm sure his head's already stuffed full of his own ideas.'

Lizzie looked alarmed. 'But that would be encouraging him?'

'So, what's wrong with that?'

'I've told you before, it's not fair because I know it can't go anywhere.' Lizzie started to cry. Cora put her arms round her and pulled her close.

'You can't be sure of anything of the sort. You need to give him a chance. So, why don't you just relax and have a bit of fun, see what happens, eh?'

To Lizzie's surprise, Steve seemed delighted when she issued Cora's invitation and on the agreed evening everything went better than she could have hoped. She didn't know what her mother had said to the twins, but Seamus and Tommy for once were well-behaved not asking awkward questions or constantly interrupting, and Sammy had gone to bed early without a murmur. At the end of the meal Lizzie had got up from the table to make the tea when there was a sudden noise overhead, a bump followed by the sounds of scratching and scurrying feet. It woke Sammy, who started screaming as if the house had been invaded and Cora flew upstairs before anyone else moved.

'What on earth?' For a moment Steve looked as if he might follow. 'I presume those are the noises you've been telling me about?'

Lizzie nodded.

'No wonder you wanted to get the house exorcised,' he said, 'though it actually sounds more like wildlife than ghosts.' He laughed. 'Not that I've ever heard ghosts.'

Lizzie smiled at that. 'Well, at least you know what I'm talking about now, though I'm sure it's nothing to be too bothered about.' She spoke with some bravado now that the noises had stopped.

'You need to find someone who can go up into the roof space to take a look,' Steve said. 'I'd offer to go myself if it wasn't for . . .' His voice trailed off as he patted his injured leg. 'But I think you're aware of how this little blighter can catch me out.' A wistful look crossed his face briefly, then his gaze switched to Lizzie and their eyes met in a sudden moment of understanding. Lizzie caught her breath and wanted to cry out, for this was exactly what she had feared. Yes, of course she knew what Cora had meant when she'd said that Steve was sweet on her – and she knew, too, that she didn't have to scratch the surface of her own feelings very hard to find out how much she liked him. But she couldn't afford to let this happen. From now on she would have to be on her guard. She stood paralysed for a moment, then carefully replaced the pot of boiling water on the hook over the fire as she tried to control her trembling hands.

At that moment Cora came downstairs with a defeated look, cradling the baby in her arms.

'I'm sorry,' she said as she brought Sammy over to the table, 'but there was nothing I could do to pacify him.'

'Shall I change him?' Lizzie offered.

'I changed him while I was up there,' Cora said, 'but then he wanted to see you and wouldn't go back into his cot.'

Sammy reached out his arms to Lizzie and pumped his plump little legs like pistons until Cora handed him over. 'When he gets into a paddy like this,' Cora explained to Steve, 'I'm afraid Lizzie's the only one who can calm him down.'

'Oh, don't worry, I've seen it many times. My sister has a baby,' Steve said, 'although, maybe it would be easier if I . . .' He half rose in his chair.

'No, please don't go yet.' Lizzie spoke up quickly but then she could feel the colour in her cheeks deepening and she buried her face, making soothing noises into Sammy's blanket. Almost instantly Sammy hiccupped and gave several sobs as he caught his breath, before his cries began to fade.

'It's uncanny,' Cora said, gesturing for Steve to sit down. 'She's really got the knack.'

It took only a few moments more for Sammy to quieten completely, his dark blue eyes gazing out at Steve over Lizzie's shoulder as his chubby arms clung to her neck. Seamus and Tommy took the opportunity to slip away from the table, Seamus racing up the stairs well ahead of his brother, shouting, 'First one in gets to run the engine!'

'I think that should really be my cue for leaving,' Steve said again. 'You ladies have your hands full.'

'Oh, no,' Cora said, smiling as she watched the boys disappear, 'please don't feel you have to rush off. Lizzie will be putting the little one to bed in a minute and then we can have a drink in peace.'

When Lizzie came back downstairs, half hoping Steve had gone, she found he hadn't and Cora had made the tea. 'There's some milk in the jug,' Lizzie said, 'please help yourself. Though I'm afraid we don't stretch to sugar.'

'I don't know anyone who does.' Steve smiled directly at her and she wasn't sure if it was an accident that their fingers touched momentarily as she handed him his cup. She didn't dare to look at him, particularly when she knew he was trying to catch her eye as he spoke.

'You know,' he said, 'you promised to come to the Rovers when you had a night off, Lizzie,' Steve said. 'I think it's high time I bought you that drink that I promised. In fact, it's long overdue. Rainchecks are meant to be cashed in, you know.' He glanced at Cora and added politely, 'And, of course, you're welcome too, Mrs Doyle.'

Cora nodded her head and smiled in acknowledgement. 'I think you'll have to count me out for the moment, what with the kids, but thanks anyway.'

'Yes, I can see how that would be a bit tricky.' Steve laughed.

'But I'd be happy to prod Lizzie in that direction,' Cora said with a mischievous grin.

'Thank you, that would be great,' Steve said, 'because I think now would be the perfect time to prove to Annie Walker that not everyone connected with the Pride is bad news.'

'Bad news? How do you mean?' Lizzie was curious.

'Well, not surprisingly our takings have been down since the Pride opened, and Mrs Walker has this notion that everyone connected to it is out to get her and should be avoided at all costs. I'm sure you can understand why, and ever since the street party disaster she refuses to go within a mile of Bob Bennett, leaving me to keep an eye on him. Someone's got to make sure he's not in a position to overstep the line again and do anything that could directly harm the Rovers' reputation or affect our customers.'

Lizzie nodded. 'I can understand that. The party business was awful, even though no one could ever pin anything on Bob. But you can't avoid the fact that the two pubs are in close proximity to each other and that . . .'

'And that Bob does have a bit of a reputation,' Steve said.

'Most likely well-founded, if any of the dealings I've seen with my own eyes are anything to go by,' Lizzie said.

'Anything specific? Steve said.

'Oh, you know the kind of things I've told you about. Deliveries arriving at all hours with mysterious-looking packages changing hands between the potmen or Bob and the drivers. Young kids hanging around the yard like they're looking for trouble. Though I'd never be able to swear to anything in court, so I can see how hard it is to pin him down and actually prove anything,' Lizzie said. 'The only good thing I can say is that whatever else he might be up to, at least his behaviour to the staff has improved. He's not been bothering me and Pat half as much since I had that problem with the gang.'

'Well, I'm pleased to hear it,' Steve said.

'But come to think of it, he has been a bit distracted,' Lizzie said. 'And we've seen rather a lot of Elsie Tanner recently. If anything, I'd say she's down at the Pride more often than she's at the Rovers at the moment.'

'I was thinking I hadn't seen her for a while,' Steve said.

'Then you're obviously out of favour. She's been too busy cosying up to Bob instead.'

'Is that right?' Steve sounded surprised. 'Not like Elsie to drift far from the Rovers. Sounds like she might have more than a drink in mind. I know she and Annie Walker haven't always seen eye to eye.'

'So I'd heard,' Lizzie said. 'At least Elsie doesn't have that kind of problem with Bob. He's always worth a few G & Ts these days, as far as she's concerned. In fact, you should see the beautiful brooch he gave her not so long ago. She's been boasting about it to anyone who'll listen.'

'You mean Bob gave it to her soon after the business with the pies? Do you think they're in cahoots?'

Lizzie hesitated. She hadn't intended to make it sound like an accusation when she had no proof of anything untoward, but she certainly couldn't deny that had been the implication behind the gossip that had been doing the rounds at the Pride.

'I'm not saying there's necessarily a connection,' Lizzie

faltered. 'It might all have been an unfortunate coincidence.'

'Then what *are* you saying?' Steve said.

'I just wondered if she'd asked Bob one too many awkward questions afterwards when it was time to settle the bill, that's all. It's possible Bob thought that a nice present would be the best way to keep her quiet.'

'Well, it's Mrs Walker I need to convince, and she's been nagging me lately to check things out and make sure Bob's not trying to take any unfair advantage. But as I told you, he always was a difficult man to pin anything on to.'

'I gather you knew him before he came to Weatherfield.' Cora spoke up.

Steve nodded. 'I won't say I *knew* him, but I did come across him many years ago in Blackpool and now here's my new boss wondering just what kind of establishment he's running in Weatherfield. So I think a visit from you, Lizzie, would be timely. It would be good to be able to show her that the bar staff at least are pretty reasonable – and reasonably pretty,' he added with a laugh and for a moment his eyes were openly flirtatious as he met Lizzie's gaze.

Lizzie could feel the blood rising from her neck to the roots of her hair and she caught her mother's eye. Cora grinned at her, a satisfied 'I told you so' look on her face.

'OK, then, I promise I will,' Lizzie said, not looking

directly at Steve now. 'Though from what I've heard it sounds like a tall order to think I could change Mrs Walker's mind on anything once it's made up.'

'That's true enough,' Steve said with a laugh.

'What's she like to work for?' Lizzie asked.

'She's fine. At least, you always know where you are with her. She leaves you in no doubts about what she expects. And let's put it this way, she makes it quite clear that she's the boss. I don't know how it's going to be when her husband gets demobbed.'

Lizzie gave a wry smile. 'I can understand that. I wonder if that's why Bob enjoys trying to take her down a peg or two?'

'The trouble is that on VE day it wasn't just a peg or two,' Steve said, his voice serious again. 'Apart from all the physical stuff, a lot of damage was done to the Rovers' reputation at that party, even though I accept that no one can prove Bob was actually involved in any of the goings-on. Thankfully I think we've managed to claw back most of our customers since then, so no long-term harm's been done.'

'I'm glad to hear that,' Lizzie said. 'Rivalry is one thing, but for me that was taking it too far.'

'So, are you going to come and visit us at the Rovers soon?' Steve looked at her directly now. He raised his brows and smiled, his head tilted to one side.

Lizzie met his smile and nodded.

*

Hilda was thrilled to have Stan home and, at the beginning, fussed around him like a regular mother hen. She tripped in and out of their two rooms with a permanent smile on her face, happily humming unrecognizable tunes. Most mornings, she flicked her feather duster at the odd pieces of furniture the landlady had seen fit to leave for them and passed the Ewbank over the thinning carpet while Stan hardly moved from where he lay sprawled on the overstuffed couch. Hilda made the occasional foray to the shops for food, but Stan made no attempt to go out, so it didn't take long before the reality of being together in such closely confined quarters began to lose its attraction.

'For goodness' sake, our Hilda, put a sock in it. Either sing a proper song or else shut up, woman!' Stan shouted one morning as she was tidying away the previous day's *Gazette* that she'd managed to salvage from the pub's bins. 'Go back to the bloody Pride – cos your constant droning is getting on my nerves!'

Hilda gasped and for a moment looked shocked, but then she smiled at him indulgently and fluttered over to where he was spreadeagled across the well-worn upholstery. She planted a kiss first on his nose, then his forehead. But her gesture had the opposite effect to what she intended.

'Go away! You're like a bloomin' buzzing bee.' He batted her away and Hilda sidestepped, protecting her face with her hands when she suddenly realized he would connect with the side of her face if she didn't move quickly enough.

Tears stung her eyes. 'I'll go and see what I've got in the kitchen for tonight's tea, shall I?' she said, somehow managing to stop her voice quavering and she disappeared behind the thin partition that separated the scullery from the main area of the living room. She glanced over her shoulder to make sure Stan hadn't followed her, then bent down to look inside the rabbit hutch of a cupboard she used for food storage. She reached in, feeling for the old biscuit tin she kept hidden at the back and brought it out carefully so as not to make a noise. She eased off the lid. She grinned then and let out her breath with relief that Stan hadn't found her hiding place. The tin still contained the coppers she'd been saving for a rainy day. Well, as far as she was concerned that day had arrived, sooner than expected. At least the money would get them out of the house for a change. And if she could pin Stan back to having only a couple of pints, then she'd be able to have a drink too. She sighed. She understood that he needed time to readjust to civilian life, but when would he start looking for a job? She wasn't sure how much longer she could go on stretching her meagre wages.

Lizzie was surprised when her friend appeared at the Pride with Stan one evening, for Hilda had been complaining that they had no money.

'I thought we could both do with getting out of the house for a change,' Hilda said, fixing her tight lips into what Lizzie recognized as a false smile. 'If you're going up to the Rovers later on, like you said, I thought we could come with you.'

'Welcome, Stan,' Lizzie said and put out her hand. 'Hilda's talked a lot about you.'

'I bet you're glad to be home.' She looked him up and down as unobtrusively as possible when she handed him a pint. He was far from the thin waif Hilda had made him out to be, with his belly spilling over the belt of his ill-fitting demob suit. In fact, everything he wore looked at least a size too small and if anything, it was Pat Evans's newly demobbed husband, Brian, who looked more like an advertisement for a POW camp.

'I might be back but I'm not sure why we bloody had to go away in the first place,' Brian said angrily when Pat introduced him.

'I'd have thought that was obvious, you were fighting for king and country.' Hilda had a smug look on her face. 'Only my poor Stan had to spend most of his time in a prisoner-of-war camp. He was in Italy, you know.'

'Huh! While we had our necks on the line out at the front,' Brian mocked.

'Aye, I'll give you that,' Stan mumbled, 'though Italy was no picnic, I can tell you.'

'And what have we come back to?' Brian seethed.

225

'What's changed? A few streets flattened and piles of rubble everywhere. Whatever happened to all the pre-war promises? That's what I'd like to know.'

At this Pat sighed and reached out to touch his arm, but he stiffened and pushed her hand away. 'They went the same bloody way all those other pre-war promises went after the Great War,' he said and he sounded bitter. 'It was no different than those poor buggers fighting for a land fit for heroes that never materialized.' Lizzie closed her eyes. She suddenly felt choked and she struggled to hold back the tears that threatened to spill. She felt a hand squeezing hers and looked up to find Hilda offering a watery smile.

'At least we've got the water and lecky back,' she said brightly.

Stan laughed. 'So long as you've got a spare bob or two for the meter.'

'Lizzie!' Bob Bennett's voice suddenly boomed behind her and Lizzie jumped as she hadn't seen him come in. 'Why are you still here? I thought you said you wanted to get off early?' He made no move towards her but she still instinctively took a step away.

'Yes, I did; I do. But Hilda came in and . . . I'm finishing up here now and then I'll be off if that's all right with you?'

She had a sudden dread that he was going to change his mind.

'Mr Bennett, can I introduce you to my husband,

Stan?' Lizzie was surprised to hear Hilda chirping up. 'He's just back from a POW camp in Italy,' Hilda said proudly.

Bob scrutinized Stan before giving a nod in his direction. 'Is that right? Well, if you're looking for work I might be able to put something your way,' he said. Stan's face flushed and he began rubbing his back. 'I must say it's tempting. But, er . . .'

'Why do you ask?' Hilda cut in, a keen expression on her face. 'Is there something going here?'

'Briefly. I'm expecting a delivery tomorrow night and some stuff will need shifting. I thought he might like to pick up a few bob, that's all.'

Hilda looked eagerly in Stan's direction and took no notice when he winced with pain.

'What time do you want him?' she said.

'Not before nine,' Bob said.

'He'll be here,' she said, 'won't you, chuck?' She turned to Stan.

'I suppose so,' Stan said.

'How about you?' Bob looked at Brian.

'No, ta,' Brian said. 'I've been and got my old job back starting Monday.'

'Wow, you lucky beggar!' Stan said. 'How did you manage that?'

'No luck about it. I went to demand it back when I heard some woman had taken it on.'

'Ooh, eh! You didn't?' Stan laughed.

'Fortunately, the gaffer soon saw sense and promised to send her packing. By heck, there'll have to be changes now that us lads are back.' Brian had a grim, determined look on his face.

'Oh, I don't know.' Bob looked thoughtful. 'I wouldn't like to be firing any of my ladies to make way for fellas. They add a bit of glamour to the place.' He turned and winked at Lizzie.

'Well, there's no glamour in my line of work. Factories are for real men, not women who think they can do a man's job,' Brian said with a dismissive gesture of his hand.

There was an awkward silence. 'I think it's time for me to be going,' Lizzie said, hanging up the last of the glasses she was wiping. 'Are you and Stan coming with me, Hilda? If so, I'll just get my coat.'

Steve felt a spark of excitement when Lizzie arrived at the Rovers and he greeted her warmly, though he was disappointed to see she wasn't alone. Since his visit to her house something had definitely changed between them and he looked forward more than ever each day to spending time with her, even if it was only short. She was different from any of the girls he'd known before; lassies like Elsie Tanner who now seemed to have turned her attentions on Bob Bennett. Lizzie was fun but she wasn't flighty. There was a sadness that lurked behind her eyes, and he wanted to take every opportunity to get to know her better.

'Lovely to see you,' Steve said with a smile and his eyes held hers as she made her way to the counter. 'I'm really pleased you were finally able to make it. What can I get you?'

Before Lizzie could respond Hilda said, 'Mine's a port and lemon and a pint of best bitter for my husband.'

Steve maintained his smile as he turned to respond to Hilda. 'Coming up,' he said, 'on the house.'

'Ta very much,' Hilda said. 'Very neighbourly of you, I'm sure,' and she took Stan's pint over to the other side of the room where he'd gone to watch a darts match.

Steve watched Lizzie as she perched on a bar stool, his gaze never leaving her face. He raised his eyebrows and spread his hands in amusement, as he followed Hilda's departure and he was gratified when Lizzie laughed. Then he put a gin and tonic down on the bar mat in front of her. 'I believe this is what I owe you,' he said. 'I hope I've got your favourite tipple right?' This time his grin was openly flirtatious.

Lizzie's cheeks reddened and she lowered her eyelids. 'You have indeed, thanks very much,' she said, 'very neighbourly of you, I'm sure.' Steve laughed out loud and they both grinned as she lifted her glass. 'Shall we drink to my very first raincheck?'

'That says to me that there might be more,' Steve said.

'Oh, I can't promise that. I just meant I've never had one before,' Lizzie said.

'It seems to me you're frightened to promise anything.' Steve lowered his voice. 'Have you had a bad experience with a fella?'

'Not in the way you might be thinking,' Lizzie said quickly. She took a deep breath. 'You know I had a fiancé?'

'Yes, and I'm really sorry.' Steve was contrite. 'I really didn't mean to upset you. That must be a very hard thing to come to terms with.' Steve was more than aware of the heartache and pain the war was causing. Everyone knew someone who had lost somebody close to them and he had seen more than his fair share of destruction on active duty.

'Joe was a great guy,' she all but whispered. 'Unfortunately he got himself killed before we had a chance to get married.'

Lizzie focused intently on sipping her drink and Steve didn't reply.

'Is it Bob? He's a bit over-familiar and I wouldn't be surprised if he'd put you off men for life. I'm sure the goings-on at the Pride can't be very pleasant. I don't mind having a word with him, tell him to keep his grubby paws off you?' Steve said after a few moments.

Lizzie shook her head and stared down at the counter. 'Don't be daft, I can look after myself.'

'Well you know I would! And you do know you

don't have to be afraid of me?' he said, lifting her chin with his finger.

'I'm not.' She looked him in the eye and smiled. 'Quite the opposite, in fact. I really appreciate you coming to rescue me. I thought you knew that.'

'No I didn't, because you've never said that before and it doesn't always feel like that. Lizzie, please tell me what more I can do? I'm trying to get to know you but sometimes it feels like you're shutting me out. I must admit I had hoped that by now we might be—' But he was interrupted once more by Hilda as she struggled to slide onto the tall bar stool beside Lizzie.

'Well, that's my husband taken care of for a bit,' Hilda said with a satisfied sigh. 'I reckon I won't be hearing a peep out of him for a while. Cheers!' She raised her glass and clinked it against Lizzie's.

'It must be good to have your husband back,' Steve turned and smiled at Hilda. 'Not like poor Mrs Walker who's still waiting for Jack to come home.'

'Of course, I'm thrilled,' Hilda said, 'most of the time.'

'Not seen you in here before.' The strident voice seemed to be directed at Lizzie and Steve turned as Ena Sharples appeared from the Snug. 'Let me introduce you to Lizzie Doyle, Mrs Sharples. She's from the Pride,' Steve said.

Ena stared at Lizzie. 'I knew I'd seen you somewhere. You're a long way from home, aren't you?' she said.

'Not really.' Lizzie laughed. 'It's my night off and I only live a few doors down on Coronation Street.'

'So you've come to scout out the opposition? Or to make eyes at the barman?'

Steve grinned. He felt sorry for Lizzie, though when he caught her eye he was glad to see she had seen the funny side.

'It does no harm to check out your rivals every once in a while,' Lizzie said, and Steve saw her give him a sideways glance as she said this, as if they were sharing a private joke.

'My friend here also works at the Pride,' she said to Ena. Without looking at Hilda, Ena splashed her empty glass on the wet counter, making several nearby drinkers jump back.

'My husband's over there playing darts,' Hilda said.

'Oh aye,' Ena said without any interest. 'Can't say as I know him or that I want to.'

'He's a good man. Got a heart of gold, has my Stan. You won't find anyone more helpful when he's a mind.' Hilda had a dreamy look on her face and didn't seem to care that her audience wasn't paying her any attention.

'He doesn't drink then is that it?' Ena said distractedly. 'Cos in my experience that's when men get mean, when they've had a skinful.'

Hilda drew her lips into a fine line of indignation.

'Not my husband. If you must know he's got himself

232

some work,' she said proudly. 'Without having some poor woman thrown out to make way for him as I've heard other folk tell.'

'Generous to a fault.' Ena's voice was full of sarcasm but Hilda didn't seem to notice.

'I don't see why any woman should have to lose her job just because the men are back.' Steve was impressed at Lizzie's spirit.

'I agree,' another voice chipped in. 'I know I don't intend to give up mine when my Jack comes home.' Steve was surprised to hear Annie Walker joining the conversation and everyone else stopped talking. 'We've always worked side by side, Jack and I, and I see no reason for us not to continue to do so. There's got to be changes after all we've been through, holding things together on the Home Front. It's important that women should be able to keep their hard-won independence,' Annie said. 'Of course the demobbed men need to get back to work as soon as possible, but surely not at our expense?'

Steve nodded and there were murmurings of 'hear, hear'.

'And what about you.' Ena turned to Lizzie. 'Will your man let you carry on working at the Pride when he gets home?'

Steve caught his breath at the bluntness of Ena's question and looked at Lizzie who had gone red.

'It's different for me,' Lizzie said eventually, her voice

soft. 'My da won't be coming home so I'm the bread-winner in the house while my ma looks after my – my three little brothers.'

Lizzie looked as if she was about to cry and all Steve wanted to do was to rush to the other side of the counter and sweep her into his arms. He could almost feel the softness of her cheek against his fingers as he imagined wiping away the tears that he could see were already forming. But she rallied quickly and, as someone shouted, 'Any service down here?' Steve turned and walked briskly to the other end of the counter, unable to trust himself not to do something foolish.

Lizzie watched Steve disappear. His place at the pumps was quickly taken by the woman she assumed to be Annie Walker. Annie put out her hand. 'You're Lizzie,' she said, and it was not a question. 'I'm pleased to meet you at last.'

'Yes, I am.' Lizzie was surprised at the friendliness of Annie's tone.

'And how are things going down on Rosamund Street?' Annie said. 'I trust Mr Bennett is keeping you on your toes?'

'Er, yes.' Lizzie didn't know how to answer. 'We've been quite busy now that the soldiers are coming home,' she said. 'I'm sure you've found the same?'

Annie frowned. 'Unfortunately they are not all home yet, though I do have high hopes my husband will be back soon.'

Suddenly there were shouts, a loud guffaw, and a thud of pint pots on the countertop as the darts players appeared at the bar, demanding attention.

'Who won?' Lizzie asked as Stan appeared.

'Oh, we're not done yet,' Stan said. Then he lowered his voice and muttered into Hilda's ear, 'Give us the price of a pint, Hilda love, will you,' as the other men began spilling silver and copper coins on to the counter. Hilda rummaged in her handbag then slipped some pennies into Stan's hand. 'You'd better make it last cos that's all I've got,' Hilda whispered and Lizzie turned away, pretending not to have heard. Steve reappeared to see if she wanted another drink.

She shook her head. 'Wow, but they're a noisy lot,' Lizzie said, nodding towards the darts players.

Steve laughed. 'If you think this is rowdy, then wait till election night next week, on July 5,' he said.

'Don't remind me,' Lizzie groaned. 'I'm sure we'll all be rushed off our feet then. Though it will also be quite a thrill. I think a lot of people are dying to get out there to vote, I know I am.'

Steve nodded. 'There's a lot at stake. It's the first chance we've had in goodness knows how many years.'

'For some of us it'll be the first time ever.' She laughed. 'A new chapter. New beginnings, after all these years of war. It's quite exciting.'

'It's what we fought the war for, after all; a change

in the old order.' Steve unconsciously rubbed the top of his leg.

'Oh, there'll be change all right. A new Labour government will soon see to that.' Lizzie rubbed her hands together and grinned.

'We don't need to go that far,' Steve said, raising his eyebrows and pretending to be shocked. 'You don't seriously think that could happen, do you?'

'Why not?' Lizzie said. 'It's about time somebody represented us working class.'

'I agree things need to be fairer. It would be nice if things could be shared out a lot more so that we all had more opportunities,' Steve said, 'but—'

'The only way to get that is to have a complete change: a new government and a new Prime Minister,' Lizzie said.

'Forgive me interrupting, but I couldn't help over-hearing and I'm not sure I agree.' It wasn't until she heard the damper in Annie Walker's voice that Lizzie realized the strength of her own feelings.

'Surely you couldn't think of voting against Mr Churchill when it's thanks to him we've still got a country we can be proud to call Britain?' Annie sounded shocked.

'I'm not denying that, Mrs Walker,' Lizzie said, not wanting to offend Steve's boss but determined to put across her point of view. 'But I feel that right now we need more than fancy speeches. If we're going to make life fairer for everyone, I think we need someone like Clement Atlee at the helm.' She had no intention of backing down.

'I suppose what you're saying, Lizzie, is that running a country in peacetime is different from rallying the troops to war?' Steve said.

'Exactly,' Lizzie agreed.

'But how do you know Churchill's not capable of doing both?' Steve said. 'Maybe you should give him a chance.'

Lizzie shook her head, aware that both Annie and Steve were eyeing her intently. 'No one wants to go back to how things were before the war. I'll be backing Clement Atlee and the Labour Party,' she said. 'By the time they've got the National Health Service they've been talking about up and running, and nationalized the railways, we'll be the envy of the world and we'll all be wondering how we ever voted Conservative. Who's going to say no to a welfare state when we're all going to benefit?' Lizzie looked up, suddenly aware that Steve was staring at her intently, a slight furrow in his brow. 'Clement Atlee will knock spots off Churchill, you mark my words,' she said, then she raised her glass and sank the remainder of the contents, aware that Annie Walker had walked away, leaving the two of them alone at the counter for a few moments.

'Blimey, Lizzie! I've never heard you talk like that before.' Steve looked at her in awe.

Lizzie smiled self-consciously and rubbed her damp palms down the side of her skirt. 'No, we don't usually talk about such things, do we?' she said.

Steve leaned across the counter so that their faces were almost touching. 'There's a lot of things we never talk about,' he whispered. 'I think that's something else that should start to change. And we don't even have to wait until next week.'

Chapter 10

'It's not like you to get all excited about politics, but you're even getting me and Hilda interested,' Cora said the following day when she, Lizzie and Hilda were sitting in the Doyles' kitchen. 'Do you really intend to vote?'

'Yes, I do. I've never been old enough before, so I'm determined to make my mark this time – and you two must as well, it's really important for everyone to vote, women especially.'

'Why should we do that, then?' Hilda looked puzzled.

'Because we can.'

Hilda rolled her eyes. 'Of course we can.'

'There's no "of course" about it, Hilda. It's not that many years since women chained themselves to railings so that we can,' Lizzie said. 'So I think we should. I feel we owe it to them.'

Hilda raised her eyebrows. 'Fancy!'

Cora shrugged. 'I wouldn't know who to vote for,' she said.

'Yes, you would. You at least know red from blue,' Lizzie said, her voice firm.

Cora shrugged. 'It's not as though my little vote could change anything.'

'Course it could,' Lizzie's voice was getting heated now. 'That's what democracy is all about.'

'There you go with your fancy words. Honestly, you don't half show us up,' Hilda said, giggling.

'But if no one voted we'd never get anywhere!' Lizzie was getting exasperated.

'And what if they all voted for the other side,' Hilda said, 'like your Steve says he might do.'

Lizzie felt her face burning. 'I hope I've made him see sense and change his mind – and he's not my Steve, Hilda, and you're not to call him that. People might take it the wrong way.'

Hilda pursed her lips. 'Well, he certainly looked like he was in the Rovers last night, so you tell me what's the right way to take it?'

Lizzie hesitated for a moment, thinking back to Steve's parting remarks when the discussion had become more personal than she would have liked. But before she could respond, there was a series of familiar scratching and scuffling noises overhead. Lizzie looked up to where the flex hung down in the centre of the ceiling and saw the solitary light bulb was swinging back and forth.

Cora went pale. 'Not them again!' she said, looking up at the ceiling.

'You should be used to them by now, Ma,' Lizzie said. 'We've heard them that many times.' Lizzie gave a laugh, glad to be able to diffuse the tension of the moment.

'We never did get to contacting the spirits to find out what it was all about, though, did we?' Hilda said.

'No, we were interrupted because your Stan had come home rather the worse for wear,' Cora said.

Hilda folded her arms across her chest with an offended look. 'I'd be perfectly happy to have another try, you know. We were only just getting started, as I recall, joining hands and trying to make contact. Nothing to stop us trying again.'

'Nothing to stop us finding someone willing to climb a ladder and poke about in the rafters,' Lizzie said, 'but for some reason we haven't done that either.'

'Hilda's right,' Cora said, ignoring Lizzie's remark. 'I think we should fix a night so that we can have another go at getting to the bottom of it once and for all.'

Hilda was delighted when Stan came home with his first pay packet. He wasn't prepared to tell her how much it had amounted to before he'd skimmed off enough to see him through the next night's drinking, but she was pleased when he handed over two crispy notes.

'What did you have to do?' Hilda asked, carefully folding them into her apron pocket. 'Was it very hard? Do you need me to rub your back?'

'Aye, that would be good. Just there,' Stan said, putting his hand on his neck by his shoulder. 'Some of them crates we had to unload were heavier than they looked.'

'What was in them? Was there a lot? Is that why you're so late?' Hilda said. 'Or did you stop in at the bar before you came home?'

'Bloody hell, woman,' Stan exploded, 'what's with the interrogation? That Bob fella had us unloading crates and cartons and a mountain of canvas bags stuffed full with goodness knows what, but if you must know he wouldn't let us start work till it was getting dark, so I couldn't see what was inside any of them. First we had to pile them in the yard and then we had to load them all up again onto another truck.'

'Us? How many of yous was there?'

'Just me and another bloke, so he had us sweating like pigs for our money, I can tell you. A mean bugger he is too. He seemed to think he was being generous cos he let us have a free pint for our troubles, when we'd finished like, but that was it. One lousy pint and not a drop more!'

'That sounds like Bob Bennett,' Hilda sighed, 'tight as a fish's behind. Maybe you should ask him if you could drive one of them trucks next time.'

'I don't think so. Somehow I don't think they were his. And there was no clues who they belonged to. No names were mentioned, not even our own. The whole thing was dead secretive. He told us we was never to talk about what we'd been doing and to forget what we'd seen. The less we knew the better for everyone, he said. So goodness knows what he's up to. Not that I care.'

'So long as it'll pay the rent,' Hilda said. 'Did he offer you any more work, that's all I need to know? For the money certainly will come in handy.'

'He said he'd be in touch if he needed us again,' Stan said. 'Now, can we get to bed cos I'm knackered as all hell!'

Steve was intrigued to hear about Stan's experience at the Pride but he wasn't sure what to make of it all when Lizzie relayed the information the following night. 'There's no doubt Bob's up to no good, though exactly what he's into is hard to tell. He's obviously buying and selling things he shouldn't, but it sounds like he's being careful about covering his tracks,' he said as they began their evening walk.

'He's certainly a tricky customer – and I'm sure he'd have some kind of fancy tale to spin if he were caught red-handed,' Lizzie said, 'so it's going to be hard to find out just what's going on.'

'You'll have to be careful,' Steve warned. 'It wouldn't do to let him know you're suspicious, and he certainly mustn't think that I know anything about his operations. I hope Hilda will tell you if Stan does get another job, for you never know where it could lead, but you don't want to be doing anything foolish or taking any chances for I reckon Bob could prove to be very dangerous if he felt cornered – and I don't want to have to be worrying about you.'

His voice was husky as he said this. He stopped walking and she suddenly felt the warmth of his hand as his fingers entwined hers. He pulled her towards him and she felt a tingling sensation ripple through her. Before she could say anything, he pressed his lips onto hers. Her immediate reaction was to kiss him back, and she wasn't sure whether it was she or Steve who was the more surprised when she did so. Lizzie gasped and looked up into his face which was intense and serious. Reeling in shock, she took a step away. She opened her mouth to speak, though she couldn't form any sensible words.

Steve put his hand to her face and caressed her cheek. 'I do worry about you, you know.' He spoke in a whisper. 'I don't know if you realize how I—'

She put her finger to his lips. 'Please don't say anything,' she said. She was breathing hard. 'I can't . . . you do have to understand . . .' She paused. 'I can't ever offer you anything more than my friendship.'

Steve stared at her, his brows creased.

'Please don't ask me to explain,' she said. 'All I can

say is that my life is not my own and I can't . . . Oh God, I feel as if I'm being torn in two!' She began to cry. 'But that doesn't mean I don't . . . It's just that I can't . . .' she sobbed.

'I'm sorry. I didn't mean to upset you.' Steve was dismayed. 'But I can't hide how I feel about you.'

Lizzie looked away as she wiped her eyes on the handkerchief Steve proffered.

'Is there something I should know?' Steve said.

Lizzie's shoulders dropped. 'We all have a story to tell,' she said, 'and you deserve to hear mine one day. But not now. It's too complicated. I'm sorry.'

'Nothing to apologize for,' Steve said. 'I'm not going anywhere. I didn't mean to pressure you and I'll try to understand.' He looked up at the light-filled sky with its first dusting of clouds streaked with orange and mauve that hinted at the slowly descending dusk. 'Let's say it's a midsummer's evening and I got carried away.'

'How's about we call it a night?' Lizzie said. Neither spoke as they walked back towards Coronation Street and Lizzie didn't object when Steve took her hand as he fell into step beside her.

When they reached number nine, Lizzie brought out her key and she shivered involuntarily.

'It's getting late, you'd better go in,' Steve said. He put his arm round her and gave her a tender embrace. 'Shall I still come for you tomorrow night?' he asked.

'If you still want to see me,' Lizzie said.

'If you care for someone, you can't let them go just like that, you know.' Steve held her again. 'And I do care for you, Lizzie, I hope you know that. I'll do my best to understand and I'm here for you if you ever change your mind.'

Lizzie savoured the momentary warmth of his closeness, but then old memories were stirred and she was too choked to reply. She pulled away, knowing that she would never be able to acknowledge just how much she cared for him.

The results of the General Election on 5 July were delayed until 26 July because voting in some constituencies was delayed because of local wakes weeks and also in order to include the overseas forces' votes in the count. When Labour's landslide victory was finally announced and Clement Atlee declared Prime Minister, Lizzie for one was delighted, if not surprised. And it was not long after, on 2 September, that the war in the Pacific finally ended. The United States had dropped its atom bombs on Hiroshima and Nagasaki in early August, forcing the Japanese to surrender, and while the devastating action divided opinion in Britain and served as a sobering bookend to the war years, the result was that the conflict was over on all fronts.

'Finally! Can you believe it?' Annie said to Steve, waving an official-looking letter in his direction. 'I had almost given up hope. But I have just got notice that

Jack will definitely be coming home soon. So now we can begin to think about organizing some celebrations.'

'For Jack, or for VJ day? What had you in mind?' Steve said.

'Why not for both?' She couldn't stop smiling. 'Though it will be nothing on the scale of what we had before.'

'I wonder what the Pride are planning,' Steve said.

'Perhaps you could find out. It would be helpful to know what kind of opposition we might be up against, so that we're not suddenly surprised or upstaged by Mr Bennett.'

'I'd be happy to pay them a visit and do a recce,' Steve said.

'Indeed. See what your young lady has to say.' Annie smiled.

'I'm not sure how Lizzie would feel being called 'my "young lady".' Steve chuckled.

'Oh, come now. There's no need to be coy. I'm sure everyone knows that you're stepping out. Besides, she's a very pretty girl and I happen to think you look very well together,' Annie said. 'You do escort her home each night, if I'm not mistaken?'

'I do usually, because there are some rather dodgy characters about, but I've hardly seen her these past couple of weeks as she's had to stay on and work late.'

'So, that's as good an excuse as any for you to go

there now. You can have a drink there, sound her out, and see for yourself what's going on.'

'Bob's not talked about doing anything special for VJ day,' Lizzie said as she served Steve a pint and, at his insistence, accepted a half-pint shandy for herself. 'And he's not here right now for me to check with him. Has Mrs Walker let you off early just to come and ask me that?'

'Well, you must admit that after the last fiasco it would help if she was forewarned. Even if we weren't ever able to prove anything, we did all have our suspicions about who was responsible for the VE day shambles.'

'The problem is, in all honesty, things don't seem to be getting any easier,' Lizzie said, 'and I worry that Bob's losing interest in the pub and concentrating too much on his sidelines.'

'That's quite possible. Serving behind a bar isn't what it used to be,' Steve said. 'You don't get decent tips these days.'

'That's the point,' Lizzie said, 'things have not got any easier for ordinary folk like you and me. Everyone is still getting by on nothing, we thought life was tough during the war, but everyone's struggling to make ends meet.'

Steve nodded in agreement.

'Anyway, whatever the reason, I'm really pleased to see you here, because I wanted to see you,' Lizzie admitted.

'Why, what's wrong? Has anything happened?' Steve

was instantly alarmed. 'He's not laid a finger on you, has he?' Steve leaned across the counter and grasped hold of Lizzie's hand. 'Because I swear I'll have his guts for garters if he has.'

'No, no. It was nothing like that, I promise you. Really, I'm fine,' Lizzie reassured him.

Steve relaxed for a moment. 'I was concerned when you said not to come because he'd asked you to work late. I should have come anyway. I did worry about what might be going on.'

'No, really, I'm all right,' Lizzie said. 'He wanted me to straighten out things for him behind the scenes, that's all. He's been out a lot recently and things had been piling up and getting out of hand. It was all a bit unnecessary, really, I'm sure he was perfectly capable of sorting things out for himself, but of course it was easier to get me to do it.'

'And he didn't try any of his old tricks?'

'Nothing I couldn't handle, or I'd have asked you to come, honestly. But thank goodness he's been a bit distracted recently, by Elsie Tanner of all people.'

'Yes, we haven't seen as much of her at the Rovers for some time, now,' Steve said. 'But I'm sure she can look after herself. It's you I'm worried about and I'm not going to take no for an answer again. I'm going to come down and meet you, whatever time you finish in future,' Steve said. 'But why did you want to see me? Something must have happened?'

Lizzie dropped her voice to barely above a whisper, even though there was no one else in the bar. 'I've been watching Bob carefully, like we said, discreetly, like and I've seen him watering down the gin. I wasn't sure what I should do about it. He's probably had a go at the beer too, but that's down in the cellar where I can't see him. Whereas up here, I actually saw him with the gin bottle, though thankfully he didn't see me.'

'Are you sure he didn't?' Steve sounded anxious again.

'As sure as I can be.'

'It could be dangerous if he caught you spying on him, let's face it, we've no idea what the hell he's caught up in.'

'I know – and there was something else.' The colour suddenly drained from Lizzie's face.

'What?' Steve almost shouted the word and Lizzie jumped.

'Those loutish lads have turned up again,' Lizzie said. 'Do you remember how they always seemed to be hanging around here?'

'How could I forget?' Steve said. 'They're not the kind of men you'd want to run into on a dark night. And let's face it, it's because of them that I started coming to meet you every night. I blame myself for not insisting I came these last few weeks. I shouldn't have left you on your own.'

'It's not your fault,' Lizzie said. 'I wanted to believe they'd really gone but since they've started popping up again I have to wonder if they ever really went away. I've often felt as though someone was watching me, and now I know I'm not imagining things because I know Stan Ogden's seen them too.' Steve received this news in silence but she could see his whole body tensing.

'And have they . . .?' Steve began but Lizzie cut him off.

'No, no!' she said. 'I promise you they've kept their distance, otherwise I'd have told you immediately.' She gave a short laugh. 'They've been kept pretty busy. Whenever I've seen them, they've been stacking cartons and dragging heavy-looking canvas bags about, either piling them up in one of the back rooms or carting them into the yard for Stan to load onto the truck.'

'Any idea what's in these bags or boxes?' Steve asked.

'Stan told Hilda he reckoned they were probably stolen goods of all sorts.'

'Really!'

She nodded. 'He said it either looked like new stuff that had fallen off the back of a lorry, or things that had been nicked, plus odd bits of good older furniture, the type of stuff that could have been looted from bombsites or from houses left empty when their owners left to go and stay in the country because of the city being bombed. Hilda's been terrified ever since she found out and she doesn't want him to take on any more work, but it's too tempting, the money's too good to turn down.'

'I bet it is.' Steve let out his breath in a low whistle.

'Stan isn't bothered – he'll do anything so long as he can get his hands on some cash at the end of the day,' Lizzie said. 'It's Hilda I'm worried about. The other day she and I found one of these bags in the kitchen and we just had to take a peak, didn't we?'

'So what did you find?' Steve wanted to know.

'Several pairs of silver candlesticks and some silver platters, but then we had to shut the bag up again fast because we heard Bob coming.'

'Did he catch you looking?'

'I don't think so. I think we managed to get it closed before he saw us. Anyway, he grabbed hold of it and we made out like we'd never seen it before. But it made a clanging noise as soon as he picked it up.'

'How did he explain that away?' Steve said.

'He laughed and said he was selling a few bits and pieces for a friend,' Lizzie said. 'Hilda wanted to go to the police, but as soon as I calmed her down she realized she didn't want to shop her own husband.'

'And she's working for the same man,' Steve pointed out, 'so how was she going to square that with her conscience?'

'Exactly. And the same applies to me,' Lizzie said.

Steve frowned. 'I'm getting worried. You're beginning to skate on thin ice, Lizzie. If he suspects you're checking up on him, this man could be dangerous. Don't forget I've come across Mr Bennett and his dodgy dealings before, even if I did know him by a different name then. But I'm concerned that he's a very slippery customer and it's always been impossible to prove anything against him.'

Lizzie drew in a breath sharply and, without warning, burst into tears.

'It's very hard to rat on someone, you must know that,' she said, a sob catching in her throat. 'Particularly when that someone is your boss. I feel so disloyal even mentioning it to you, because, after all, Bob does pay my wages.'

Steve pulled a white cotton handkerchief from his pocket and handed it to her across the counter. 'I'm sorry, Lizzie, and believe me, I do understand, but you mustn't think of it as ratting. This could be serious and you don't have to feel guilty.'

Lizzie shook her head. 'Honestly, I would have left here before now if I didn't need this job so badly, but jobs for women are not that easy to come by now that all the men are starting to come back.' She sniffed and wiped her nose. 'And someone's got to look after my ma and my – my brothers.' She gave a long hard blow into the handkerchief. 'Though I don't know how much longer the Pride will be able to stay open anyway.'

'Are you serious?' Steve was surprised.

'I am,' Lizzie said, the tears running down her cheeks again. 'I don't think it's living up to Bob's expectations.'

'Really?' Steve said.

'All that razzmatazz and the promises he made at the beginning? They seem to have come to nothing. And now he's away from the pub more than he's here, so I do worry about the future.'

'Hmm,' Steve said. 'You mean the pub's future?'

'And mine. I don't know how much longer he'll be able to pay our wages.'

'That bad? How come you've never mentioned it before?'

Lizzie shrugged.

'Well, I don't know what the answer is at the moment. But I do think that you must be extra vigilant and not take any unnecessary risks.'

Lizzie nodded. 'The cabaret acts they've been getting in on a Saturday night are second-rate and takings must be down because customer numbers have certainly been falling off. Why don't you come and see for yourself?'

'That sounds like a good idea. Maybe I could even engineer a chat with Bob. In the meantime I must report back about VJ day because that's what Annie Walker really wanted to know.'

Lizzie put her hand to her mouth in horror. 'Does that mean you'll have to tell Mrs Walker everything I've told you?' she asked.

'No, of course not,' Steve reassured her quickly. 'I'll only tell her what I think she needs to know.'

Chapter 11

Autumn 1945

By the time Jack Walker finally received his discharge papers and Annie was officially informed that he was on his way home, the euphoria of VE day was a distant memory. All thoughts of the street parties and celebrations that Annie had so enthusiastically recounted in her letters were now confined to the past along with the patriotic bunting. A Union Jack, its edges well frayed, feebly fluttering from an upstairs window, acted as a solitary reminder. Even the memories of the VJ day festivities following Japan's surrender in August, were beginning to dim as Jack trudged home, his mind wading through a sea of images, sounds and smells that didn't seem to belong in this northern street. How life had changed since the war started. During the last few years he had been exposed to so many new experiences that he no longer knew what was real and what was not. Like now, when he felt decidedly alien in civilian clothes and a part of him wished he could be back in his army uniform. He felt uncomfortable and distinctly out of place in the scratchy material of the one-size-fits-all demob suit he'd picked up with his discharge papers.

The limited daylight from the overcast sky barely illuminated the mud-smeared cobbles of Weatherfield as he plodded steadily homeward, and Jack could feel the chill as the light drizzle began to seep through the cheap material of his coat. He stopped to take his bearings when he drew close to the viaduct, looking to see if the war had inflicted any noticeable damage on the landscape since the last time he'd been home. To his relief, all he could see as he spun in a complete circle were the familiar sights he'd grown accustomed to during the two years he had lived there before the war. He had written to Annie as soon as he knew he was coming home and he fixed his mind on the image of her face as he continued through the grey streets, ignoring the weight of the kitbag slung over his shoulder, and the inflamed soreness of his neck where the unyielding shirt collar had rubbed against the weathered skin.

It was dinnertime when he arrived at the Rovers Return, and he stood for a moment, unsure whether to go in through the front doors of the public house or enter directly into their private quarters at the back. But as he reached the main entrance he bumped into someone he recognized as an old regular. It was Albert Tatlock, heading towards the bar for an early drink.

At first Albert peered at him, then he rocked back on his heels. 'Well, well, well! If it isn't Jack Walker? By heck, but you've lost weight, I hardly recognized you.'

'Well, I haven't exactly been at a holiday camp, you know!' Jack couldn't help snapping.

Albert ignored him and stared up at Jack's glasses that kept slipping down his nose. 'It's good to see you, anyhow. Your missus's been talking about your home-coming for so long I was beginning to think you'd changed your mind.'

Jack gave a sardonic laugh. 'No chance of that,' he said.

'By gum, but it's great that you're safely home at last.' Albert patted him on the back then shook him by the hand, 'though Mrs Walker never let on you was actually arriving today.'

Jack frowned. 'Well, I did tell her,' he said, but before he could worry further Albert pushed him forwards as he held open the double doors.

The warmth and people-smell combined with the fug of cigarette and pipe smoke assailed his nose almost as soon as he crossed the threshold, but the first thing he saw was the comforting sight of Annie pulling a pint and he stood for a moment, wanting to hold the snapshot in his mind's eye. She didn't look up immediately, but when she did, she almost dropped the glass. Her cheeks flushed and she suddenly looked flustered. But then she quickly signalled to the young man beside her to take over. She made no further public show of emotion as she grasped Jack's arm and, with a tight-lipped smile, ushered him through the door that led to their private rooms. Then she turned to face him, arms extended. 'Jack! Oh, Jack!' she said and she buried her face in his coat.

Jack put his bag down on the tiled floor and took hold of her gently by the shoulders, a smile twitching on his lips. 'Here,' he said, 'let's be having a look at you, then. Eh, you've not changed a bit, lass, I'm pleased to say.'

Annie touched her hand to her hair in a gesture he fondly remembered and he smiled as he pulled her roughly towards him. Cupping her chin in his hands he held her face close to his in a chaste kiss for several moments. Then he clung to her in a tight embrace as they stood together in the middle of the room, his eyes closed. When he finally opened them again he found he was looking over her shoulder at a young boy who was standing by the sink, helping himself to a glass of water from the single tap. Jack's eyes widened involuntarily.

'Billy?' he cried and, letting go of Annie, stepped towards the boy, his arms wide in expectant embrace. Billy, tall for his seven years, stared at him for a moment while a brief flash of fear crossed his face and he took a step back.

'Who are you?' Billy demanded, frowning.

'Don't you know?' Jack was taken aback.

'No, stupid, or I wouldn't have asked, would I?' Billy said. 'So keep your thieving mitts off me.'

Annie gasped. 'Billy, what language! Just you apologize to—' But Jack interrupted. 'Don't you recognize me from my pictures, Billy? Didn't your mother tell you I was coming home? Annie, tell him,' he entreated as he made a move towards the boy, his arms still outstretched. But before Annie could open her mouth, Billy shouted, 'No!' and threw the contents of the glass at Jack before running out of the back door.

Jack could only stare after him in disappointment and confusion as water soaked through his shirt. That was not the kind of greeting he had expected. Then a movement by the door alerted him to a little girl who was playing quietly with her dolls on the floor. She was undressing them and putting them into a tiny tin bath that was on the rug in front of the hearth. When she saw him, she jumped up and with her hands over her ears ran crying to her mother's side where she buried her head in Annie's skirt.

'Don't let him touch me! Tell him to go away,' she whimpered to Annie imploringly. She backed away till she was almost behind Annie, then twisted her body so that she was still clinging to a handful of material while peeping out at Jack at the same time. Once or twice she half-heartedly kicked out at Jack, who stood still. He didn't dare approach the child, let alone consider kissing or cuddling her. This was not the welcome he had dreamed of.

To his surprise, Annie laughed and smoothed her hand over her daughter's hair. 'This is Daddy, darling. Remember the pictures I showed you? I told you he would be coming home soon. Well, here he is. Safe and sound, at last.'

Joanie stuck her thumb in her mouth and turned her head away, though she continued to peek out occasionally at Jack from behind Annie's back. Each time her face appeared, Jack raised his eyebrows and said, 'Boo!' in as bright and cheerful a voice as he could muster, though he was careful not to shout too loudly or to make any movement towards her while he watched Annie continue to soothe her.

'Well, Jack darling, welcome home,' Annie said with a warm smile, eventually turning back to her husband. 'I'm glad to see you even if nobody else in this house is!' She laughed. 'In fact, I've been longing to see you.' And with a gentle movement of her hands she stood Joanie to one side and gave Jack the kind of welcome he'd dreamed of when he'd thought of coming home.

It was Lizzie's day off and, at Steve's, invitation she went to the Rovers in the evening. She was surprised to find Elsie Tanner was there, for she had been patronizing the Pride for months now, and she was enjoying a quiet drink with her neighbour when Jack Walker finally arrived home. She could probably have guessed from the sight of his ill-fitting demob suit and the oversized kitbag on his shoulder as he heaved his way into the bar, but it quickly became clear who it was. So, this was Annie Walker's beloved husband, Lizzie thought; the name that was painted above the door. Bob had talked a lot about the homecoming of the man he considered to be a serious rival, once his imminent demobilization had become common knowledge, and not unnaturally he was concerned about what that might mean for the Pride. However, when Lizzie first set eyes on Jack she hardly marked him as a man to be feared. Certainly not in the way Annie's sharp tongue was to be feared, though Lizzie had to admit Annie had done a good job holding the fort during the years her husband had been away.

When Lizzie saw the way Annie's face lit up the moment Jack walked through the door, she couldn't stop a lump rising to her throat, and for a moment she felt quite choked. She was sad to think that her father would not be coming home to be greeted like that by Cora, and neither would she be embracing Joe . . . But having heard young Billy's shriek, and Joanie's fearful cry when they saw their father for the first time in years, it made her think of the effect demobilization had on the rest of the family and she couldn't help wondering how the twins or even Sammy might have reacted if their da had suddenly reappeared after so many years. She forced herself to shut her mind to such thoughts, though she couldn't prevent a few tears trickling down the side of her nose and she brushed them impatiently away, but not soon enough, for Elsie had already noticed.

'Cheer up, love, there's worse things happen at sea, as my mam used to say. And talking of the sea, I can tell you I won't be shedding any tears over my Arnold not coming home,' Elsie said gaily.

Lizzie was surprised. 'What do you mean? Have you heard from him?' She felt immediate concern, even though she had never met the man. 'He's not been hurt, has he?'

'Nah,' Elsie said. 'Last I heard he was fit and well enough to be demobbed, but I don't think that coming back to live in Coronation Street with his wife and kids is part of his future plans.'

'Oh dear, I'm really sorry about that,' Lizzie said.

'You needn't be, I'm certainly not,' Elsie said. 'Good riddance to bad rubbish is all I can say. I won't be able to get rid of him fast enough.'

Annie was thrilled to have Jack back at home again, and at first she revelled in the way that he insisted on spoiling her. It had been a long time since anyone had brought her cups of tea in bed or insisted she put her feet up in the middle of the afternoon. While she had been in sole charge, every day had brought its problems and though Annie had always risen to the challenge, she had often felt uncomfortable.

'You don't have to worry about those sorts of things now I'm here, love,' Jack insisted when she confessed her pet hates to him and, in the beginning, she appreciated him looking out for her wellbeing. Then she noticed he was going out of his way to relieve her of the regular duties he considered to be onerous, until soon there seemed little for her to do.

They had always worked well together and Steve fitted beautifully into the team as Jack had promised he would. As time went on, though, Steve and Jack between them began to take on more and more duties while Annie, almost without her realizing it, gradually relinquished the additional responsibilities she had had to assume during the war years. So it was quite a shock for her one day when she suddenly became aware of just how little there was left for her to do. She knew she would have to discuss the matter with Jack and deliberated for several days on how to broach the subject without hurting his feelings.

'Do you think perhaps you're overdoing it a little?' she finally asked him one day. She kept her voice as light as possible, though she couldn't help feeling anxious. 'You know, it really should have been me pampering you all this time.' She gave a little laugh before adding in a more serious tone, 'After all, you're the one who's been through the really dreadful difficult times. So I think you're the one who most deserves to rest more.'

Jack regarded her solemnly. 'You've had more than your fair share of difficulties to deal with, while I've been away, Annie my love, don't think I don't know that,' he said. 'This is my way of saying thank you for stepping in so bravely at such short notice, and keeping things going so valiantly. It can't have been easy, no matter what you said in your letters.' He wagged his finger at her as he said this and then laughed. Annie blushed coyly, thinking of several other things she had said in their somewhat lively correspondence, and she didn't contradict him.

Jack might have got back into the swing of work at the Rovers so that it wasn't long before he felt as if he had never been away, but it took him much longer to settle back into the kind of family life he had dreamed of while he'd been fighting in the Pacific. It was hard for him to understand the effect his absence had had on both Billy and Joanie during the greater part of their young lives, and he didn't seem to realize that it would take some considerable time for them to accept the return of their father after he had been absent for most of their formative years, so there was often an uncomfortable atmosphere in their private quarters behind the bar of the Rovers that neither he nor Annie seemed to know how to dispel.

Joanie was the first to accept that he really was her father, the same person as the image that Annie had tried so hard to keep alive, and she gradually came to believe that Daddy was not just a name on a flimsy blue envelope or an unrecognizably fuzzy face. It took several weeks, but finally, to Jack's delight, Joanie climbed on his knee with her favourite book one afternoon and asked if she could sit on his lap while he read her the story. After that, Jack did his best to spend as much time as he could with her and was gratified that whenever she asked Annie to help her with her drawing or show her how to write the letters of her name, she was happy to be referred back to Daddy. Billy, however, was not so easily won over and he continued to ignore Jack whenever he could, and to shrug off his touch if Jack tried to reach out to him. It took several months before he grudgingly acknowledged that Jack really was his father, and then it was only because he had a burning desire for a new sledge so that he could toboggan down Coronation Street with all the older boys when the heavy snow that had been forecast finally arrived.

Annie had been so concerned behind the closed doors of their private quarters about building the children's relationship with their father that it took some time before she became aware of how her own role within the Rovers Return was subtly changing and that Jack was now firmly back at the helm. So she was not prepared for Jack's question one morning when he said, 'You know, love, I've been thinking – you should be reducing your hours. There's really no need for you to push yourself like you have been doing. So why don't you take next week off?'

She looked at him in astonishment. 'Why would I want to do that?' she said.

'Because you deserve a break, and I thought you might like to use the time better, as it's not that far from Christmas.' Jack's cheeks reddened as he said this, and he looked down at his shoes. 'I hate the thought of you trying to do two jobs at once like you have been doing, when there really is no need. Steve and I are perfectly capable of managing.'

Annie was too surprised to fully process his words and their implications immediately. Since he'd been home, she'd appreciated being able to put her feet up for the odd afternoon and had even taken the occasional evening off. Who wouldn't enjoy a little break? But the idea of not working for a whole week? Was he really saying he didn't need her help in the bar any more? Did he really intend to shut her out?

'We're hardly mad busy at the moment and it's not as though we're anticipating a great rush this week, is it?' he persisted. 'Of course, it will be different once we have to start thinking of Christmas, but for the moment I just thought you might like to have a few days to yourself. I know you're not fond of snow so I thought now would be a good time before the bad weather sets in.'

When Jack had disappeared into the army, Annie had taken on every aspect of the management role to ensure the smooth daily running of the place and she certainly had no wish to become marginalized now. It upset her to think that that was what Jack might be implying. She had come to think of herself as the beating heart of the Rovers and the Rovers was, after all, in her eyes, at the very heart of the local community, far more so than the Pride could ever hope to be. She hadn't appreciated before just how much fun she had had being in charge at the pub while Jack was away. Yes, at times she had found it difficult to juggle the full-time work with motherhood and having enough time for the children, but the idea of Jack carrying on running the pub without her was not something she had ever contemplated. She had been closely involved ever since they had first taken over the tenancy before the war, when she and Jack were newly married, and she realized, as soon as Jack said the words, how resentful she would feel if she allowed herself to be pushed out to the sidelines now.

'It seems to me now would be the perfect time for you to step back a bit, so why don't you take the opportunity?' he said. 'You could do something nice with the children after school for a change, or meet up with one of your friends.'

Annie stiffened as she suddenly realized how much being the acting boss at the Rovers Return had meant to her. She hadn't thought about it before, but she had really enjoyed being in the limelight, just like she'd loved being centre stage in her heyday in amateur dramatics all those years ago. And yet here he was, virtually asking her to step down.

Unsure how to react, she was conscious only of needing to respond, so Annie did what she always did when faced with a difficult situation: she smiled to cover her confusion while she tried to think of the appropriate words. 'Now that is such a very kind thought, Jack,' she said eventually, 'but why would I take all that time off now, when I'm needed here?'

Jack came to join her behind the counter and put his arm round her. 'But that's my point. What I'm trying to say is that you don't have to split yourself in two. You don't have to do everything yourself any more. You're not on your own. So you can take your time sorting things out behind the scenes while I take charge here. It would be best to make the adjustments now, while we're not too busy, because before we know it things will start hotting up for Christmas and it will literally be all hands to the pumps and we won't have a minute for anything other than pulling pints.' Annie took a deep breath as if she was about to speak but didn't actually say anything. Jack pulled her close and gave her a squeeze. 'I can manage here, you know,' he said, looking round. 'I do remember what to do and how to do it. It's all come back to me.' He laughed, but Annie didn't join in.

She turned to look into his face, her smile frozen. 'Thank you, my love, I really appreciate the thought but now isn't the best time for me to have time off. And I'm sure Billy will be too involved with his friends to want to go anywhere with his mother and his little sister. And I'm also sure that if you asked Joanie she'd say she would rather curl up on the rug by the fire with a book as she usually does.

'Besides, I think Steve could still benefit from my supervision. He has told me on several occasions how much he appreciates the advice I've been able to offer. You won't want to be bothered with those kind of details while you're still finding your feet, now will you?' Annie gave a little laugh as she threw back her head in the movement she had perfected when dealing with difficult customers.

'So, thank you for the offer, my love, but maybe I'll be in a better position to take advantage of it some other time,' she said. 'In the meantime, I shall continue to take a few odd hours here and there as I have been doing and know that you will be able to manage very well without me.'

Hilda had never missed a day at the Pride since she and Lizzie had started to work there, bar the VE Day aftermath, so when she didn't come into work one morning and sent a message that she was ill, Lizzie was concerned. She rushed over to Charles Street as soon as she could to find out what was wrong.

She rang the doorbell and was aware of a curtain twitching on the first floor. It took several minutes before Hilda finally appeared and opened the door a tiny crack.

'I wanted to make sure it was really you,' Hilda said as she admitted Lizzie into the dark hall.

'Why? Did you think it might be an imposter?' Lizzie laughed, but when Hilda turned to face her she wished she'd held her tongue, for Hilda's left eye was various shades of black, purple and yellow and the lid was so swollen it remained half-closed. Without another word, Hilda led the way upstairs.

'Let me make you a cup of coffee,' Hilda said. Lizzie looked at the almost empty bottle of Camp on the kitchen table. 'I've just had one, thanks,' she lied, 'so why don't you come and sit down and tell me what happened?'

'There's nothing to tell,' Hilda said, trying to smile. She did sit down and immediately began playing with the uneven edge of the red and white oilcloth that was spread over the table. 'I walked into the cupboard door,' Hilda said. 'I stupidly must have left it open.'

'Now come on, Hilda,' Lizzie said, 'you can do better than that. It's me you're talking to, not one of your nosy neighbours. You're neither stupid nor blind. So tell me what really happened. It was Stan, wasn't it?'

She could see Hilda was clenching her teeth and sealing her lips together as tears began to drip silently from the end of her chin.

'He didn't really mean it. But he'd had a drink or two before he came home and . . .' Hilda sighed. 'You know how it is.'

'But it doesn't have to be like that,' Lizzie said, shocked.

'He did say he was sorry almost straight away, but when I looked in the mirror when I got up this morning and saw this . . .' She lifted her head and stared at Lizzie through tears that were pouring steadily now. 'I knew I couldn't go into work. What could I say to Bob? Not that I can afford not to work, but I didn't want anyone to see me like this.' Hilda looked down into her lap again.

'What sparked it?' Lizzie said. 'I presume it wasn't only the drink?'

Hilda shrugged. 'It was all so silly, really,' she said. She was staring ahead of her now, not looking at Lizzie. 'I'd gone to the butcher's, special like, cos he said he fancied a bit of hotpot but all I could get was ground beef. At least, that's what the butcher said it was. All I know is, it used up my coupons and most of my money. There was just a little bit left to buy a few spuds and an onion and I wanted to try to make it tasty.' Hilda had to stop for a moment then as her voice was cracking and the tears were flowing freely. 'But in the end,' she said, 'he barely got to *see* the blooming thing, never mind eat it.'

Lizzie put her hand on her friend's arm and said nothing.

'By the time he came home,' Hilda began again, 'it was all dried out, wasn't it? It didn't even look fit for a dog – if we'd have had one.' She began to sob. 'I would have eaten it myself rather than waste it if I'd have known he was going to come in that late, but as it was, it was fit for no one by the time he pitched up.'

She continued to sob quietly for a few moments, then she said, 'You know, money doesn't stretch like it used to when there was only me to buy for.'

'No, of course it doesn't,' Lizzie said soothingly. 'Don't forget the army's always taken care of Stan.'

Hilda stared at Lizzie. 'I never thought much about that cos I always had an extra bob or two in my pocket and the time to spare to spend it how I liked. Not like now, when not only have I got to spend time looking out for him as well, but I can't seem to make ends meet, no matter how hard I try.'

'No, it's quite different when you've got someone else to consider. Well, you think about it,' Lizzie said. 'The army has paid for his board and lodging, and for his clothes, for all the years you've been married so it's no wonder you can't make your wages stretch for two.'

'But Stan's got a job. Bob has him loading trucks most nights.'

'Yes, but what does he give you out of it?'

'Well, he has to have his fag and beer money, it's only right, so there's not really a great deal left.'

Lizzie gave an ironic chuckle and Hilda looked as if a light bulb had suddenly been turned on.

'You know, you're right,' Hilda said. 'I never really thought about that before.'

'I suppose Stan accused you of being a poor manager?'

'Well, let's just say he doesn't think I'm very good with money. And he's right, for I'm not really, truth be known.'

'Hilda, no one could make a wage that was barely enough to support one person stretch to pay for two. And with all due respect to you, cleaners are not paid the highest wages in the land.'

Hilda let go of the oilcloth and sat back, a relieved expression on her face. 'Oh, but at least now he's got a proper daytime job, thank goodness, maybe things will change. It's nothing to do with Bob Bennett or the Pride of blooming Weatherfield. I haven't had a chance to tell you.' For a few minutes she began to talk like the old Hilda, with pride shining through her voice. 'He's going to be driving one of them huge pantechnicals and he'll be going great long distances. Sometimes he'll be so far away he'll have to stay overnight.' She stopped and smiled at that.

'I presume the firm pays for the stopover?' Lizzie said.

'Oh, it doesn't cost anything. He can lock himself in the cab then snore away to his heart's content,' Hilda said. 'While here it'll be lovely and quiet again, like it was before. At least I'll get a bit of peace.' She gave a wistful sigh.

'So, now you really will have his wages to top up yours, then?' Lizzie said. 'That's a relief.'

There was a pause. 'Not all of them,' Hilda said. 'As he says, he's got to keep a few bob in his pocket in case he has to pay his way and buy a round for the lads. You know how it is. He can't lose face in front of his mates.' Hilda looked embarrassed.

Lizzie did know how it was with Stan, but she couldn't bear to hurt Hilda's feelings by saying so.

'So what happens now?'

'Oh nothing,' Hilda said quickly. 'I'll just have to make sure I don't burn it next time.' She put her fingers gingerly to her face wincing as they touched the bruises. 'He only lashed out a little swipe really, and he did say he was sorry.'

Chapter 12

Winter 1945

Steve had never been to the Pride on a Saturday night and for the first time he was going to see their live cabaret. He arrived late, close to the time the show was about to begin, and despite what Lizzie had told him, was surprised to see the place was only half-full, although customers were still trickling in, gradually filling up the seats around the small tables.

He nodded a greeting to a few Rovers' customers and some looked a little sheepish, but Elsie Tanner, seated at the bar, seemed too engrossed to notice him at first as she was mooning up at Bob Bennett. She and Bob were deeply engrossed in conversation, but they stopped when he approached.

'Well, if it isn't the opposition,' Bob greeted him as Steve ordered a pint.

'I'm just looking for a quiet night out,' Steve said, nodding to Elsie and pausing to add a word to Lizzie before going to sit with his drink as far away from the stage as possible. He noticed Bob had left Elsie at the bar and had disappeared behind the scenes while, at the same time, a pianist came out from backstage. Settling on the stool in front of the piano he began flexing and stretching his fingers. Steve was sitting back, taking a sip of his beer, ready for the show to begin, when suddenly he heard raised, angry voices and he looked up to see a young woman of about Lizzie's age almost fling herself at Elsie. She'd grabbed handfuls of Elsie's jacket and was shouting in her face. Everyone in the audience stopped what they were doing and turned to watch the extraordinary scene, although nobody tried to intervene.

'Where did you get that brooch?' he heard the young woman yell as she clawed at the unusual floral spray of pearls clustered round a small diamond on Elsie's coat. Making a grab at the tweedy material that the brooch was fastened to, she pulled at it until it grazed Elsie's cheek.

'It's none of your business and you can get your thieving mitts off it. It's mine,' Elsie cried, trying to prise open the woman's fingers and release her grip.

'Not bloody likely!' the woman shrieked. 'It's mine.'

'It was given to me!' Elsie shouted back, pulling desperately at the woman's hand.

'I'm telling you it's mine!' the woman continued to scream.

'Gerroff!' Elsie tried to bat the woman's hand away, but the woman clung on.

'Then tell me where you got it.' The woman almost spat the words out.

'It's none of your bloomin' business. It was a present.' Now it was Elsie's turn to scream.

'It is my business because it was my mother's bloody brooch!' the woman said. There was a collective gasp in the room. 'But it disappeared, didn't it? Soon after the bomb dropped on our house. You nicked it, didn't you? So now you can give it here.' The woman tried again, unsuccessfully, to snatch at it, then she stood back glowering, arms akimbo as if preparing another strike. Then she seemed to think better of it and took a deep breath. 'Give it back to me now and no more will be said.' She tried a more conciliatory tone and she put out her hand in readiness.

Elsie shook her head. 'I don't nick things and I know nowt about your mother or any bombs, except them as got my family, so get lost,' she said. Her voice was quieter now.

'I know you didn't know my mum, but I'm telling you, you've got her brooch. So give it back.' She was staring at the brooch again and looked as if she was gearing up to make one more attempt to grab it.

'Clear off out of here,' Elsie said and she took a nip of gin.

But the woman was not letting go so easily. She took a step closer to Elsie, not taking her eyes off the brooch. 'Our house,' she said, her voice cold and deliberate, 'or what was left of it, was looted before any of us could get there. And I'm telling you, that brooch was nicked.' She pointed to it dramatically, her hand within touching distance. 'Couldn't wait to get in there, could you? And it wasn't the only thing that was stolen, so where's the rest of it?'

'How dare you!' Elsie went pale, but she showed no other signs of weakening. At that moment Bob appeared from backstage, shouting, 'What's going on here? What's all this noise about?'

Elsie looked relieved to see him and even grinned at him, opening her mouth as if about to speak, but Bob walked past, ignoring her. He went straight to the other woman, grabbing hold of her hands and latching his fingers tightly onto her wrists.

'I must ask you to leave,' he said, his voice low and menacing. 'I can't have people accusing my customers of looting without one shred of evidence.'

The woman squirmed uncomfortably, trying to free her wrists. 'Let go of me, you bully!' she shouted. 'How do you know I've got no evidence?'

There was a moment's silence while she drew breath and seemed to be gathering her defences. Then she began to scream again. 'It's my brooch, I'm telling you. And she's a thief.'

'Then prove it,' Bob said his voice low but steely.

The woman glared at him. 'I don't have to prove it,' she said although her voice was weaker now. 'I'm telling you it's mine.'

'Just as I thought,' Bob said. 'Wild accusations. Now kindly leave before I call the police.' He sounded anything but kindly but he let go of her wrists and pushed her towards the door.

'Oh, I'll save you the bother,' she said, rubbing the circulation back into her fingers as she backed away from the bar. 'I'll be happy to call them as soon as I get out of here. I shall be very interested to see what *they* have to say.' With that she turned and strode out through the swing doors.

The conversation levels peaked almost immediately as a buzz of excited chatter flashed around the room. Elsie looked visibly shaken and got up to follow Bob into the kitchen behind the bar, but he pushed her away. 'I'm sorry, Elsie, love,' he said, 'but I've no time right now. I'm in the middle of some rather delicate negotiations. But I'm sure you have nothing to worry about.' And with a shout to Lizzie to give Elsie whatever drink she wanted, on the house, he disappeared.

Almost immediately the pianist struck up several chords on the piano and the singer who'd been given star billing came onto the stage and started to sing. It was as if nothing had happened.

It wasn't until the end of the evening, when Lizzie was collecting the dead glasses, that Steve had a chance to talk to her.

'Well, that was a bit of entertainment and a half,' Steve said. 'Do you think Elsie needs an escort home?'

'She's slipped off earlier,' Lizzie said. 'Said she didn't want any fuss. But I don't think you have to worry about Elsie. She won't be intimidated easily. She's made of sterner stuff.'

'Any idea what it was all about?' Steve said. 'Did you know the woman?'

'Never seen her before,' Lizzie said. 'And I don't think Elsie had either. But that was the brooch that Bob gave Elsie after the VE party, remember?'

'Of course,' Steve said. 'I didn't immediately make the connection. The woman was right though, it wasn't Elsie's brooch.' He rubbed his chin thoughtfully. 'Amazing, isn't it, how all roads lead back to Bob? I did tell you never to trust him, didn't I?' Steve said. 'Goodness knows what he's been up to.'

'I suppose the next question is: where did he get the brooch from?' Lizzie said slowly, as though not wanting to put voice to the words.

'Exactly,' Steve said.

Lizzie shuddered. 'You don't think he could have had anything to do with looting that house, do you?'

'Who knows?' Steve said. 'But I think perhaps we should be the ones to go to the police in the morning.'

Lizzie lowered her eyes. 'You're serious, aren't you?' she said softly.

'I am. I think the time has come for us to tell them all we know.'

Lizzie looked thoughtful. 'Unfortunately, we don't have any actual proof of how it got from that woman's house onto Elsie's coat, do we?'

'No, we don't,' Steve said, 'but I think that's for the police to find out.' He stood up. 'And right now we need to get you safely home. On the way I can tell you what I know about a man called Dave Elliott . . .'

Lizzie could hardly believe what she was hearing as Steve unfolded his tale about the man from Blackpool she knew as Bob Bennett. But there was no time to ask questions, for when they reached number nine they found a black police car was already pulled up outside the house next door.

Cora Doyle opened the front door almost as soon as Elsie Tanner knocked. She had just come back from seeing the boys off to school and hadn't even had time to say hello to Lizzie or even to take her coat off.

'I'm sorry the police had to bother you an' all last night, especially as it was so late,' Elsie said as Cora closed the door and ushered her inside. 'But they asked me if any of the neighbours had been in the Pride and witnessed what had happened so I had to tell them about Lizzie. They were determined to talk to her immediately and didn't seem to care what the time was.'

'You don't have to worry about that, Elsie love,' Cora said. 'Come and join us for a cup of tea and tell us what they said to you. There's only me and Lizzie here now, thank goodness, but I've had the devil's own job getting the boys off to school after last night's excitement.'

'I didn't think they'd be up so late as to hear what was going on. It was you and Lizzie I was feeling sorry for,' Elsie said.

'Seamus and Tommy got woken when the police arrived because they didn't spare the knocker with their banging, and then, being young boys, they had to sneak to the top of the stairs and listen to everything, didn't they? Even though I scolded them to go to sleep.'

'Of course, they woke Sammy with their racket,' Lizzie said, 'and it was all we could do to shoo them back into bed after the police had gone.'

'Naturally, they were dead tired and didn't want to get up this morning,' Cora said, although she was the one who looked exhausted. 'They wanted to see the policemen, they said, they were convinced they were coming back. Even Sammy didn't want to go to nursery, did he, Lizzie? Though he usually can't wait.'

Cora pushed aside the children's toys that were cluttering the chairs. 'Here, have a seat at the table, Elsie,' she said, 'Lizzie's just putting up a pot of tea.'

'Actually, it was a good job you steered the police in this direction,' Lizzie said, 'because Steve was still here and it saved him a journey. He'd decided it was time he talked to them about Bob and he was planning to go down to the station this morning.'

'Steve often pops in nowadays after he walks her home from work, you know,' Cora whispered to Elsie, a look of pride on her face that made Lizzie roll her eyes heavenwards.

'They don't think it had anything to do with the Rovers, do they? Like Annie Walker trying to upset their rivals?' Elsie said. 'Only they were asking what Steve was doing at the Pride.'

'He was chasing Lizzie, that's what he was doing,' Cora said with a grin. 'He's sweet on her, you know.'

'Now, Ma! I've told you before not to go spreading daft rumours,' Lizzie protested.

'Don't "now Ma" me. I've told you before. You could do a lot worse.'

Lizzie sighed.

'As it's turned out, they definitely suspect Bob of doing something crooked and they were looking for witnesses,' Elsie said. 'But all the bloomin' questions they asked me made me feel like I was the criminal not him. And let's face it, he was the one that gave me that damned brooch in the first place.'

She pulled a packet of Craven A from her skirt pocket and offered them round. Cora took one and went to get a spill that she lit from the fire. Elsie took a long draw on the cigarette. 'How was I to know where he got it from?' Elsie said. 'That's hardly the first thing you ask when someone gives you a present, now is it? It was pretty and I liked it, so I said, "Ta very much".' She shook her head. 'But I can tell you, I gave it straight to the police last night. Told them I never wanted to see the damn thing ever again.' Elsie shuddered. 'I think someone's just walked over my grave,' she said. 'Maybe it was that poor dead woman whose brooch it was in the first place. And if it did belong to her, then a curse on whoever stole it from her, but it certainly wasn't me.'

The three sat in silence for a few moments, sipping their tea, Elsie and Cora puffing on their cigarettes, when there was a knock at the door and this time Lizzie got up to answer it.

'I hope it's not too early to come calling?' Steve said. 'But I wanted to make sure you were OK after all the goings-on last night.'

'Thanks, that's very kind.' Lizzie smiled. 'And I'm fine.' She opened the door wide. 'It wasn't me that was in the firing line, but thankfully Elsie's fine too and she's here already. Why don't you come in and join us? We're just having a drink.'

Steve greeted Cora and Elsie and accepted the tea Lizzie offered.

'Is there any news?' Elsie asked as Steve sat down.

'Have you been down to the police station this morning?'

'There seemed no point,' Steve said. 'I doubt they'd be able to tell me anything that I didn't already know from last night. It's an ongoing investigation as far as they're concerned, but as you'd expect the street's buzzing.'

Elsie laughed. 'Naming no names, I bet the usual rumour-mongers are having a field day.'

'Any sign of Bob?' Lizzie wanted to know.

'No chance of that,' Steve said. 'It seems he's gone on the run, so he'll be long gone. Folk like him always manage that once the whistle's been blown. It's amazing how they can save their own skin, and then somehow manage to set up in the next place and start again.'

'You sound like you've come across him before?' Elsie was taken aback.

'Let's put it this way, I knew someone called Dave Elliott ten years ago and he was not a very savoury character. Not one I ever wanted to be associated with again.'

'This sounds good, tell us more.' Elsie was interested now.

'Dave got up to all sorts of what the police refer to as "criminal activities",' Steve said.

'Like what?' Elsie asked eagerly.

'Well, I know for a fact that he was involved in selling stolen goods before the war, a business which hotted up during it, what with supply shortages. Looting bombed-out buildings, I believe, was one of his specialities, as they made for very easy pickings, particularly for gangs who already had established fencing operations so that they could sell things on.'

Now Elsie looked agog. 'And what's this Dave Elliott got to do with Bob Bennett?'

'Dave Elliott *is* Bob Bennett,' Lizzie said, with a grim smile.

'Are you sure it's the same feller?' Elsie asked.

'Oh yes. I'm sure,' Steve said. 'But I have to be very careful what I say, because up till now no one's come up with any actual evidence to make an accusation stick – though I think the police might be able to finally do that now.'

'Do they know it's the same man?' Elsie asked.

'Oh yes, though he's been very clever at covering his tracks, has our Dave,' Steve said, 'but this time he may have gone a step too far.'

'You mean that brooch could nail him?' Lizzie said.

'With any luck,' Steve said.

'All they have to do is catch him.' Elsie gave a wry smile.

'That would be a good start,' Steve agreed.

'But surely Bob or Dave or whatever he's called didn't do the actual looting?' Elsie frowned.

'I doubt it,' Steve said. 'Not personally. But he doesn't need to get his hands dirty. There's always gangs of young lads available to see to that side of things.'

'Like at the VE day party,' Lizzie said, nodding her head as she recognized how the pieces of the puzzle were coming together.

'The police seemed to be in no doubt that he was behind that,' Steve agreed. 'I believe they may have some proof as well – some of the younger ones' parents forced the kids to own up.'

'But I thought he was supposed to be a comedian before he came here, and a bit of a magician with a stage career behind him, not a blooming crook?' Elsie said.

'Oh, but he is,' Steve said. 'That's what makes him such a smooth operator. But all the stage stuff is just a front. The fact that he's good at it helps to make the whole thing credible.'

'Goodness! What a story.' Elsie stubbed out her cigarette and shook her head. 'I hate to leave when it's all getting so exciting,' she said as she stood up, 'but I'm afraid I've got to go and see to the kids. Lizzie, you'll let me know what happens won't you, cos I doubt I'll be hearing from Bob.'

'Of course,' Lizzie said and she stood up to see Elsie out.

'The police must have been pleased to talk to you,' Cora said to Steve as Lizzie came back into the room.

Steve shrugged. 'All I did was give them a statement. They don't give much away, so you can never tell what they're thinking. That's why I was surprised they said so much about the street party.'

'So, what will happen to the Pride, do you think, if he's run away and abandoned it?' Cora said.

'I've no idea,' Steve said. 'If Bob has gone missing completely then no doubt the brewery will step in, but whether they'll want to close it down or try to get a new tenant landlord, only time will tell.'

Lizzie drew in her breath sharply. 'There is the possibility of me losing my job, then,' she said, paling at the thought.

'I suppose that would be up to the brewery,' Steve said.

'Blooming heck,' Lizzie said. 'What a mess.'

There was another knock on the door, a more urgent-sounding one this time that made them all start.

'Who can that be?' Cora frowned. 'We're not expecting anyone.'

'There's only one person it could be,' Lizzie said as she got up to answer it. 'Have you forgotten about poor Hilda in all this? This is about the time she usually clocks in to work, so she's probably only just found out about last night. I bet she's frantic to know what's going on.'

Cora's hand flew to her mouth. 'Good gracious you're right. I wonder whether the Pride was even open for her to get in – and in this weather too. Have you seen? It's started to snow?'

Cora hovered by the window. There was an icy blast

when Lizzie opened the front door and Hilda almost fell inside with the wind whipping the snow all around her.

'Come in quickly,' Lizzie said. 'Gosh, the street looks so treacherous it's a miracle you didn't fall.'

'I know, it's very slippery. I was frightened to go too fast,' Hilda said.

'Come in and get warm,' Lizzie said, 'you must be fair clemmed.'

'I am a bit. It wasn't this bad when I set off, but you'll never believe what happened when I got to work this morning – or should I say, *didn't* get to work,' Hilda said, and she went over to the fire where she immediately began warming her hands. She looked so agitated and upset that Lizzie didn't even try to respond. 'The whole neighbourhood's buzzing with it,' Hilda said, 'and my head's buzzing too, although no one really seems to know what's up. But I had to come to tell you right away, because it's awful, and I didn't know where else to go – but I think we might both be out of a job.' She paused to draw breath and stared at Lizzie as if to gauge the effect of her words. So far she had paid no heed to any of the others in the room as she was so anxious to tell Lizzie her story and she began talking quickly again, not even stopping when she stumbled over her words.

'I daren't go home and tell Stan,' she said, 'so I thought I'd best come and tell you first, Lizzie. Well, the Pride was all locked up with no sign of Bob and there was a bobby outside the front door, making sure no one tried to get in.' She put on a deep voice, '"You can't go in there," he ordered when I tried the front door, but when I told him I had to because I worked there he told me to go and talk to this other man who was wanting to speak to the staff. I'm sure he'll want to speak to you later, Lizzie. Mr Warner, the man said his name was, from the brewery, though I've never seen him before, but he had a very smart coat on and he tipped his hat to me, and spoke quite posh.' She suddenly giggled and paused to take a breath. 'I wasn't sure if I should curtsy to him or what, but in the end all he said was that he didn't know when they'd be open again for business as the police had to search the place for evidence.' Here she hesitated, her forehead wrinkled. 'Though evidence of what he didn't say. All he did say was, "We'll be in touch with all the staff as soon as we can".' And she deepened her voice again in imitation. 'But that was it as far as he was concerned, so I've still no idea what's going on and there was no one else to ask so I didn't know what to do . . .' Her voice trailed off now. 'So I came here.'

'Well, now you're here you can sit there and have a cup of tea and try to calm down,' Lizzie said taking hold of Hilda's hands and guiding her to the only empty chair at the table.

Hilda looked round as though seeing the others for the first time. Her face reddened as she touched her hand to her headscarf that was only half hiding her curlers and she self-consciously pulled together the edges of her thin coat in an attempt to cover her overalls. She cleared her throat. 'You'll pardon me in my working clothes, won't you?' she said looking at Steve and Cora now. 'But I wasn't expecting to be going visiting.'

'It's not as though you're visiting strangers.' Lizzie put a cup of tea down in front of Hilda. 'And you've come to the right place, because *we* do know what's up,' she said and Hilda's eyes widened as Lizzie began to give her the gist of the events of the previous night. 'So now you know as much as we do,' Lizzie said finally, 'and you can see that you're not the only one still in the dark, for none of us knows exactly what's going to happen next.'

Hilda drank the tea quickly and stared into the bottom of the cup as though expecting to tell someone's fortune. 'You're right,' she said, 'but maybe we could have known if only we'd gone ahead with our little séance.' She giggled. 'I kept telling you we should have got rid of those restless spirits. I'm sure it's them as keeps bringing bad luck into this house. It's the last straw if you're going to be out of work, Lizzie, so it seems obvious to me that they're still here and we need to exercise them.'

'That's a thought, Hilda,' Cora said. 'We were interrupted the last time we tried. Do you think maybe we should try again?'

'Well, it's never too late, you know,' Hilda said, 'and you're going to have to do some serious thinking about the future, so it might be a good time to clear away any bad omens from the past and get rid of any polter-thingies.'

Then Steve said, 'How do you know they're still here, these bad spirits, have you heard anything recently?'

Lizzie was about to say no, but Cora said, 'I wasn't going to say anything but . . .' She looked across at Lizzie. 'But I think whoever they are, they've been active again.'

'When was this?' Lizzie frowned.

'You're out most evenings, Lizzie,' Cora said, 'but when I've been here on my own of a night I've heard the noises again almost every night.'

'You've never said.' Lizzie looked doubtful.

'There seemed no point in telling you since you never seemed that bothered to do anything about them,' Cora said. 'But now I'm sure they were definitely trying to tell us something.'

'That the Pride's closing down.' Lizzie chuckled. 'And won't that please Annie Walker, though?'

'Not necessarily,' Steve said. 'There's nothing like a bit of honest competition to keep you on your toes in any business, you know.'

'So long as the competition is honest,' Lizzie said. 'The problem here is that it seems as if Bob was totally dishonest right from the start.'

As the others nodded, Cora suddenly turned to Steve. 'Maybe you should go and have a word with this . . . Mr Warner, or whatever his name was,' she said. 'If he's from the brewery that owns the Pride you could put yourself forward as a good, honest, potential land-lord who's ready and willing and more than capable of taking over the tenancy. That would keep Lizzie – and Hilda – in their jobs.'

Steve laughed. 'My future ambitions go far beyond Weatherfield, I'm afraid. Besides, I don't think Annie Walker would like to have me as her rival,' he said, 'any more than she liked having Bob, and imagine how she'll feel about him if he proves to be guilty once they've actually caught him.'

'He must be guilty,' Lizzie said. 'His running away proves that, surely?'

'Yes, but no one seems quite sure of exactly what,' Steve said. 'It's still possible he wouldn't be convicted in a court of law; it depends what evidence the police have managed to unearth. He only needs to find himself a good barrister and it's amazing what he might be able to get away with.'

'But surely Warner's could still sack him, couldn't they, even if he wasn't proved guilty?' Lizzie said.

'I'm sure they could always find some pretext if they

really wanted to get rid of him,' Steve said. 'But who would want to follow in the footsteps of someone who left under such a cloud?'

'I suppose in one way it doesn't really matter what happens to Bob Bennett,' Cora said. 'Hilda's right, we could at least try to exorcize any spirits that might be bringing bad luck directly into this house And then maybe Lizzie might not lose her job.'

Lizzie looked at Steve, her eyes full of laughter, and she was relieved to see he looked sceptical too.

'I suppose anything's possible,' Steve said, 'if you believe in it firmly enough.'

Cora rubbed her hands together and laughed. 'Sounds like a good idea to me. I bet we can get rid of any restless spirits – and even if not, we can certainly have some fun trying,' she said and she grinned at Lizzie. Then she looked across the table. 'What do you say, Hilda? Maybe we can do something different this time and it will be up to you to tell us all what we have to do.'

Chapter 13

A few days later, Hilda arrived at the Doyles' armed with several sheets of paper on which were special words that she thought she ought to use in the summoning of the spirits, just like she'd heard Madame Arcati do in the film. It was another dull and bitterly cold day. A fresh deposit of powdery snow had covered whatever had begun to thaw the previous day and then iced over and she had slipped twice on her way to Coronation Street on the glass-like slides some of the young children had made.

Hilda's hands fluttered nervously as she tried to keep the papers in order. 'If we're all here, then there's no reason for us not to start,' she said.

'We're just waiting on Steve,' Lizzie said. 'I invited

him as he said he'd like to come and I promised we wouldn't start without him.'

Two minutes later there was a knock at the door.

Hilda smiled nervously as she watched Lizzie take Steve's coat and hat and she shuffled her papers one more time. 'Then I'm ready if everyone else is,' Hilda said and she let Steve go first as they climbed up the stairs to the small hall landing. A ladder into the loft was already in place and she shook it to test its steadiness, her face creased into a frown. 'It will work best,' she said, 'if I can say the words while standing as close as possible to the place where the noises were coming from.' But she didn't volunteer to actually climb the ladder. Instead she let Steve climb the first few rungs and then watched as he reached up and removed the loft cover. She looked up at the hole that he had uncovered in the bedroom ceiling.

'By heck, but it's draughty up here.' Hilda stood back to allow Steve to come back down the ladder and to make room for Lizzie as she came up the stairs to join them. 'Are you sure you're going to be all right climbing that, Lizzie?' Hilda asked.

'I'll be fine,' Lizzie said, 'so long as you and Steve hold on to the sides to stop the wind getting at it.'

'Brave girl! You wouldn't catch me climbing up that.' Cora remained downstairs and looked up gingerly. 'I can't be doing with heights.'

'Me neither,' Hilda said from her position at the foot

of the ladder by the bedroom door, her voice already trembling slightly. 'This is as far as I go.'

'And Steve is too big to negotiate the gap so thank goodness I don't mind, then,' Lizzie said. 'Now, ladies and gentleman, when you're ready?' And she started to climb.

Lizzie was glad Steve had accepted their invitation to join them, for she hadn't realized what a tight squeeze it was going to be to get into the roof space and she was grateful for his steadying grip as she climbed. When she was in line with the opening she reached down and Hilda passed her a lighted candle.

'Be dead careful with that,' Cora shouted up from downstairs, 'we don't want the whole house going up.'

'Oh, Ma, honestly!' Lizzie said, not trying to hide her exasperation. 'The house can't be *that* jinxed. She stretched her arm as high as she could over her head and watched the flame flicker and splutter as it illuminated the section under the roof closest to the entrance hole. She wasn't sure what she had expected to see, but it wasn't the large number of bags that were strewn between the beams, covering a significant portion of the uneven floor and leading away into the darkness of the roof. Most were tied up with thick rope and were the same type of bags she had seen in the yard at the Pride; the same bags Stan had been loading onto the trucks. In some places she could see them more clearly as there were small patches of light where she could see through to the sky and feel the wintry wind whistling through the gaps. She instantly dismissed any thoughts of the supernatural, for even in the poor light she could see that some of the roof tiles were at odd angles as if they had been moved in order to create spaces for the bags to be dropped through and then had been replaced haphazardly to keep out the rain and the snow; a manoeuvre that would certainly have had to involve human intervention.

She leaned into the space as far as she could and tried to look in different directions but whichever way she looked, all she saw were bags. 'What's going on? What can you see?' Hilda's voice sounded distant as she called up to her. 'Can I say the words yet?'

Lizzie didn't reply because at that moment, to her horror, several smallish animals with long tails flashing like whips shot across the floor in different directions in front of her, and then the wind snuffed out her candle. Lizzie felt the ladder rock backwards and she practically lost her foothold, but she managed to grasp onto the rim of the loft's opening until Steve steadied it from below and she began to inch her way down so that her head was once more clear of the hole. She was glad Steve was there although she hoped that he wouldn't have to catch the full weight of her.

'You can save your breath, Hilda,' she called, trying not to look down. 'I don't think there's any kind of spirit life going on up there.' She came down the final rungs with less confidence than she'd gone up, for her legs were trembling and she was never more relieved than when her feet touched the bare floorboards of the landing.

'Well, I don't want to be uncharitable, but you certainly look like you've seen a ghost,' Steve said, 'so what is actually up there if not some kind of poltergeist?'

Lizzie tittered, glad to be able to break the tension, but she couldn't speak immediately.

'What did you find? Don't keep us in suspense,' Cora begged as she came half way up the stairs. 'Could you see anything before the candle blew out?'

'It was pretty dim even with the candle,' Lizzie said at last, 'but I could see a little way in.'

'And you actually saw a ghost?' Cora said with a catch in her voice. 'So should Hilda start chanting?'

'I don't think that will be necessary,' Lizzie said. 'I'm pleased to be able to tell you that it's not ghosts or spirits who've been moving around up there all this time. It's more likely to be rats and human beings.'

Hilda gasped and Cora's hand went to her mouth. 'Human beings?' Cora said. 'How on earth could anyone manage to get up there?'

'That's exactly what me and Steve are going into the back yard to find out,' Lizzie said. 'But I think we have the answer as to where Bob and his lot have been stashing at least some of their stolen goods. So, in the meantime, Ma, you'd best get down to the phone box to call the police.'

Bob Bennett was apprehended by the south coast police as he tried to board a ferry that was crossing to France. He was brought back to Manchester, pending investigation, and ultimately he was charged with several counts of robbery and looting as well as the fencing of stolen goods and was sent for trial. The brewery didn't wait for the verdict. They soon made it plain that, whatever happened, Bob Bennett would not be coming back, and that there was the likelihood that the Pride would be closing down. In the meantime the police would not allow anyone into the premises until they were satisfied that their forensic experts had gleaned all the available evidence.

'I don't understand what they're hoping to find there,' Annie Walker said when Steve and Lizzie were sitting with them in the back parlour at the Rovers. They had gone to explain the situation to Annie and Jack and to fill in the details about what had happened to their rival.

'There seem to be so many different rumours flying around I don't know what to believe,' Annie said.

'Didn't they find a load of stolen property in sacks in the roof space at yours?' Jack said, looking at Lizzie.

'Yes, but that was only a small part of Bob's operation.' It was Steve who replied. 'It was mostly the smaller gear, the jewellery and personal items that he and his gang had looted from bombed-out buildings over the years. It was the kind of stuff that didn't weigh too much, so it was easy to move around. And the police found more in the lofts of some of the other houses along Coronation Street as well.'

'I can't imagine how on earth they managed to get all that stuff into such a small space,' Jack said.

'It was quite a skilful operation getting it up to the roof in the first place,' Lizzie explained, 'but they had kids who were good at shinning up drainpipes and hopping across the rooftops. They looked for patches of slates they could easily shift and lowered the bags down into the loft space. Then they'd send the smaller kids in after them, to clamber about on the beams and spread the weight of the bags. They'd replace the slates when they'd done. It was a miracle none of them ever fell through the gaps – and what they'd have done once it snowed seriously, goodness only knows.'

'And the police also have lists of larger pieces of furniture that people have reported missing,' Steve said, 'which they're convinced are being stored elsewhere, including at the Pride.'

'I know for a fact that some of the things they couldn't move on immediately ended up there,' Lizzie said, 'at least for a short while. I remember seeing different pieces that kept appearing but weren't there for very long. I even challenged Bob about some of the bits I saw once and he said he was selling them for a friend.'

'I always knew he was a wrong 'un,' Annie said with a shudder, 'but I'd never have guessed to what extent. It seems he's an out-and-out villain and I hope he ends up in jail as he deserves.'

'He certainly didn't care who he stole from, that's for sure,' Jack said. 'From the sounds of it, he hardly waited for the dust to settle after a bombing raid than he was sending in one of his looting teams. It seems like he was almost pulling the jewellery off the poor people before some of them were even cold.' He shook his head sadly.

'And he didn't seem to care who he gave things to, either,' Annie said. 'I don't know what he was thinking of, giving away such a recognizable piece of jewellery to someone who was so close to home.'

'Imagine, we'd almost convinced ourselves that our house was haunted when all the time it was real people doing dreadful things,' Lizzie said. 'Who'd have thought?'

'It really is quite an extraordinary story,' Jack said, 'and thank you very much for coming to tell Annie and me.' He peered at his watch. 'Looks like it's opening time now, so no doubt we'll be hearing a few more lies and yarns about all the goings-on. But I'm glad we know the truth.' He looked at Annie who nodded in agreement. 'Come and have a drink on the house, Lizzie,' Jack said.

'That's the least we can offer you.' Annie beamed her a smile. 'I'm really sorry you've lost your job.'

'That's very kind of you, thank you,' Lizzie said and she followed them out as Steve led the way into the bar.

Lizzie hadn't seen Hilda since the day the police had interviewed them both following the discovery in the roof and she was surprised to see her now in the Rovers. Far from looking miserable about the fate of the Pride and losing her job, Hilda was looking at her pretty best, her hair free from headscarf and curlers, and she greeted Lizzie with a broad smile.

'Lizzie! The very person I was hoping to see,' Hilda said. 'I called at the house but your ma said you and Steve were out and about.' Hilda winked and Lizzie felt her cheeks flush.

'We came to make sure Mr and Mrs Walker heard the correct version of events,' Lizzie said. 'There's so many rumours flying around at the moment that even I have trouble keeping track of the truth. It all seems so unreal. It's not something that happens in a place like Weatherfield. But tell me, how are you managing? Does Stan know yet about the Pride?'

To her surprise, Hilda smiled and nodded. 'Yes, he does. He couldn't say owt because he's lost his evening job and all, don't forget. And he had to convince the police he didn't know that the stuff he was handling had been stolen. But he's still got his driving job, thank goodness. And what's more he's done me a favour.'

'Oh, how?'

'You know how he drinks mostly at the Docker's Arms where his mates hang out? Well, he told me he thought I could do a better job of cleaning than the young lass they had working there. She was straight from school and it seems she can't scrub a sink to save her life.' Hilda laughed as she smoothed her fingers over her hair and preened in the mirror on the wall at the side of the bar as she enjoyed again Stan's unexpected compliment. 'So I marched down to the Arms the next morning, just like you and me did, Lizzie, when we asked for a job at the Pride. Of course, they knew about the goings-on at the Pride and it seems nobody was surprised to hear about Bob. Turns out he was well known in that part of town as a bit of a rogue. Any road, I told them what my Stan had said and they only offered me the job on the spot! It seems they'd been thinking of firing the young girl anyway. A month's trial, they offered me, but as the bossman said, "You can't be any worse than the last one, so I'm sure the job's as good as yours."' Hilda clapped her hands with delight. 'I start in the morning.'

'Well, I'm very pleased for you, Hilda, I really am,' Lizzie said. 'I bet Stan's relieved too that you're not having to face a long period out of work.'

'He is for now, though I don't think he's realized yet that that'll mean I might have a fancy now and then to go drinking at the Docker's Arms an' all. And then

I'll be able to keep an eye on how much he's putting away.' She laughed out loud. 'You know, you need to do something like that, Lizzie,' she said. 'Go and get yourself a new job. It'll make you feel tons better to know you've got a wage coming in.'

Lizzie looked thoughtful, for it was something she had been worrying about and intended to discuss with Steve.

'Oh, but I'm not suggesting you go to the Docker's Arms,' Hilda said quickly. 'Good heavens no, you're far too classy for them.' She laughed again. 'But how's about asking for a job here in the Rovers? I could see you alongside Annie Walker at the bar. And just think, you'd be able to see Steve all the time, too.' She lowered her voice as she said this and turned her look knowingly in his direction. 'I bet they must be busy now that their rivals have gone, so they could do with an extra pair of hands.' Lizzie began to wonder if maybe Hilda had 'the gift' after all, for she had been thinking about making just such a move, though she had no intention of rushing into any hasty decisions before she'd had a chance to speak to Steve. The next morning she made up her mind and she hand-delivered a note to Steve asking him to drop in at number nine on his way home from work that night.

Chapter 14

'Ma's gone next door to have a chat to Elsie,' Lizzie said when he arrived.

'That's cosy.' Steve gave her a flirtatious look as he came into the kitchen, then he gave her a friendly hug and brushed his lips across hers before jokingly peering behind all the furniture. 'No stray twins lurking?' he said. 'Or a baby? Don't tell me all the boys are in bed?'

Lizzie felt the warmth of a blush heat her cheeks. 'Of course. But that doesn't mean we can do anything but be on our best behaviour.' She smiled as she wagged her finger at him, enjoying the banter, wishing it might go further but knowing she could never allow that to happen.

'As if I would dare!' he said, his voice teasing.

'Sorry about the rather formal message, but it's not so easy getting hold of you nowadays, now that you don't have to see me home from work any more,' she said.

'Does that mean that you miss me?' Steve looked at her provocatively for a moment or two longer than necessary until she had to look away. Of course she missed him, but she could never tell him how much.

'I suppose we do have an odd kind of relationship nowadays,' she said.

'Do we really have a relationship? That makes it sound like more is happening than in reality,' he said.

Lizzie's cheeks were burning now and she was almost sorry she had asked him to call.

'I suppose . . . I wasn't really thinking . . . I . . .' she began and realized she didn't know what to say.

'I know we at least have a friendship,' Steve said as if she hadn't spoken, 'although you've made it very clear that I'm not to hope for more. I take it you've not changed your mind?'

She couldn't avoid looking at him, for he was gazing directly at her now and she knew she must have coloured even more deeply than before.

'You know I can't . . .' she said.

'No, I don't know that. I only know that you *won't*, for you've never actually said what's getting in the way.' He paused and she had to look away. 'If it's another man, then you're certainly keeping him a well-hidden secret. Unless you asked me here to talk about him now?'

Lizzie shook her head. 'I'm sorry if you got the wrong end of the stick. And I hope I'm not about to spoil our friendship in any way.'

'Now, how could you possibly do that?' he said and he pulled her down to sit beside him on the couch.

'That's what I wanted to talk to you about.' She pushed away from him and then turned to face him. 'I wanted to ask how you would feel if I applied for a job at the Rovers?'

Steve looked disappointed. 'But there isn't a job going at the Rovers!' He sounded puzzled.

'No, I know that, but I need to work and my guess is you could do with an extra pair of hands there. So I thought it would be a good idea to put myself forward now.' She told him about her conversation with Hilda, and about her friend's new job. 'But I wouldn't even approach Mr and Mrs Walker if you didn't think we could work together. I'd hate to be stepping on your toes.'

Steve didn't speak for a few moments. His brow wrinkled and he looked very serious as he said, 'Please don't ask them for a job. I don't want you working at the Rovers.' He stopped, looking very uncomfortable, and began to go red from the neck up.

Lizzie was taken aback, for that was not what she had expected him to say. 'Would you tell me why not?' she said. 'Is there something wrong with the Rovers? Or with me?'

'There's nothing wrong with the Rovers, or with you.' Steve hastened to assure her. 'On the contrary . . . It's me, I'm getting fed up with this friendship business and I–I don't . . . I don't actually intend to stay there very much longer.'

Steve squirmed in his seat for a moment and then took hold of both her hands. 'Look,' he said, 'I wasn't planning on saying anything yet. You're the first person I'm telling this to.'

But Lizzie was hardly listening. She felt as if she had been punched in the stomach and was still reeling from the blow. She let go of his hands and slid across the couch, putting even more space between them so that she could take in the impact of his words. Weatherfield without Steve. She had never considered that and it wasn't until he had said the actual words that she realized how unthinkable it was.

'Why . . . Where . . . What . . . Oh goodness, listen to me. I don't know what question to ask first,' she said.

'That's all right,' Steve said. 'It's for several reasons. One, I think it's time to let the Walkers have the place to themselves. Since Jack's come home they can't seem to agree who's the boss in the pub, who I'm supposed to answer to, or even whose job it is to look after the children. They need time and space to sort themselves out.'

Lizzie laughed. 'Oh dear! And they've not got the easiest two kids to take care of, have they?'

'Let's just say they're enough to put anyone off having children of their own.'

'Have they put you off?' Lizzie said flippantly.

'I'm just starting out in my career, so I certainly wouldn't want to have any children cluttering up my life right now, however good they were.' Steve's answer sounded quick and decisive and Lizzie was surprised. 'I need to get established first,' he said. 'I want to get on in life, and I can see how children could seriously hold me back.' Lizzie bit her lip and didn't reply.

Steve cleared his throat. 'The other reason I won't be staying is because I've been offered another job. You may remember that I've told you how I've always dreamed of having my own pub, in the country, down some leafy lane somewhere, full of horse brasses and county types.'

Lizzie laughed. 'Yes, of course I remember. You described it in such detail I actually believed it existed.'

'Well, it does, though I didn't know that when I first talked about it. But that's what I've been offered, my own tenancy at a country pub in Cheshire. It's got beautiful grounds, room for tables outside, and very attractive living quarters.'

'You mean you've already seen it?'

Steve nodded. 'Honestly, it's almost too good to be true.'

'But you've not told the Walkers?'

'Not yet, no. The whole thing only came up a few days ago. I've not even given the brewery my answer yet. I'm still mulling everything through.'

'You're not thinking of refusing, are you?' Lizzie sounded surprised, though her heart was pounding to think that he might still change his mind.

'No, but it's all been a bit of a whirlwind. They're giving me a few days to make up my mind so that I'm sure. And – and there are one or two things I need to get sorted before I accept.'

Lizzie didn't want him to see how his news had affected her so she tilted her head to one side and asked, as lightheartedly as she could, 'Like what? It makes sense to me that this is the next step to take on your career path. From what you've said about your mother I'm sure she'll be delighted and she won't stand in your way, will she? Surely, you don't have anyone else to worry about?'

A strange look crossed his face and Lizzie was aware of a moment of uncomfortable silence. She looked into his face, trying to work out if she had said something wrong. His tongue curled round his lips and she was shocked to see that his eyes had filled. His voice cracked as he said, 'Yes, I do have someone else to worry about, for I don't want to go alone.' He was looking directly into her eyes now as he said, 'I've been wanting to ask if you'll come with me.'

Lizzie's eyes opened wide and she stared at him. 'Me?

I don't understand. Why me? How would that work out? Where would I live?'

Steve put his hand inside his jacket, then paused. 'Gosh, this is a whole lot harder than I imagined it would be, though I must admit I've not had time to plan things out properly. I thought all this wasn't going to happen for a few weeks yet.'

Lizzie watched in astonishment as he drew out a small cream-coloured box from his inside pocket.

'You'd live with me, of course,' he said. He dropped to the floor in front of her on one knee. 'I don't know if you realize, even though I've been trying to tell you for some time, but I love you, Lizzie Doyle.'

Lizzie opened her mouth to speak but no words came out as she stared down at him.

'I'm asking you to marry me and come with me as my wife.'

Lizzie drew in a sharp breath. It was the question she had most feared.

'I know I've probably surprised you,' Steve said quickly. 'Whereas for me, this is something that's been on my mind almost since the day I first met you. I've thought of nothing else for months. But I accept that you'll need time to think about it.'

Tears filled Lizzie's eyes as she looked at Steve's eager face and for a moment she had images of how it might feel to be his wife. But then she thought about the implications and possible ramifications of what that might mean and she sat for several minutes until her breathing steadied again and she was sure her voice wouldn't break. 'It's a beautiful thought, Steve,' she said eventually, her voice soft, 'and I don't want you to think I'm not grateful. In fact, I want to thank you from the bottom of my heart, but I can't go with you and I can't marry you.'

'Why not, for Heaven's sake?' he said. 'Is it my leg, has it put you off?'

'Oh, Steve!' She put out her hand instinctively towards him. 'No, no! You'll never know how much I want to say yes. But truly, I can't. I can't leave my ma and . . .' she hesitated, 'and I certainly can't leave the boys.'

Steve frowned. He got up from his knees and sat beside her on the couch again. 'Won't you even consider my offer, think about it at least?'

Lizzie shook her head. 'It won't make any difference,' she said. 'I won't change my mind. I'm very flattered to have been asked, but I can't go.' She had hardly looked at the small diamond ring that she now saw sitting on a blue velvet cushion in the tiny box but she shut the lid and closed his hand round it. 'Save it for the right one,' she said.

'But *you're* the right one for me,' he said. 'That's what I've been trying to tell you for ages, only you don't seem to hear me.' His shoulders dropped and he looked defeated as he stared down at his hands. 'I guess that means that you don't love me.'

'I didn't say that, Steve. But there are . . . complications, other considerations. Please just accept that I can't marry you.'

Cora was shocked by Lizzie's appearance the next morning when she came down to breakfast. Sammy was already in his high chair, chattering away in his baby-style jargon that made no sense to anyone but him. Lizzie responded to him with an automatic soothing comment as she always did but for once she didn't seem aware of what she was saying. She looked distracted, her face blotched pink as if she had been crying all night.

'I was surprised you'd gone to bed by the time I got back last night,' Cora said. 'I wasn't home late and I expected to see Steve. Didn't he come?'

'Yes, he came.' Lizzie began setting out the breakfast things, sharing out the coarse bread she'd bought yesterday, but she couldn't hold back the tears for long. Cora sat her down and put her arms round her. 'Lizzie, love,' Cora said, 'what on earth is the matter?' Then her eyes widened as Lizzie began to tell her the whole story of what had transpired the night before.

'So you told him a definite no?' Cora said eventually.

'Yes, of course I said no.' Lizzie's manner was impatient as she began to feed Sammy his morning cereal.

'Why "of course" when you took no time to consider?'

Cora snapped. 'Really, Lizzie, I do sometimes wonder if you actually want things to change.'

'What was there to consider? I've known him for quite a while now; don't you think the possibility of him proposing at some point had crossed my mind? Though I must confess I didn't think it would be so soon.'

Cora shook her head. 'I'm never sure what goes on in your mind, love, especially not when it comes to men. You've never shown any real interest in anyone since Joe. I was beginning to despair, but I was hoping that it might be different with Steve.'

'Yes, I know you like him, Ma, you've made that very plain.'

'Don't you like him?' Cora said, a look of surprise on her face.

Tears filled Lizzie's eyes again and spilled onto her cheeks. 'Yes, I do, I do,' she said quietly, 'but how can I even think of . . .'

'Well, it's obvious he loves you,' Cora said, putting out two plates for the boys, 'and that's worth a million in most people's book. They'd be queueing up to say yes.'

Lizzie looked off into the distance. 'Sometimes I even think I love him,' she said, gazing dreamily for a moment. But she was brought back to the present by a shout from Sammy as he grabbed the spoon and spattered cereal across the table.

'Oh, Lizzie!' Cora said, ignoring the wet patches in her attempt to embrace her daughter. 'You know I want what's best for you. But you only have one life and you really shouldn't throw it away. You can't go on grieving for Joe for the rest of your life. It's not good to live in the past and I'm sure he wouldn't have wanted you to.'

'I know,' Lizzie began but Cora interrupted. 'And you can't spend the rest of your life looking out for me and the boys.'

'Well, I can't just up and leave you,' Lizzie protested.

'You'll have to one day, and believe me, we'll be fine. And so will you. The world will not fall apart. But you can't sacrifice your whole future because of mistakes you've made in the past.' She reached out and covered Lizzie's hand. When Lizzie didn't respond Cora said, 'We all have to follow our own paths, you know. I shall encourage each of the boys to go off and tread theirs when the time comes. It's only right. So you must go off too. I'd hate to be the one to hold you back.'

'I know that, Ma, and you're not holding me back, honestly. It's just that I don't want to live with any more lies.' Lizzie looked directly at Cora. 'At the back of my mind I'd always be worrying about things that might be said in anger, what secrets might be revealed, So I've either got to tell him the whole truth, or let him walk away.'

Cora looked at her sadly. 'But we went to such pains

to make sure that the truth could never come out. As far as I'm concerned it's all in the past and we shouldn't even be thinking about it any more. To me, our life is our life as it is now and I can't think of it in any other way.'

'But it isn't really, is it?' Lizzie challenged. 'Because the past happened and things were very different then, and that's how it still feels to me. I can't base a marriage on secrets and lies.' She gave Cora a brief hug then she picked up Sammy and said, 'I'll go and get him ready for nursery,' and as he gurgled with laughter she carried him up the stairs.

Lizzie paced up and down outside the Rovers, waiting until the lights in the bar had been switched off. This is not a night to be out on the street, she thought staring at the toboggan tracks that had been carved out on the road. Fresh snow continued to fall and she realized she was in danger of sliding across the cobbles. The soles of her shoes were so thin the cold struck right through them from the freezing stones. She shivered and pulled her hat well down, winding her scarf more tightly about her neck as she tried to keep warm while she kept an eye on the front entrance.

'Hello, what on earth are you doing here?' Steve said in obvious surprise when she emerged from the shadows as soon as he appeared. 'You look frozen. Why didn't you come inside?'

She shrugged her shoulders, taking comfort from the fact that his face had lit up for a moment when he had first seen her.

'What's with the cloak and dagger?' he said.

'I–I was hoping we could have a private chat,' she said, 'though I think I could have chosen a better night.'

'Have you come to tell me you've changed your mind, like they do in films?' he said. 'So we can disappear into the distance and live happily ever after?'

Before she had time to reply, the moment of eagerness in his eyes was replaced by a hardened expression that she hadn't seen before and she wasn't sure how to read now.

'No,' she said, as they began to walk, 'I told you I won't change my mind, but I did feel that I owed you an explanation.'

'Oh?' was all Steve said, though she was aware he kept casting glances in her direction.

'I don't think it was very fair on you the other night, me saying "no" like that without telling you why I can't marry you and why I can't leave Weatherfield,' she said.

'I presumed you're still hankering after that serviceman. What was his name?'

'Joe,' she said, unable to keep the catch from her voice. 'He was a Canadian airman who sadly got himself killed. But that's only part of it and I feel I owe it to you to tell you the rest. But it's too cold to talk out

319

here.' Her breath was vaporizing like she was exhaling steam into the frosty air. 'Why don't we go to my house? Ma will be in bed so we'll have the place to ourselves and at least we'll have the embers of the fire to keep us warm.'

A few minutes later as they drew two chairs close to the kitchen hearth, Steve said, 'I don't suppose I'd ever be able to live up to your airman's memory, so I apologize for ever thinking I could.'

'You don't have to apologize for anything, and that's not what I've brought you here to say, but you've a right to know everything,' Lizzie said, stirring the coals with the poker. 'I don't suppose anyone will ever really be able to replace Joe but I'm sure I'll come to terms with that, given time. We were going to get married and he gave me a pretty little diamond ring that I shall always treasure. It sits on a blue velvet cushion in a cream box . . .' She paused. 'We had to get a special licence because he didn't get leave very often and we had the date booked with the local vicar for a small ceremony the next time Joe was due back in Weatherfield.' She couldn't look at Steve now, so she stared at her hands, which were still red from the cold. 'But Joe never made it. It took some time to get the details and by the time we found out as much as they could tell us, I realized that I was almost five months pregnant.' She heard Steve's sharp intake of breath but still kept staring down into her lap. 'I kept trying to pretend it wasn't happening . . .' She had to pause to clear her throat. 'And by then it was too late to do anything about it in any case.'

Steve turned sharply to look at her. 'Would you really have considered . . .?'

'I honestly don't know. I'm only thankful I never had to answer that question. But I did know I couldn't just give the baby away.'

Steve frowned and turned to her. 'So, what did you do?' He sounded puzzled. 'I don't . . .'

'That was when my ma stepped in,' Lizzie said. 'She was wonderful.' There were tears rolling unheeded down Lizzie's cheeks now and she made no attempt to stop them until Steve produced a white cotton handkerchief. 'She arranged for us all to go down south for a few months.' She said, dabbing at her cheeks. 'The boys were too young to understand what was going on so she packed them off to stay with her family who live in the country while I went to a special home just outside London to have the baby. They tried to get me to give the baby up, but I refused and ma stood by me.' Lizzie blew her nose in Steve's handkerchief. 'By the time we came back to Weatherfield, as far as the rest of the world was concerned, the boys and I had a new brother.' Her voice cracked and she had to stop.

Steve drew in a large breath. 'That's some revelation.'

'Yes, it is,' Lizzie said, as she pulled the edges of her large woollen cardigan more tightly together. She didn't try to look at Steve's face as she said, 'So, as you'll have realized by now, I can't let you go on thinking Sammy is my baby brother, when in fact it's time to acknowledge that he's my son.' She paused, letting the weight of the words sink in as she actually spoke them out loud for the first time. 'I hope you can understand now why I can't go off and get married, because I love Sammy and I couldn't bear to part from him. The shame of having an illegitimate child is difficult enough to cope with, but a marriage based on lies would be worse.'

For a few moments Lizzie's voice gave way to sobs. But when she finally wiped away the tears, she cleared her throat and sat up straight, looking directly at him. 'Do you know what?' she said, her voice suddenly stronger. 'You're the only person in Weatherfield who knows the truth about Sammy, right now, apart from my ma. But you've made me realize that I'm tired of all the lies and having to keep everything secret. I don't want to keep on denying who Sammy is, or who I am. I want to be a proper mother to him and the only way I can do that is to admit to the world that he is my child.'

She didn't know how to interpret Steve's continuing silence and she willed him to say something so that she could at least understand the impact of her words. But the look on his face told her that he had been shocked by her bombshell and didn't know how to respond.

She stood up. 'So you don't have to worry about me any more,' she said. 'And thanks for that.' She stuffed the handkerchief into Steve's hands. 'Now let me get you a drink at least – there's still some water heating over the fire.'

'No thanks,' Steve said. 'I think I'll be getting off home. I appreciate you telling me and I shall respect your confidence. Don't worry, no one will hear about Sammy from me.'

He stood up and put on his coat. Then Lizzie watched as he strode off into the night, taking no heed of the wind tossing his hair back and forth, or the snow glistening treacherously underfoot. And as she closed the door behind him she sank down onto the cold lino floor and let the tears flow unchecked.

Lizzie was glad she had told Steve the truth about Sammy, although she was disappointed that he had made no move to contact her in the days that followed her revelation.

'It was obviously too much for him,' Cora said when Lizzie told her about Steve's reaction. 'As it would have been for most men, I suppose.'

'But he kept telling me how much he loved me, so I stupidly thought he might be different.' Despite her best efforts, Lizzie couldn't help crying.

'And you loved him,' Cora said, coming over to give her daughter a hug. 'Of course you were going to believe him.'

Lizzie nodded her head vigorously, not trusting herself

to speak. 'It was far better to have told him now than to have carried on pretending it – it would only have grown more difficult as time went on to maintain the lie,' she said eventually.

'You didn't have to do it at all, you know,' Cora said.

'Yes, I did,' Lizzie said. 'I couldn't have gone on living a lie. And I didn't want him to go away to Cheshire without knowing the truth. And now I feel as though it doesn't matter if the whole world knows. Let's face it, at the moment people have so much on their minds that my little bit of tittle-tattle will be nothing more than a five-minute wonder.'

'Fancy!' was Hilda's first comment when they met together at the Pride for the last official staff meeting. Lizzie had taken her aside to tell her the facts surrounding Sammy's birth. 'But I have to tell you that I'd suspected as much.'

'Really?' Lizzie was surprised.

She was astonished to think that their carefully hidden secret might not have been so secret after all. But Hilda made no judgement and Lizzie was encouraged to tell her about Steve's marriage proposal and her refusal.

'Now that's a shame,' Hilda said, 'because you make a lovely couple, you know. I was only thinking that the last time we was together in the Rovers.' Hilda sighed. 'It would have been lovely,' she said, a dreamy look in her eyes. 'I always like a nice wedding. But I understand you sticking up for the little 'un. Are you going to tell other folk too?' Hilda wanted to know.

'I think it's time,' Lizzie said.

'I'm right by your side if you need me,' Hilda said, linking arms for a moment with Lizzie. 'Because, you know, you'll have to learn to take no notice of some of the nasty things folk can say, for there's bound to be some that will give you a piece of their mind.'

'I know,' Lizzie said with some regret. 'I remember at school how some kids who didn't have a da – for whatever reason – used to get bullied. Poor little Sammy . . . though no doubt he'll soon learn to toughen up. I'm sure his brothers will help him stand up for himself. Or maybe I should call them his uncles,' she said, and she couldn't suppress a smile.

'He'll be all right, you won't have to worry about that,' Hilda said, and she sounded so positive Lizzie wanted to believe her.

'It is a shame Steve's leaving the Rovers, though; he'll certainly be missed, you know,' Hilda said. 'He's been good for Coronation Street, I reckon. I wonder what it will mean for the landlady?'

'Well, they'll certainly be short-handed behind the bar,' Lizzie said, 'so I was hoping now might be a good time to go and ask if they've got any extra hours going.'

Hilda didn't answer immediately, then as if she hadn't heard she said, 'You know, I think you and me should go back to yours for a cup of tea right now.' She gave a chuckle. 'If you don't mind me inviting myself. But I think it's high time I read your tea leaves.'

'Why now?' Lizzie laughed.

'Because it would be a good idea to do it while we know for sure there's no harmful spirits hovering about number nine. I have a feeling that I'll only see good signs for the future and little Sammy's story will be a definite omen for the good.' Hilda suddenly became very perky. 'You mark my words, only good can come of this now.'

Steve knew that his answer to the brewery would have to be yes, even though he had been devastated by Lizzie's rejection and revelation. But the new job offered everything he had ever dreamed of and it would be foolish to turn it down. He had felt a glimmer of hope when Lizzie had sent him the note asking if they could meet, but he could tell from the determination in her voice and the set look on her face that she was not going to change her mind. All that was left was for him to hand in his resignation to the Walkers as soon as possible and prepare to make the move, alone.

He waited until shortly before opening time the next day to tell the Walkers of his intentions and Jack's first reaction was to clap him on the back. 'Well done, old boy!' Jack said, looking genuinely pleased. 'That's a great step up for you career-wise, though we'll really miss having you here.'

'Congratulations!' Annie said, her voice more restrained. 'Cheshire's gain is our loss. Though it's amazing to think they've offered such a tenancy to someone who's still so young and comparatively inexperienced,' she said with a stiff smile. 'And they didn't even ask us for a reference.'

'Obviously the work you've done here has impressed the brewery, without us having to spell it out,' Jack said to Steve.

'And it will leave us short-handed, at least for a while,' Annie added. 'I wonder if the brewery has thought of that?'

'I'll work out my full notice,' Steve offered, 'and I'll do a bit extra if it helps. I don't intend leaving you in the lurch.'

'That's grand,' Jack said, 'and now that the Pride's shut maybe Lizzie might be glad of some casual hours?'

Steve felt his face suddenly getting hot at the mention of her name and had to look away. That was one discussion he didn't want to get involved in.

'You know, you should count yourself very lucky,' Annie said, 'these opportunities in such desirable locations don't come up very often.' She gave a tinkling laugh. 'I should know. Running a country pub in Cheshire was long my dream, wasn't it, Jack dear?'

'It was indeed one of your aspirations, my love.' Jack chuckled. 'For many years. Until I pointed out the impracticalities of us living in the country with our two young nippers, not to mention all the hard work that had gone into building a reputation for ourselves right here in Weatherfield.' He turned back to Steve. 'So, go well is all I can say.' Jack put out his hand. 'We will certainly wish you all the best when the time comes. And let us know if there's anything we can do to help with the move.'

'Thanks, Jack, thanks for everything.' Steve shook Jack's extended hand, but before he could say anything to Annie, he realized she had already disappeared into the bar.

Lizzie was feeling wretched and despite Cora's chivvying she found it hard to raise a smile. She hadn't seen Steve since that fateful night she had told him about Sammy and she was missing him more than she would ever have imagined. She went to the window and peered up at the sky that was making the day look as dismal as she felt. There had been a forecast on the radio for more snow before the day was out and the clouds did indeed look laden. A group of children were revelling in the previous fall which had already made the whole street white, squealing with delight as they went slip-sliding from lamppost to lamppost in a form of rounders. But she was thinking about the words Mr Warner had used at the meeting yesterday, when he had advised all employees officially that the Pride would be closing down. Lizzie sighed. Now would be the time for her to seek a job at the

Rovers but she was hesitating. Of course she desperately needed the money, but the last thing she wanted was to bump into Steve.

She looked up when she heard the tooting of a car's horn, an unusual sound on Coronation Street, and she turned back to the window. She looked out and saw that the children had stopped their game and were running alongside the car as it cruised slowly down the street. Lizzie couldn't see who was driving and she was astonished when it pulled up outside number nine.

'What's all the commotion out there?' Cora called from the scullery.

'I can't tell,' Lizzie called back. 'But this car's stopped outside our front door.'

Lizzie remained glued to the window and was astonished to see Steve get out of the driver's side. There was a loud rap at the door and Lizzie ran back to the scullery and pushed Cora forward to open it.

'Good morning, Mrs Doyle,' Lizzie heard Steve say.

'That's a very fine car, if you don't mind my saying,' Cora said.

'Glad you like it. It's a Hillman Minx, the lovely new car that goes with my lovely new job.'

'Congratulations on both counts,' Cora said. 'You know I wish you well,' she went on.

Lizzie was pleased her mother hadn't invited him inside. 'Have you started working in your new pub yet?' Cora asked.

'Next week,' Steve said, 'but the brewery are happy for me to be driving it, to help with the move.'

'Is that where you're off to now?' Cora said.

'So long as the weather holds; I'm moving in a bit at a time.'

'Have you come to say goodbye, then? Shall I be calling Lizzie?' Cora said. 'I'm sure she wouldn't want to miss seeing you before you go. Why don't you come in.'

Lizzie froze.

'Actually, I was hoping she'd be at home, for it's Lizzie I wanted to see,' Steve said, and peeping from behind the door she could see him as he stepped over the threshold. Lizzie's stomach began to churn.

'Did I hear you say you're off today?' Lizzie asked, forcing her voice to sound as normal as possible, though she couldn't look him in the eye. 'I wish you well in your new life.'

'Actually,' Steve said, removing his hat as he stood in the hallway, 'I haven't come to say goodbye at all.' He looked down at his hat which he was nervously passing from one hand to the other. He cleared his throat and said, 'I've come for you.'

'For me?' Lizzie said. 'I'm sorry, I don't understand.'

'I overheard the Walkers talking about offering you a job,' Steve said, 'and I knew I couldn't let you accept it.'

'W–what do you mean?' Lizzie said.

'I've made a mistake. I've stayed away when we

should have been together, talking things through, and now I don't know if you can forgive me?'

'I – I . . .' Lizzie began, but Steve hadn't finished.

'That was quite a bombshell you dropped about Sammy, and I don't think I dealt with it very well. I thought if I kept away it would be better for both of us, but I've found that I can't, Lizzie – I don't want to live without you.'

Lizzie was finding it difficult to breathe and stood rooted to the spot, by the front window where she had been gazing into the street, watching the car pull into the kerb when he'd arrived. She was not sure if she was hearing him correctly.

'I've come to ask if you would still consider marrying me and if you would come and live with me. You and Sammy, that is, because I totally understand that you couldn't leave him behind; I wouldn't want you to.'

Lizzie opened her mouth to speak, and no sound came out, though Steve didn't seem to notice for he continued speaking. 'So I stopped off to see if you would do me the honour of taking a trip out with me this afternoon, weather permitting of course. Because I thought it might be a good opportunity for us to have a look at our new home. Sammy's welcome to come too, if you think he'd like to come along for the ride.'

Lizzie was dumbfounded. 'Me and Sammy?' she said. 'I didn't think you wanted kids until you were established in your career.'

'I know I said that and I was being an idiot. What I didn't realize when I said it was what I'd be in danger of throwing away.'

'I think you should both come into the sitting room,' Cora intervened, taking Steve's hat from his hand.

'Are you sure you mean this is really for the two of us? Not just for this afternoon but for the whole . . .'

'Forever,' Steve said. 'And yes, I'm very sure. I've never been so miserable as I have during these past few weeks without you. It's been agony not seeing you or even hearing your voice.' He took a step towards her and drew her to him, touching her lips lightly with his before opening out his arms and wrapping them tightly around her.

'Me too,' Lizzie whispered, though she hardly dared to voice the words. But suddenly being held in his arms like this felt like the most natural place to be.

'I promise I'll always love Sammy. Secretly, I think I already do,' Steve whispered into her ear. 'And I'll bring him up as if he were my own. But if you don't want to be a publican's wife and spend your life pulling pints behind a bar, then you don't have to. You can go back to college and become a teacher if you want. I promise to love and support you whatever you do.'

Cora was still standing by the door as though afraid to make a move, but when she caught Lizzie's eye she winked and grinned. Just then there was a knock at the door and Cora answered it.

'It's Hilda,' Cora announced as Hilda stepped inside her eyes wide.

'I saw that amazing car outside and I was too nosey to pass the door without coming to find out who it belonged to,' she said with a cheerful grin.

'I hold my hands up – it's mine,' Steve said.

'Very nice,' Hilda said.

Lizzie extricated herself from Steve's clasp and indicated Hilda should sit down. 'Steve's come to take me . . . us. We're going to see our new home in Cheshire.' She couldn't help grinning as she said it and Steve was smiling broadly too. 'We are indeed. And I don't think I'm jumping the gun if I tell you we're going to get married just as soon as we can organize it.'

'I don't know about that,' Lizzie began, but Hilda beat her to it. 'Oh Lizzie!' Hilda cried going over to hug her friend. 'That's the best news ever. I'm really happy for you both.'

'Now, if you'll excuse us,' Steve said, 'we have to get going – and you,' he said pointing to Lizzie, 'have to wrap up warm as we don't have the luxury of a heater.'

Lizzie embraced Hilda in a parting hug and then gave one more wave as her friend set off for home. She watched with a lump in her throat as Hilda, in her thin-soled shoes, carefully picked her way down the icy street.

Then, with a nod to her mother, Lizzie disappeared upstairs and when she came down she was wearing her winter coat and Sammy was bundled into a navy-blue boiler suit.

As Lizzie opened the front door there was a blast of cold air and, as if by magic, Elsie appeared in the doorway.

'My, you look cosy,' Elsie said. 'Where are you off to?'

'Nowhere if this stuff sticks,' Lizzie said, stepping outside, and she laughed as she pulled off her gloves and held out her palms as the first snowflakes began to fall. Dennis and Linda pushed past their mother as they ran into the street, shouting, 'More snow! Here it comes!' Billy Walker and Kenneth Barlow were scooping up the remains of the previous snow fall, pelting each other with small compact balls. 'We're off to Cheshire for the afternoon,' Steve said.

'And we'd better go soon before it really begins to come down,' Lizzie added and she laughed as the twins ran into the street joyfully pretending to catch the large flakes.

'Well, have a nice time,' Elsie said.

'We will. And we'll look forward to seeing you at the wedding,' Lizzie said. Elsie stared at her in astonishment, looking quickly from Lizzie to Steve.

Lizzie grinned. 'No doubt Ma will tell you all later,' she said.

Steve held open the car door as Lizzie ducked inside with Sammy in her arms. He turned over the engine and as the car slowly pulled away several of the children abandoned their games and began to run after it. They were screaming with delight as it crept over the cobbles and the fistfuls of snow they hurled at the vehicle spattered across the boot and the back window.

'You must tell me more, Cora,' Elsie said. 'Isn't that wonderful?'

Cora clapped her hands together in childish delight as the two women went back into the house.

'It's more than wonderful,' Cora said. 'It's like a miracle.'

'There's no question about it, is there?' Elsie said. 'The luck at number nine has definitely changed.'

THE END

Jean Alexander – Would the real Hilda Ogden stand up please?

Jean Mavis Hodgkinson was better known to British television viewers as Jean Alexander, the actress who played *Coronation Street*'s much-loved and long-enduring character Hilda Ogden. She was born in October 1926 in Toxteth in Liverpool and lived with her mother Nell, her electrician father Archie, and her older brother Kenneth in a terraced house with no indoor toilet – not unlike some of the early fictional houses of Weatherfield.   She attended St. Edmund's College for Girls in Princes Park, Toxteth. Jean caught the acting bug at an early age, initially while staying at a guesthouse in Barrow-in-Furness where her father was working at the shipyard. There she saw twelve little girls practising their dance routines in the back yard and suddenly she saw herself performing for an audience. Her resolve to go on the stage was strengthened by the variety acts she saw at Liverpool's Pavilion theatre, and from then on she became dedicated to achieving her newfound ambition. It was not that she was aiming to become famous – all she wanted was to find opportunities that would help her develop her acting skills. Even marriage was not part of her long-term plans.

As a teenager, she joined the Playgoers' Club, an amateur theatre troupe where she spent most of her spare time, and it was there she became adept at stage management, set building and prompting. She tried to obliterate her native accent and signed up for elocution lessons. These were only partly successful for though she did manage to refine her speech, several years later someone still asked, 'What did you say, scouse?'

When she was about fifteen, Jean began to hone her skills more specifically as she and a friend took turns to read the speeches from all of Shakespeare's plays. Her acting career didn't begin until 1949 when she was hired for £5 a week by the Macclesfield-based Adelphi Theatre Guild. She made her professional debut in Somerset Maugham's *Sheppey* as Florrie. However, it was not a success and she received her first and worst-ever review. Undeterred, she continued to play minor character parts in rep at theatres in Oldham, Southport and York during the 1950s, even playing the front end of a pantomime horse. She also worked as a wardrobe mistress and stage manager.

At the end of the decade she headed to London where she made her TV debut in *Deadline Midnight* and she appeared in the popular police series *Z Cars* and *Emergency Ward 10*. Several other minor TV roles followed, and in 1962 she appeared in *Coronation Street* as Mrs Webb, a kidnapper's landlady.

Hilda was first introduced into the soap by Granada TV in 1964 when, in an effort to improve ratings, a new family was brought in – the Ogdens. Husband Stan, a lazy, hard-drinking layabout was played by Granada continuity announcer Bernard Youens while the role of his down-trodden wife Hilda offered a career break-through to thirty-seven-year-old Jean Alexander. On-screen the pair battled daily while off-screen they quickly established a good rapport and often learned their lines together over a friendly game of scrabble.

Hilda Ogden was a dreadful gossip and general busy-body and she gradually developed into a much-loved comedic character, unconsciously injecting humour through her malapropisms such as famously calling the mural on the living room wall her 'muriel'. In many ways Hilda typified the residents of *Coronation Street*, and her name becoming synonymous with a certain type of working-class woman: feisty yet long-suffering, badly done by but persistent. Despite her many clashes with her good-for-nothing husband Stan, Hilda was constantly defending his ill-advised actions. Hilda worked as a cleaner in *Coronation Street*'s main pub the Rovers Return, though she was disdained by her employer Annie Walker and many of the pub's regular clientele. With her hair permanently in curlers and covered with a headscarf she looked as if she was preparing for some grand event, the invitation to which hadn't yet arrived. Often misguided, she was always trying to do her best, even though she usually failed, and viewers quickly warmed towards her.

Initially, aspiring actress Jean had expressed concern to her agent that taking on such a role might 'blight her career', but despite her shortcomings, Hilda, the nagging wife and gossiping char with the whiny voice, soon found her way into the hearts of millions of Corrie's enduring audience – even though Jean was not always aware of the scale of her popularity. In her 1989 autobiography, *The Other Side of the Street*, Jean was always careful to distance herself from her famous role. Indeed, she said that once she took out her curlers and folded her pinny at the end of each recording session, the character ceased to exist for her and she was able to leave Hilda behind as Jean stepped back into the real world.

Hilda continued to be adored by the nation's TV fans even after the fictional demise of her TV husband Stan, following the sad loss of her friend Bernard Youens in

1984. Her performance in the show as his grieving widow, thrown into despair, is often cited as one of the greatest soap scenes ever, and in 1987 when she decided to leave the show fans started 'Save Hilda!' campaigns, not realising that Jean had made her own decision to depart. Her final scenes in the programme were aired on 25 December 1987 and attracted nearly 27 million viewers, the highest number in the show's history. In the script, she was invited to move to the country to keep house for the widowed Dr Lowther, and her departure made front page news. The *News of the World* headline read 'TA-RA CHUCK!' as Hilda left the street and Jean Alexander began to seek new challenges.

In 1988 Jean was invited to make a guest appearance in the BBC's long running sitcom, *Last of the Summer Wine* and she appeared as Auntie Wainwright, a money-grabbing local junk shop owner. She made a second guest appearance in 1989, and in 1992 became a regular, remaining in the show until the series ended in 2010. Jean also took on several minor roles in TV dramas and comedy shows and her film credits included playing Christine Keeler's mother in *Scandal,* the 1989 film about the Profumo affair. Such variety is a true tribute to her virtuosity as an actress.

Jean lived for many years in Southport, Merseyside, where she was a regular visitor to the Southport Flower Show. She also endeared herself to the locals when in 2009 she joined in the successful campaign for a temporary library in the town while the central library was being refurbished.

She announced her retirement in 2012, two years after her last television appearance, finally pulling down the curtain on an acting career that had spanned more than 60 years.

But her achievements had not gone unnoticed. In 1985 she won the Royal Television Society Award for Best Performance for her role in *Coronation Street*, and in 1988 she was nominated for a BAFTA TV Award for Best Actress. In 2005 the UK TV Times poll voted her as the Greatest Soap Opera Star of All Time.

Jean Alexander celebrated her 90th birthday on 11 October 2016 but was taken ill and died three days later in Southport Hospital.

The actress, known to millions as the down-trodden, loveable Hilda Ogden, is sorely missed, but her last words bring comfort to friends and family.

'Not bad for a poor girl from Liverpool.'

If you've loved *Snow on the Cobbles*,
read Maggie's other novels in the
Coronation Street series, available now
in paperback and on eBook.

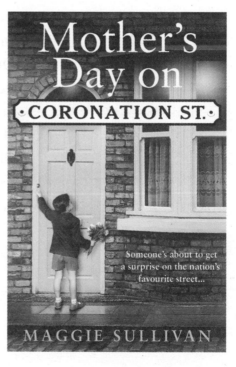